She bel...   ...ildren.
She als... ...ved in herself ... and was
willing to fight for the independence to be
someone in her own right.

DR. CHARLES ENGERS
Exciting, charming, a plastic surgeon with a
brilliant career, he was all she had hoped for.
Until she realized that he expected her to
sacrifice her life for him.

JAY PRESSLER
The real estate tycoon who gave her a start in
business . . . and a love that sustained her in
the climb to success.

ELLIS GIBBONS
An unscrupulous attorney who had the power
to help her, for a personal price she refused to
pay.

MOIRA JOHNSON
The other woman in her husband's life—a
Hollywood starlet who loved for what she
could get.

Other Avon Books by

Neal Travis

MANSIONS
PALACES

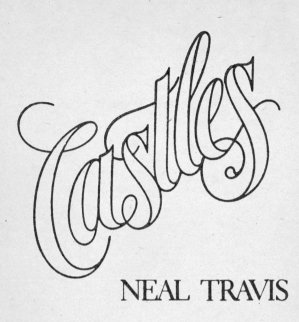

NEAL TRAVIS

 AVON
PUBLISHERS OF BARD, CAMELOT, DISCUS AND FLARE BOOKS

AVON BOOKS
A division of
The Hearst Corporation
1790 Broadway
New York, New York 10019

Copyright © 1982 by Neal Travis
Published by arrangement with the author
Library of Congress Catalog Card Number 81-70582
ISBN: 0-380-79913-8

First Avon Printing, June, 1982

AVON TRADEMARK REG. U. S. PAT. OFF. AND IN
OTHER COUNTRIES, MARCA REGISTRADA, HECHO EN
U.S.A.

Printed in the U.S.A.

WFH   20   19   18   17   16   15   14   13   12

For Elaine

Chapter One _____

MITZI. THAT DAMN NAME.

She could still remember the first day of school in Pittsburgh, running home crying because of the ridicule that name had brought down on her. Her father must have been watching for her from the window of their second-floor apartment because suddenly there he was in the dingy street, scooping her up in his huge arms.

"There, there, little one," he crooned to her as he carried her up the stairs, past the smells and sounds of the neighbors, stepping carefully over the tattered hall carpet and into the bright clean rooms that were home for the two of them. He put her down on the faded green sofa and knelt on the floor beside her, his head cocked to one side. He studied her like that until her tears had stopped, his bright blue eyes intense.

"It was that bad, huh?" he said gently. "First day of school almost always is. Why, I remember back in Hungary my first day—"

"No, Daddy," she broke in. "School was all right at first. But then we had to stand up and say our names. When I told the teacher I was Mitzi Christgau, she said Mitzi wasn't a real name, and what was it short for? And I said that it *was* real because it was my name and she said I was snippy.

1

And then at lunchtime the other kids were laughing at me and one of them pushed me. I hate school!" She began to sob again. "If I have to go back tomorrow, please can I have a new name?"

Conrad Christgau lifted her up into his arms then and began pacing the sunlit room, her tiny form fitting snugly into his shoulder, his big hand gently patting her back.

"It's a very special name, Mitzi," he said. "Your mother and I picked it because it seemed so American and so fitting for you. You were lying in your mother's arms, fours hours old, so fair and pretty and your mother said, 'She's a Mitzi, if ever I saw one' and I said, 'Where did you ever see a Mitzi?' and we both started laughing because we were so happy to have you. And that night, after your mother went to heaven, all I had to keep me going was the thought of little Mitzi. And it's kept me going these five years. Working nights in the mill, in all the heat and noise, I'll suddenly think of my Mitzi and start to smile. Why, there couldn't be a better name for you."

But that didn't make it any easier. Even without the other kids' jeers, she learned soon enough that she wasn't a "Mitzi" and never would be.

"Mitzis" were pretty and blond and bubbly. She was quiet and shy. She had to wear those ugly wire-framed glasses until she was ten and her teeth, though white, protruded slightly. She was decidedly not pretty. She was, to the children at school, "Mitzi Rabbit" and "Mitzi Four-eyes" and she wished every day for a name like Jane or Mary, something that wouldn't draw attention to her.

She was naturally withdrawn, anyway, and the teasing made her more so. During recess, she read. She was the best reader in the class and near the head of the class in most other subjects. She had plenty of time for reading. Her father always worked the night shift at the steel plant so that he could be at home to send her to school in the morning and welcome her back again. She would pretend to be asleep as he left in the evenings, but she read late into the night. It stopped her from being lonely. Mrs. Vittorio, the widow downstairs who had been watching out for her since she was a baby, still supposedly "sat" with her nights but the two of them soon came to an understanding and left each other alone, Mitzi to her reading and Mrs. Vittorio to her cleaning and cooking downstairs.

The best time was Sunday. It was their special day together and Mitzi and her father developed a ritual, making breakfast in the little kitchen and studying the real-estate section in the Sunday paper. Together they would decide on a house, or houses, to be inspected, then set off on foot. In Hungary Conrad had been a carpenter and it was their dream that one day they would build their own house. In the meantime they inspected other people's homes, and Conrad would whisper comments, usually critical, to her as they trooped through the houses.

"A house is the most important possession any of us will ever have," he told her one summer evening as they sat in the apartment sipping lemonade after a hot day trudging through a housing development and a faded mansion. "A house will embrace you, keep you safe and warm, shelter you for all your life and the lives of your children. But it must be the right house for you. It must speak to you like a friend the moment you meet it."

She nodded gravely. Over the seasons of their

walks he taught her most of what he knew about building and told her what to look for. She knew not to buy a good house in a bad neighborhood, but to look for the real prize, a run-down place in an area that was rapidly being improved. A house could always be fixed up, assuming that it had been solidly built to begin with, but a neighborhood was almost impossible to salvage, and no one person could save a neighborhood by himself.

She understood that it would be a long, long time before they could have a house of their own, but it was fun looking and dreaming. When Mitzi was twelve, her father greeted her at breakfast one morning with great excitement.

"Last night, at work," he said, "one of the men told me about a piece of land he owns in the mountains, just twenty miles from here. He doesn't want to do anything with it and will sell it for a reasonable price. Next week we can go and see it and if we like it . . . then you and I shall build our own house in the woods. This place," he said, sweeping his arm around the apartment, "will be only our town house. We will be like rich Americans, with a place in the city and a country house for weekends. And when I retire and you are through with school we will live in the country all the time."

They borrowed a big old Packard for the trip to the mountains. Conrad had driven very little and was tense, but they made the journey without mishap, taking an hour to cover the twenty miles. They saw a few other cars, families just out for Sunday drives. But she and her father had a mission.

It was a parcel of ten acres in a wooded valley, the mountains continuing their rise all around. A

4

stream ran right across the property and they left
the car on its bank, took the picnic hamper she had
packed, and began to work their way along the
water. The only sounds were the breeze in the tall
trees surrounding them, the water on the stones in
the stream, and an occasional bird. They rounded
a bend in the stream and stopped. The stream
suddenly broadened into a lake. Just a pond,
really, but they would always think of it as their
lake. Her father released her hand and silently
pointed across the water to where a deer, dappled
in the sun and shadow, stood drinking. They
stayed absolutely still for ten minutes until the
deer was finished and had stepped delicately back
into the trees.

"We will build our house over there, on that
rise," he said to her. "And every evening we will sit
on the deck and watch the animals come down to
drink from our lake."

Even with the help of his friends from the mill, it
took three years of spare-time labor to complete the
house in the woods. But it was a task the two of
them loved, and the time flew. By then Mitzi was
totally occupied in caring for her father and
running the apartment. After his first protests
that she should be out playing with friends, they
had settled into a comfortable routine. It was Mitzi
who organized the housewarming party.

She wrote invitations to all who had helped build
the house, asking them to come on the last Sunday
in September. She bargained with Mr. Fratzos at
the local deli for a huge order of cold cuts, salads,
and beer and soda. On Saturday, before the party,
they transported the food up to the house in the
Ford pickup her father had bought when they
started building the house. They spent the day

setting up makeshift tables in the big bare living room and on the deck that surrounded the house. It took more time than it should have because they both kept stopping to admire their new home. There was her father's room and her own and a bedroom for guests, all leading off the living room, which was big and open and beautiful with natural timbers. There was a bathroom, as glistening and modern as anything she had seen on their tours of the Pittsburgh mansions. The kitchen might have come out of *The Saturday Evening Post*. And there was the view of the lake and the woods and the mountains.

At dusk she brought a beer for her father and lemonade for herself and sat with him on the deck. It was cool and quiet and the fresh timber of the deck smelled like the forest around them. They could hear the plop of small fish in the lake and all the forest sounds. She stood up and went to her father and hugged him.

"I'm so happy here, Daddy," she said. "I don't ever want to leave. You'll get your pension soon and I want to leave school and live here and keep house for you."

He took a deep pull of his beer and wiped his moustache with the back of his hand. He smiled into the dusk.

"I would like nothing better than that, my dear," he said. "But even as we move into this house we must be making plans for your future. You can't devote yourself to an old man. I have been very selfish letting you play house when you should be with people your own age having fun. You're a good student and we must start to plan college for you."

"I don't want to go to college, Daddy," she said,

and she meant it. "I just want to be with you, always."

"But I won't be here forever, little one," he said. "I'm already getting to be an old man. You will need something to occupy your life, Mitzi." His voice was gentle and he was searching for just the right words. "You are a lovely girl and I adore you, but . . . you are not pretty in the way the girls are that men chase after. That's why I want you to go to college, so that you will be able to take care of yourself after I'm gone."

In bed that night she thought about what he had said. Not pretty. Well, she had never had any illusions about that. She knew she wasn't beautiful like the women she saw on the movie screens, not like her namesake, Mitzi Gaynor, for example. She wasn't as pretty or as popular as most of the girls at school. But still it hurt to hear her father say it, no matter how kindly he meant it. She got up and looked in the mirror. Not much to work with, but she did have good bones, and her blond hair was quite nice. She would have to get some help.

The housewarming was a wonderful, exuberant affair that began at ten in the morning when the first car came bumping up the dusty lane, its horn blaring. Soon there were a dozen cars there, about forty people in all, the men from the mill and their wives and girlfriends. They brought chicken and pies and bottles of wine and huge coolers of Iron City beer and gaily wrapped gifts for the house.

By noon the temperature was in the nineties and many were splashing in the pond while others fanned themselves on the deck and waited for the afternoon breeze. The wine and beer flowed and after they were through eating, the floor in the living room was cleared for dancing. The records placed on the little portable player were as diverse as the company—Hungarian folk songs, Irish ballads, Ukrainian dances, Italian love songs. Everyone danced to all the music, stomping around the floor as if to test the soundness of the new house.

Mitzi had worked hard all day to make the party a success and by late afternoon there was nothing left for her to do. She was snuggled in a corner watching the grown-ups boisterously enjoying themselves when a large hand reached down to clutch hers. Pete Brennan was looming over her. He was, next to her, the youngest there, a robust twenty-five-year-old who had spent more time helping build the house than anyone else from the mill. He was quiet and shy but she knew somehow that he had a crush on her. His bright blue eyes seemed to follow her everywhere and now, thinking again of her father's remark of the night before, she was glad.

"Come on, Mitzi," he said. "You work too hard. It's time to dance."

She blushed. "I can't dance," she said. "I never learned."

"It doesn't matter," he said. "Just follow me." And she allowed herself to be dragged onto the floor and caught up in a wild Irish reel. She loosened up as he whirled her around the floor. At least half the dancers knew as little about dancing as she did. Pete asked her for four more dances, and each time they danced her confidence grew. She felt romantic. She felt grown up.

At dusk she and her father waved to the last of their guests and started tidying the house. It was dark when they were finished and they sat awhile on the deck, enjoying the night sounds and the cool air.

"That was the nicest day I've ever had," she said, "and this is the best house in the world. It's our own castle in the woods."

He laughed. "You'll see many grander castles than this, Mitzi. And many happier days, I pray. The whole world is just beginning for you." He grinned at her. "Young Pete danced with you a lot. I think he likes you."

"Oh, Daddy!" she said. "He was just being nice. I bet he's got a million girls his own age. He's so handsome."

"We'll see," her father said. "I don't think he hangs around me just because I'm such terrific company. Maybe in three or four years . . . He's a good man, strong and hardworking."

She fell asleep on the drive down the mountain and he had to nudge her awake when they reached the apartment. She stumbled up the stairs, kissed her father good night, and fell asleep at once.

The next afternoon she got out her bicycle and pedaled across town to the home of her only close friend, Julie Haydon. Julie's father was a manager at the steel works and they lived in a large and comfortable house. Julie herself was one of the prettiest and most popular girls in school and it was a source of continuing amazement to Mitzi that they were friends. What did Julie see in her? Of course, Mitzi was able to help Julie with her homework, and if that was why Julie liked her, Mitzi didn't mind. More and more lately she had found the need for a friend, someone in whom she could confide the things she couldn't tell her father. Julie seemed so mature. She had guided Mitzi through so many of the agonies of growing up—her first period, buying her first bra, what to wear to a school dance.

Mitzi found her friend behind the house, lying on a blanket on the smooth green lawn, reading *Photoplay*. Julie was wearing a two-piece bathing suit, the top undone, exposing her finely tanned back. Mitzi was, as always at summer's end, bright pink and peeling.

"Julie," she said, "my dad says I'm not pretty and that I'd better go to college and make something of myself. Do you think there's any hope for me?"

Julie rolled over on one elbow and looked at her. The swimsuit top fell away from her small, firm breasts but she made no attempt to cover herself.

"Not pretty . . ." she said. "Yes, I can see why a father might say that." She laughed at Mitzi's crestfallen look. "But fathers don't know everything," she added quickly. "With just a little work you could be quite pretty indeed. Look"—she riffled through the *Photoplay*—"here're Debbie Reynolds's beauty tips. Now, she's not really beautiful, just cute, but she knows what to do with herself. With a little makeup and the right hairstyle you could look a lot like her." Julie stood up and fixed her top. "Come on up to my room and we'll see what we can do for you. This is going to be fun."

Julie's bedroom was all pink and white, the kind of room Mitzi longed for but could not envision for herself. Stuffed toys fought for space with pictures of Eddie Fisher and Dinah Shore. Julie's clothes overflowed from two large closets, and the bottles and jars of cosmetics with which she was constantly experimenting covered the surface of her glass dressing table.

"Take your dress and slip off and sit in that chair in front of the mirror," Julie ordered.

Mitzi did as she was told, feeling awkward and a

little embarrassed in her sensible white pants and bra. Julie glanced at her and giggled.

"Those are the first things that will have to go if you want to be glamorous," she said. "Those undies! Okay for school, but a girl needs special *lingerie* (she drawled the word, making something special and mysterious of it) if she's going to feel her best." She looked at Mitzi closely. "I take it this project is being done to attract some particular boy?"

"No," Mitzi said quickly. "I just sort of want to know whether there's any hope for me."

"Well, you've come to the right place. Now sit quietly and let me work miracles." Julie began to circle the chair, studying her. "First, the hair. You've got naturally curly hair and there's no sense trying to hide that. So we'll put it in tight rollers and give you a nice Judy Holliday look. You really need a blond rinse as well, to bring out the highlights."

Julie worked on her for an hour, mostly in silence, fixing Mitzi's hair and applying various shades of powder and lipstick and mascara until she got just the look she had in mind. Mitzi was afraid to sneak a look at herself in the mirror but as the session progressed she found herself actually enjoying being the center of attention.

Finally, it was done. She gasped when she saw herself. Her hair, lifted away from her face in tight little curls, revealed a smooth, glowing skin. Her blue eyes were highlighted and seemed to sparkle. Julie had done something to bring up her cheekbones and soften her jawline, and bright pink lipstick formed her mouth into a bow.

"It's . . . it's perfect," Mitzi said as she gazed at herself, stunned.

Julie stood back, grinning, admiring her creation. "Stand up," she said. "I'm going to do the rest of you." She rummaged in a chest of drawers and returned with a handful of wispy garments. As Mitzi stood there meekly Julie stripped her of her bra. "Put this on," she said. "It's a push-up and it'll make you look like you've got more than you have. And this," handing her a lacy garter belt and sheer nylon stockings. "You've got to feel glamorous from the skin out."

Soon Mitzi was standing in the unfamiliar garments, staring at the new figure in the full-length mirror. The person looking back at her seemed almost beautiful, older, and far more confident than Mitzi felt.

Later, in her own small, familiar room, Mitzi studied herself in her mirror for a long time. Then she took off all the makeup and brushed out her hair. Whatever Julie had done, it had not been right. It was a nice surprise to know she could look that way, but the face Julie had created had nothing whatever to do with Mitzi and never would.

Chapter Two _____

OVER THE NEXT MONTHS, MITZI BEGAN TO DATE a little, but always in groups. There was no real involvement, just group sorties to the movies or bowling. She didn't have all that much time anyway, what with schoolwork, keeping house in the city, and making occasional winter visits to the house in the woods.

Pete Brennan became a steady visitor to the house and as the cold weather closed in they spent warm, happy Sundays around the big log fire, Pete and her father talking while she sat quietly gazing into the fire. She caught Pete looking at her and, although he never so much as tried to hold her hand, she felt that he was in love with her.

She thought it all out over a period of weeks and decided Pete might be the solution to her future. If she married him after high school they could all live together and she wouldn't have to leave her father. Her teachers all thought she should go to college. She was an excellent student and they assured her she would have no trouble getting a scholarship. But there was her father. She could not bear to leave him.

On the third of January in her eighteenth year, a dreadful, cold night, she got a call from the mill where her father worked.

The voice at the other end sounded terribly harassed.

"Miss Christgau," he began apologetically, "I'm afraid I have awful news for you. Your father . . . we had an accident this morning. Your father was killed, your father and two other men. We haven't had a major accident here in years . . . but . . . I'm sorry," he said. A pause. "Are you there?"

"Yes," she said softly. "I understand. My father is dead."

"Of course," he said rapidly as if he had rehearsed his speech, "both the union and management will assist you through this tragedy in every way. We'll send a welfare worker over later to talk to you. In the meantime, is there anyone who should be notified? Relatives?"

"No, there's no one but me," she said.

The funeral affected her hardly at all. Her father, that big, laughing, gentle man, had nothing to do with the grave site, the mourning steelworkers uncomfortable in shiny dark suits, or the stone-faced man who chauffeured her, all alone in the back of the large black limousine, to the grave and back to the apartment.

Later a union lawyer and a man from the mill came to the apartment and spelled out to her precisely what her father was worth dead. Twenty-three thousand dollars would be held in trust for her until she turned twenty-one. The union lawyer was the executor named by her father in his will and he would make disbursements to her. It all went very smoothly and soon Mitzi realized that the authorities would not interfere with her life just because she wasn't quite of age. Apparently no one cared. She was deeply relieved.

She found that keeping busy was the only way to

contain her grief, and she studied hard and made plans. There was no difficulty about selecting a college. Mitzi was adamant that she did not want a scholarship. She could pay her own way. Julie was going to Northwestern, and Mitzi's application there was quickly accepted. She would surrender the lease on the apartment at the beginning of summer and move into the house in the mountains. After that she would spend all but the summer months on campus in Evanston, Illinois.

Her plans clearly dismayed Pete Brennan, who had been calling on her once a week. He was too shy to visit more often than that. He took Mitzi to the movies, or to dinner, even on several occasions to a basketball game in the high school gym. Quiet amusement was her classmates' reaction to Pete.

"He's good-looking," Julie pronounced solemnly. "All that curly brown hair and those wild Irish eyes. He could put his boots under my bed anytime."

Mitzi smiled uneasily. Why couldn't *she* see that way? She knew she must let Pete down as gently as possible. If Mitzi did fantasize about a lover, it wasn't Pete Brennan. She saw Pete as a big brother, kind and strong and so eager to please. The fact that he was in love with her was a slight embarrassment but that was all. After the summer, she would be gone and he would forget her.

His time was running out by late August. It was the end of a fiercely hot day, one on which thunder had been growling around the horizon for hours. Pete had invited himself up to the house in the woods, to swim and barbecue. Julie and her current boyfriend were supposed to be there too, but Julie had come down with a summer cold.

It was a pleasant, lazy day, made all the better

for the fact that Pete didn't nag her about their future together. But he was attentive and cheerful, doing the barbecue by himself and thrashing happily in the pond. Night fell and it was time for him to start down the mountain when the storm finally crashed down through the darkness, coming out of the west, lashing through the trees. Lightning flashed and thunder rolled over them as a savage wind made the house tremble. Sheets of rain were flung sideways against the house. The storm's ferocity stunned them and they sat huddled in the living room, waiting for it to ease. Great trees crashed in the forest and they worried about the roof. The electricity went out after an hour and Mitzi groped for the candles, hoping for a slackening soon. But the storm continued to build. The whole house creaked and groaned like a ship in heavy seas. Sometime after ten o'clock, it became apparent that there would be no trip down the mountain for Pete that night.

"I'll make up the guest room for you, Pete," she shouted above the din. He said something she could not hear and his eyes flashed at her in the guttering candlelight. She made up his bed and then crawled into her own bed, pulling the blankets up high to shut out the fury of the storm.

It took her ages to fall asleep. Dreaming, she felt a huge, warm creature—a bear?—snuggling up to her. It was not an unpleasant dream and she smiled in her sleep as the big animal caressed her. Then all at once she was awake and screaming. He put his big hand over her mouth.

"Please, Mitzi, please don't be afraid," Brennan whispered. "Please. I have to do this."

She struggled but he was far too strong for her, his weight crushing her down on the bed. His mouth clamped hers and he tugged at her pajama top. She felt a button rip and then his hand was feverishly massaging her breast. She managed to tear her mouth away from his.

"Stop it! Stop it, Pete!" she cried. But he seemed not to hear. His hand tore at the waistband of her pajamas and pulled them down over her thighs in one strong motion. The hand forced itself between her legs and she shuddered. He was thrusting his whole body against her and she felt his huge nakedness hammering at her. She continued to struggle, wrenching herself from side to side, but he entered her easily, brutally, and she fell back in exhaustion, just wanting it all to be over. The pain was terrible and almost instantly she felt her blood begin to flow, but he continued to thrust himself into her. She felt nothing at all then, no emotion, just a little pain. After a few minutes, a shudder ran through his body, and he was spent.

He rolled off her and lay beside her in the dark, panting.

Then he began to speak, and she was shocked to hear that he was sobbing.

"I had to," he gasped. "It was the only way I knew to keep you. To stop you from leaving me, Mitzi. I've loved you for so long and waited so patiently. And it would have all been for nothing if you'd gone away. Now you'll have to marry me."

She said nothing. Lying there, letting her bruised body rest, she knew she should hate him for what he had done to her, but she didn't hate him. She had always felt a little guilty about his love, his devotion to her. The rape at least removed the guilt. He had hurt her, and that made it much easier to do what she had planned on doing all along.

"Just go back to your room, please," she said quietly. "This hasn't changed anything. We're not going to get married. If I ever did anything to encourage you to think we were, I'm sorry. But you can't make what you have done to me all right. I don't ever want to see you again. Please don't be here in the morning." She felt him sidling out of the bed and listened to him bumping across the room. She thought she could still hear him sobbing as he went back to his room. When he had gone she pulled the pajamas all the way off her and made her way to the bathroom. There was no hot water and she shivered in the dark as she found a towel, dampened it, and tried to repair the damage he had done to her. She fought off a wave of nausea and went back to the bedroom. She did not want to sleep between the same sheets, so she piled all the spare blankets into a little nest on the floor.

Pete and his car were gone when she got up in the morning. The storm had passed, leaving branches and other debris cast up against the house. She made a quick inspection tour and decided no real damage had been done. She still felt weak and sore but she guessed no real damage had been done to her, either. There were only a couple of days to go until her period, so she was not too worried about being pregnant. She studied her face in the mirror and saw tiredness there but no other signs.

But it would be two years before she again put herself in a position where a man could think he loved her.

Chapter Three _____

SHE HAD SEEN HIM AROUND THE CAMPUS, OF course. The tall, rumpled figure of Charles Engers was everywhere during her sophomore year. He had long since graduated and become a plastic surgeon, but he kept returning to Northwestern, where he was a popular and inspiring speaker. Engers was virtually the conscience of the campus, exhorting students to get involved, to use their privileged position to change the system.

At first Mitzi had thought him a bore, an aging— he was almost twenty-nine then—radical. She had little patience with reformers. She was a serious young woman, in college to get a good job later. Radicals never looked serious to her.

Actually it was Julie who had the crush on him. They were roommates and still best friends after over a year at the university and they shared secrets, although Mitzi had few to share.

"I've just spent the most fulfilling evening of my life," Julie announced importantly one evening in late fall as she came into their room and dropped on her bed. Mitzi, working on a term paper about Herman Melville, frowned and went on writing. "I went to the clinic Charles Engers runs on the South Side," Julie said. "It's amazing what he's doing for poor black people. Most doctors don't care about anything except getting rich, but this man is in the real world, using his skill as a surgeon to help burn victims and people in crashes. He's fitted out this storefront clinic like a little hospital. Do you think many plastic surgeons know how to fix black skin? He knows how to get things done in medicine *and* politics. He was an organizer for Jack Kennedy."

Mitzi sighed loudly and closed her book but Julie went on, oblivious. "He's done so much with his life already. He has wonderful ideas about our potential, about how America is finally flowering and what it can give to the world. You've got to meet him, Mitzi. Charles could change your life."

Mitzi laughed. "Look, I've seen him around and I can see why you'd be attracted to him. But don't give me that bleeding-heart stuff. People live for what they can get out of life and that's the way people just *are.*"

"That's your trouble, Mitzi," Julie said hotly. "I don't think you believe in anything."

The two girls glowered at each other. "Listen," Julie said suddenly, "I'll make you a bet. You come to the clinic with me for an evening and watch Dr. Engers with his patients. Then tell me nobody cares. He's the most caring person I've ever met."

To her surprise, Mitzi agreed. To her astonishment, she went to the clinic again and again and gradually she found herself being of real help to Charles. She would soothe the younger patients, make coffee.

She had never seriously expected love, not for her. Love happened to the real Mitzis of the world. But from the first time she watched Charles Engers in his clinic something took hold of Mitzi, something with an undertow. Tall and rangy, he stooped politely to listen to an old woman's story, knelt to talk solemnly to children before taking blood from them or changing their bandages, always very gently. It did not occur to her to wonder whether he saw her, waiting in the shadows or working at the edge of things. It was enough that she was there and that he was.

It was at about the end of her second week when they finally got to talk for more than a few moments. He stood up from his ramshackle old desk, brushed a shock of brown hair out of his eyes, and came over to the table where she was working. He was six feet five, more than a foot taller than she, and he had to bend down low to speak to her.

"I'm sorry we've been keeping you so busy," he said. "You must have schoolwork to do."

"After seeing your work here, classes seem unimportant. This matters so much more than getting a degree."

"I don't know," he said. "You need the tools to get the job done. Do you have plans for after college?"

"Teaching, I guess."

"That's good," he smiled, the blue eyes glowing. "There's nothing more important than teaching, especially if the kids are from ghettos like this one. If these kids don't start off with a good, caring teacher, we've lost them forever." Suddenly he dropped his grave manner. "If it's not too late for you," he said, "I'll take you for a drink and some of the best jazz you'll ever hear. Tony Scott is playing just down the street."

The jazz club was noisy and smoky and exciting. Mitzi hardly noticed that apart from Scott, the clarinetist, they were the only whites in the place. Charles seemed to know most of the people there.

They were taken to a booth, and cold beers appeared immediately. At the end of his set Tony Scott appeared at the booth and she listened, entranced, as he and Charles talked about jazz and politics and Asia, where Scott had been touring. It was past one when Charles got her back to the dorm.

She increased her visits to the clinic. Julie had dropped out as soon as she saw the effect Charles was having on Mitzi.

"I'm not going to get in your way," Julie had told her. "I think something very special is happening. Good luck."

Mitzi's relationship with Charles was shifting rapidly from their being co-workers to being a couple. It was soon routine for him to drive her home from the clinic, and they usually stopped somewhere for a late supper and drinks. That went on for a month before he first kissed her, parked in his car and talking about a film they had just seen. The kiss was passionate and disturbing and she longed for more.

His mouth was close to her ear but he spoke so softly that she could hardly hear him.

"Mitzi," he said, "Mitzi, I love you."

After that they were together every day, at the expense of Mitzi's coursework. Charles was attached to Illinois General Hospital and she often drove down there to have lunch with him. Then there were their nights together after the clinic, and of course the joy of working together. She knew it was only a matter of time before their kisses, growing ever more passionate, led to sex. She was afraid.

It worried Mitzi that Charles never pressed her to go beyond kissing, walking arm in arm, or sitting close together in his car. She knew the time would come when she would have to tell him about Pete. She didn't want to. She desperately didn't want to, but she was afraid of her own reaction to sex with Charles—with any man—and she would have to let him know what was bothering her.

But Charles continued not to pressure her. She was glad, really, because she thought it meant that he was very serious about her, serious enough to want to wait. But she was also a little impatient because she had to tell him about Pete sometime, and she needed to find out how she would respond to sex again.

It was soon time to meet his family. There was to be a party for his parents' thirtieth wedding anniversary a little after Christmas, and Mitzi would spend the weekend at their home on Chicago's North Side.

Her first glimpse of the family home did not put her at ease. The sprawling Tudor mansion, surrounded by equally imposing houses, was just like the places she and her father had inspected, with awe, on their Sunday walks in Pittsburgh. At least her clothes were suitable, for she'd come a long way under Julie's tutelage. But Mitzi felt like an imposter as Charles guided her up the gray stone steps to the wide oak door. She didn't know what to expect, perhaps a butler, but they were greeted by a smiling, gray-haired woman who kissed Charles and took her hand.

"Mitzi," she said, "I'm Emily. I've been so looking forward to this. We've hardly seen Charles for the past three months but he does manage to phone occasionally, and you are all he talks about." She turned to her son. "Put Mitzi's bags in

the guest room. You're in your old room, if you can
still find your way there." She took Mitzi's arm and
led her away. "Come into the kitchen and we'll
talk. Oh, it's so good to have young people around
the house again. I know Charles has to live close to
the hospital but I do miss him so. His father's
never here. He's either working or on the golf
course, finding new and ever richer patients."

The kitchen was a big, bright room with a red-
tiled floor and sparkling white stucco walls. Mitzi
found herself happily carried along on the tide of
Mrs. Engers' conversation. It eased Mitzi's nervousness. She nodded when Mrs. Engers held up
the coffee pot. "You're probably feeling shy now,"
she said to Mitzi when they were seated at the
butcher block table. "Meeting parents is such an
ordeal, isn't it? I remember—God, I was only
nineteen when I had to meet Henry's folks. Mitzi
. . . such a pretty name, how did you get it?"

Now thoroughly at ease, Mitzi found herself
pouring out her life story to this nice woman.
Emily listened quietly and when it was all told, she
patted Mitzi's hand.

"You poor child," she said. "You've been so
alone. I think you're very brave."

Mitzi blinked at her. She couldn't find a thing to
say. Emily Engers had warmed her. As had happened when she first met Charles, Mitzi felt something take hold of her.

The following night's party was brilliant, the
women all impossibly elegant, the men handsome
and strong in their dinner jackets. A band played
for dancing, and uniformed maids slipped easily
through the crowd, dispensing champagne and
hors d'oeuvres. Mitzi had several glasses of champagne and finally began to relax. Her strapless

midnight blue taffeta gown was just fine, she decided. Her hair was swept up, the first time it had ever been long enough for that.

"You are beautiful," Charles told her as his arms encircled her for yet another waltz. "You look so fresh and genuine, not like these people," he said, glancing around the dance floor.

"Don't say that," she protested. "Your parents are wonderful people and I'm sure their friends are just as nice."

"They've all got too much money," Charles shrugged. "They spend all their time worrying about how to hang on to it. My father once wanted to be a good GP, helping people. Now he's the eminent heart specialist who never sees anyone but wealthy patients—and wealthy friends."

"There's nothing wrong with being successful, Charles," she sighed, but he didn't seem to be listening. He never responded when she said things like that. Holding her tightly, he steered her off the dance floor and toward the library, shutting the door carefully behind them. The sounds of the party died. When he turned toward her, he looked awkward.

"Mitzi," he said abruptly, his broad shoulders twitching, "will you marry me?"

She moved quickly into his arms. Tears began smarting. "Of course I will," she said with a laugh as she felt him clumsily thrust a tiny box into her hand. They kissed and then her hands were shaking so much she could not open the box. He had to open it for her.

The rest of the evening was a blur of shouts and applause and toasts, of dancing, of being kissed and hugged. It was three o'clock before Charles and Mitzi, wonderfully giddy from the excitement

and the champagne, could break away. He led her
up the stairs and down the long corridor to her
room. At the door they stopped and then kissed
longingly. There was a noise on the stairs, and
Charles reached behind her and opened her door
and they both slipped inside.

Mitzi caught a glimpse of the two of them in the
long mirror across the room. Charles was so tall
and handsome. She wanted to be in his arms. So
when she felt his hand move from her bare shoulder to her breast, she pressed against him. All
her fears were gone. Her mind had cleared of
Pete Brennan.

He shifted the hand to the inside of her dress and
her nipples hardened at his touch. She lay her head
against his chest and then quickly the dress fell to
the floor. He was struggling with clasps and
buttons, kissing her all over her body. She pulled
him up off his knees and together they got him
undressed. They crossed to the bed.

This time there was no pain, only the most
intense pleasure. He was a gentle lover, entering
her slowly and tuning himself to her pace. They
moved together in harmony, slowly, gracefully,
until she felt a tide begin to swell in her. Their
movement increased and suddenly wave after
wave of the most exquisite sensations flooded
through her. She heard Charles gasp just as she
was struggling to restrain her own cry. They lay
together then, at peace, in love, until the first light,
when it was time for him to go to his own room.

She watched him dressing. There was a little
smile on her face when he bent to kiss her. "Thank
you," she said. "Thank you for making it beautiful. I was so afraid."

Then she began to cry, the tears dampening his

dress shirt, and all at once she told him about Brennan. Charles held her tightly until the tears stopped.

"Put it out of your mind," he said. "It never happened."

They set the wedding date for five months later, in June, and Mitzi spent as much of that time as she could getting to know her new family. They were so important to her because, as much as she loved Charles, she also loved the sense of belonging that Emily had inspired in her. Charles's father wasn't there much but he was a charming, cordial man and seemed to like her.

"You know," Emily said to her about a month before the wedding, "if anything goes wrong between you and Charles, you and I can still be friends."

Mitzi smiled. "Thank you, but nothing will go wrong with Charles and me. He's such a generous, loving person."

Emily smiled too, but wryly. "He also has the potential to be an SOB, and don't ever forget that," she said. "He's a lot like his father, charming but spoiled. Don't let this public service blind you to all the rest of Charles."

"Oh, but Emily," Mitzi protested, "his need to help others is what first attracted me to him."

"Well," Emily said with a smile, but her light blue eyes were serious, "just remember you've always got a friend here."

And Mitzi was so touched that she decided not to be shocked by Emily's . . . well, her disloyalty toward Charles. If that's what it was. Mitzi didn't want to think about it.

Chapter Four _____

THEY WERE MARRIED ON JUNE 16 AND SHE WAS pregnant by September. They hadn't meant for her to be—Charles's fourteen thousand dollars a year seemed to go nowhere. And besides, they were joyously, selfishly in love, and the baby would interfere. But they hadn't really taken any precautions against it. Charles wouldn't let her use the pill, considering it too new and unproven, and she often forgot her diaphragm.

After the initial shock, their joy seemed even greater.

"One thing it means," Charles said firmly, "is that you'll have to forget about getting a job."

The job was the only thing they had found to fight about so far. Mitzi had been happy to drop out of college when they married but had been determined to go to work. He had been opposing it.

If the job was out, there was still one other important task for her. They had moved into an apartment near the hospital but it was far too small to raise a baby in, and it was a cold, impersonal place, a box next to more boxes. She was determined to get them out of it. She spent the hot early fall combing Chicago, checking out advertisements, dogging realtors, talking, talking,

talking to anyone who seemed to know about houses.

It was early November, cool and pleasant, when she finally found what she wanted. That evening she waited for Charles in the hospital parking lot, smiling broadly as his tall figure came loping toward her. He smiled when he saw her standing by the car.

"Sweet surprise," he said, kissing her and gently running his hand over her filling belly. "You're just the person I need to see at the end of a day like this one."

"I've found it!" she crowed. "Our place."

Charles's smile faded a little. He had been humoring her throughout her search for a new place, but he was really quite happy where they were.

"Really," he said, "all I could face right now is a long, cool drink and a back rub. I'm bushed."

"Just jump in the car and I'll drive you there," Mitzi said. "You're going to love it."

She eased them across town and onto Lake Shore Drive. Lake Michigan was dark and cool beside them. She drove for half a mile along the lakefront, then turned into the driveway of a big new condominium block. Construction was not quite completed and there was cement where the lawns would be. The windows that looked out onto the magnificent lake had white crosses daubed on them. But already the building had a rich, solid look about it.

He followed her out of the car, protesting.

"Mitzi," he said, "forget it. I know what the price is on stuff on the lake. We can't afford anything like this. And if you think I'm going to borrow from my parents—"

She stopped him. "Please, Charles," she said. "Just come and look at what I've found. That can't hurt."

It was a ground-floor apartment and she let him in through the sliding glass doors that would eventually open onto a private garden overlooking the lake.

He whistled in appreciation when she turned on the single unshaded light.

"It's going to be beautiful," he said. "Small but beautiful and exclusive."

She led him through the apartment.

"Two bedrooms, two bathrooms, good kitchen, big living room," she rattled off. She knew the place as well as if she had lived there for years. "But the important thing is going to be that little garden, all to ourselves and the baby," she told him. "That garden is going to make this place one of the most desirable apartments in the building."

"But how much?" Charles sighed wearily. "Eighty thousand? More? There's no way we can spring for it."

She smiled at him triumphantly and walked him back out to the garden-to-be. Out on the lake they could see the lights of a string of barges.

"We can get this place for forty-five thousand," she announced. "I found it through an agent I've been seeing a lot of. The developers have sold all but three apartments and they want to wrap this project up and move on. Most people won't look at this ground-floor apartment. They want to be high up for the view. I've studied the prospectus and the thing is that, with title to the garden, we'll be buying twice as much space as anyone else in the building for less than half the price! You do love it, don't you?"

He put his arm around her shoulder and squeezed her.

"It's really beautiful, Mitzi, and it is a steal," he said gently. "But even at forty-five thousand we can't afford it. Not as long as I work for hospital wages. Someday I'll make it all up to you and the kid," he said, stroking her stomach again, "but for now we're just going to have to stay where we are."

She laughed and kissed him.

"I've talked to the bank and your insurance company. The bank will give us twenty on a personal loan, and the insurance will pick up a first mortgage for the rest, with your life insurance as collateral."

"But that's crazy," he cried. "I can't go mortgaging my life insurance. It's there to protect you and the child if anything happens to me."

"Don't be so stodgy, Charles," she said with a laugh, scenting victory. "Life insurance is a rip-off, anyway. Real estate's the thing to have if you want security. This place will double in value within two years and appreciate 20 percent every year after. Match your life insurance against *that*."

"Okay," he snapped, and she realized quickly that, in her excitement, she had forgotten to play the role she was supposed to. "But the payments are still going to cost us an arm and a leg. I can't take on any more worries at this stage of my career."

"I'm sorry, honey," she said. "I didn't mean to rush you like that, to present it all cut and dried. But you are so busy at the hospital and the clinic that I didn't want to bother you with all the details." She took his hand. "I've gone over all the figures. It will cost us only two hundred and fifty a month more than we're paying in rent, and we get a tax deduction on the interest and maintenance payments, which will save about a hundred and forty a month. Please say you'll think about it. I know we can do it."

Two days later he agreed, still gruff because she had gone ahead without him. Still, he seemed proud of her ability. She ought to be in real estate, he told her on the day they closed.

It was snowing the day they moved in and Mitzi, enormous by then, was grotesquely bundled up in coats and scarves and rugs to keep out the bitter wind sweeping in off the lake. But there was warmth in the apartment among their boxes and crates, and Charles held her close to him. The apartment seemed to wrap itself around them, as if they were just the young family it had been waiting for.

The baby was long and thin and dark, just like Charles. She cried when she held him for the first time. To have two Charleses to love!

Charles had hesitated whenever they talked about names. He had no way of knowing whether she wanted to name the baby after her mother or her father. When his son was born, he kept a wary eye on her face, wondering whether she would say anything about her father, but she didn't. If he'd thought about it, Charles might have wondered more fully at her reticence to mention Conrad Christgau. But Charles didn't wonder much, and when the baby was a day old and nothing had been settled, he said, "Mitzi, if you want to name him after your father, I—"

"Oh, nothing like that," she broke in forcefully, almost fearfully. *Was* it fear? he wondered.

"I don't . . . want to do that, no." She rushed ahead. "I was thinking of calling him Charles, so that I could have two of you."

He smiled. "Not a 'Junior,' Mitzi. Besides, I like 'Dane.' It's such a strong name. What do you think?"

She didn't think anything except that Charles was obviously set on "Dane," so Dane it was.

On their first normal day, when Charles was back at the hospital and she and the baby were at home, Mitzi allowed herself a moment's recollection of that conversation. Conrad. Of course she hadn't wanted to name the baby after her father! Didn't Charles know that there would be only one Conrad, ever? How could he have thought . . . but it was nice of him, she told herself firmly. Nice of Charles.

If only he might have known, though. If only he had guessed her feelings. But he hadn't.

Dane was at first a quiet and gentle baby, easy to love. She passed her days dreamily, napping with him, carrying him with her when she moved around the apartment, timing their day, with its high point being Charles's return from the outside world.

"You've got to snap out of this, you know," Julie Haydon told her one afternoon. "You're too young to sink into motherhood. The world's still going on out there. You have to keep involved."

"No," Mitzi said. "I'm just so content. I'll leave the political activism to you. And to Charles. My job is to make a home for him."

"Don't kid yourself, kid," Julie said. "Husbands may think that they want a quiet little homebody, but as soon as they're sure they've got her, they start looking around for something more exciting."

Mitzi changed the subject without bothering to be subtle about it.

"Have you decided what you're going to do after graduation?" she asked.

"Postgrad work, I guess," Julie said, pushing back her thick hair. "I want to have a lot of spare time next year to get involved in the presidential campaign. It looks like that insane bastard Goldwater is going to be the Republican candidate. My dear father thinks Mr. Goldwater is just wonderful. What about Charles?"

"I don't know," Mitzi said. "It's funny, but we never talk about politics anymore. Of course, Charles is obsessed with his work. I don't like to tax him with talk when he comes home. Mostly we just play with the baby." She looked at her friend and smiled. "You're right, Julie. Just listening to myself then, I realized what you were warning me about. I will make a real effort to become the 'vital, interesting, aware young woman' he married."

When Dane was six months old she became pregnant again. Charles was pleased but she was secretly disappointed. It was too sudden. She was just looking forward to a life beyond diapers and it was all going to start again. Still, if it made Charles happy . . .

Shana—Charles's choice again—was nothing like her brother. She cried constantly, angrily, and there seemed nothing Mitzi could do to calm her. The new baby also unsettled Dane and he quickly lost his sunny disposition. He always seemed to be looking for ways to upset her. Her days were endless periods of cleaning up after him, soiled clothes, broken things. Somehow, though, she always managed to restore order by the end of the day, and both she and the children were scrubbed and quiet and smiling when Charles finished his weary way home. It was as if there were a conspiracy, she and the children in a state of siege through the day and declaring a period of truce while the master was in the house.

"I never tell him how awful it seems," she said to Emily as they sat in the garden, Shana asleep in her cot and Dane crawling in the dirt and grabbing at plants. "He works so hard and his work is so important. I want him to see the children and me at our best, so I put on a happy face. But sometimes"—she paused and glanced at her mother-in-law—"sometimes I get so down. Yesterday I started screaming at Dane. He'd spat up his lunch and flung the bowl at the wall. I wanted to hit him."

"So?"

"With a chair?"

"Oh!"

"Emily, I do love the children but I get scared sometimes. I think what it was like without them and I start to feel that they've locked me in a prison. They are going to escape one day but there'll be no release for me. It's not right for a mother to feel that way."

"Oh, yes it is," Emily said, laughing. "Half, maybe three-quarters of bringing up babies is just sheer hell. You find yourself praying that the little monsters will fall asleep early. You're tired all the time and you fight a constant, losing battle to keep ahead. And there's no one to sympathize with you because the father, no matter how much of a partner he thinks he is, doesn't *really* take what you're doing seriously. Playing house all day sounds like fun to him. You know," she said with a smile, "when Charles was a baby he actually drove me to drink. I kept a bottle of vodka in the kitchen and when things got too bad, after I'd screamed, 'Shut up, you little bastard' for the tenth time, I'd take a drink to calm me down. Hell, I was sloshed for most of the first year of his life. Henry never noticed but, fortunately, my doctor figured out what was going on. He switched me to Valium. I'm not sure that was such a good idea, but I coped that way. So I know what you're going through. The thing is to *do* something about it." She thought for a moment. "What say I hire you a nurse?"

"Oh, no, Charles wouldn't hear of it," Mitzi said. "He won't take anything from you and Henry. But thanks for the offer. God, it would be great to be able to get away from them for a while."

"Why does Charles need to know?" Emily said. "Bring the children over to our house and I'll have the nurse there to take care of them. Two or three days a week, whatever you like. If Charles asks, say you're visiting me. He'd like that."

She used her secret time for all of them. The lakeside apartment would soon be too small. They needed a real house now. She went back to Jan Spelling, the agent who had handled the condominium purchase.

"I'll have no trouble selling your place," Jan told her. "Lakefront property is going out of sight. I can put it on the market for a hundred and get you ninety for sure on a quick sale. But the problem is, where do you move? Everything else has gone up, too."

The two women spent months looking together, rejecting house after house. In the end it was Mitzi, by herself, who found the perfect place. She had driven out to Oak Brook to check out a new town house development on the former Cooper estate. The town houses were disappointing, but as she was driving away she spotted it set back in an enclave of trees. It had been the gatehouse to the estate, a two-story Victorian place looking like a gingerbread cottage.

"It just might work," Jan told her after looking into the situation. "The developers don't know what to do with the cottage. They've already built all the units they're allowed under the zoning plan so the gatehouse and its land have to stay as they are. I think they'd be happy to take any reasonable offer."

She managed to get Charles to inspect the house with her on a Sunday morning. It hadn't been lived in for a couple of years and it was dirty and dank. He shook his head adamantly the moment they entered it.

"Try to see it the way it could be," she pleaded. "We'll open up the downstairs into one huge area. Bedrooms and another bathroom upstairs, a garden room out back—oh, Charles, we could turn this into a wonderful home."

"Mitzi," he said wearily, "I'm too busy to get involved in converting derelict cottages into homes. Later on, when I've made it, I'll buy you anything you want. But I can't stand any disruption right now."

"You won't have to do a thing," she begged. "I'll look after everything. I promise you this: When I've gotten everything ready, you can leave the apartment in the morning and drive home here that night. All you'll have to do is learn a new telephone number. Nothing else. I promise."

He held her to it. He took no interest in the gatehouse beyond signing the papers she put in front of him. The apartment was sold for ninety-seven thousand, the cottage bought for one hundred and twenty-five, the renovations completed for twenty-two thousand more. Their monthly payments would be what they had been for two years.

"I can't believe it," Charles said a few months later as he stood in the white-walled hallway, gazing around the newly opened living area. A fire glowed in the grate, gently reflecting the soft red of the exposed brick walls, throwing its light into the open kitchen and bouncing off the copper pots and quarry tiling. The children, already at home there from their many visits during the restorations, were safely stashed away in the upstairs playroom.

"It's ... it's amazing what you've done," he marveled, putting his arm around her. "I know I've been selfish, preoccupied, Mitzi," he said gently. "I didn't want to think about this move. I was scared you were getting us in over our heads, or that this place was beyond saving, but you've done it! You're wonderful!"

Later, the children asleep in their new bedrooms, she and Charles made love on the rug in front of the fire. Filled with love and sex and her achievement, she found it one of the happiest times of their marriage.

"I have to go to New York," Charles said a month later. "Patingay, the Brazilian, is giving a set of lectures for a handpicked group of us. Ten days of intensive talks, just ten of us from around the country. The hospital's very proud that I was invited."

"That's wonderful," she said. "I'm very proud for you, too. When is it?"

"A week from tomorrow," he said. "Maybe you should move in with my folks while I'm away."

"No, I'll be fine," Mitzi said. Indeed, Charles had been out of town often in the past year, to conferences and seminars and lectures around the country.

"But then you were safe in the apartment," he said. "Out here in the woods, I don't know. I'd feel safer if you and the children stayed with my parents."

"I know what to do," she said, grinning. "Why don't we send the kids to your parents' place and why don't I come to New York with you? Second honeymoon." Her small, alabaster face lit up at the prospect.

"That's out of the question," he said gruffly. "I'm not going on some social outing. It's going to be nothing but work all day. And at night we'll sit around talking over what we've all learned. You don't understand, Mitzi. These things are vital—a chance to learn from a man like Patingay! I can't afford to be worrying all the time about what you're doing."

"I think I could cope, Charles," she began, then stopped. "But if that's the way you feel . . ."

She didn't tell him how much she wanted to go, to be with him, to get away from the children and the routine, to be lovers again in a new place.

"You go to New York," she said. "We'll keep the home fires burning here. Don't worry about us."

After all, there was nothing else she *could* say.

Julie called her. It would have to be Julie, of course it would.

"So what's it like being married to a celebrity?" she crowed, the kids' howling in the background making her shout at Mitzi, who could hear perfectly well. Anyway, she was tired of Julie's hidden meanings, never really hidden, and the insinuations that always followed the mention of Charles's name.

"Julie, I'm up to my ears in things and I have to call about getting rid of the mice. What are you talking about?"

"Aaron Gold's column. That was a nice mention Charles got. Bound to be good for his career, right?"

"I haven't seen anything, Julie. Is that the *Trib*?" Mitzi sounded less impatient. It was nice of Julie to call, really.

"The *Trib*," she said, and they hung up after a few minutes.

The "Tower Talk" column was datelined New York, which it often was. This had Gold at a Broadway opening night, and two paragraphs were devoted to one Moira Johnson, who had a small part in the play, which had closed the night after opening.

But our own Moira, she of the tall, dark, beautiful presence, received excellent personal notices for her opening performance and then again at the opening-night party at Sardi's, where she entered on the arm of tall, dark, and handsome Charles Engers, Chicago's impor-

tant young plastic surgeon. If only Dr. Engers could have given the play a face-lift.

Just then Shana screamed. Dane had hit her on the head with a spoon. Mitzi smacked Dane hard on his bottom and he started screaming too. She put her hands over her ears and burst into tears, ran into the bathroom, and locked herself there until all three had cried themselves out.

He was very jaunty when he returned from New York.

"I hear I made the gossip columns," he said with a laugh as he watched her unpacking his suitcases. "My one night off from the lectures and I have to be dragged along to the worst play to open on Broadway in twenty years."

"I didn't know you knew that actress, Moira Johnson," Mitzi said casually.

"Oh, sure," Charles said. "Her brother and I were in college together. I even took her out a couple of times. Of course, she was just a kid then. She called me in New York and asked me to come to opening night. She knew the play was a bomb and I guess she wanted a little hometown support when the critics savaged it."

"How was the rest of your trip?" Mitzi asked, also casually.

"Wonderful," he said. "Patingay has some fascinating techniques. I got to talk with him a lot. You know, he's been pictured as a publicity hound, a man who wastes his skills in glossing the beautiful people, but he's a lot more than that. He made me see how a surgeon can have the best of both choices—the rewards that come with being the best, and the satisfaction of serving people who really need you. He says the fees he gets from his celebrity patients allow him to devote time to the poor and to difficult cases."

"But you've always worked for the poor, Charles." She sounded bewildered and he gave her a quick, hard glare. "I mean the impossible cases . . . the horrible scars and—that's your life."

"But it's not what I expected!" he shouted, as much surprised by his outburst as she was. He sat down, folded his large hands and, staring down at the rug, struggled after words.

"I spent so many years learning newer and newer ways of grafting, ways of avoiding scars and discolorations. It never occurred to me not, not to trust everything." He rushed on. "When the woman from the car explosion—Remember? She had an extra gallon of gas in the trunk of her car?—when I worked on her I had everything I needed, the right timing, the right fluid balance, the best people at the center. She came along better than I could have prayed for. That woman was everything I *ever wanted* to do with a burn case."

He stopped talking but didn't take his eyes off the floor. Suddenly he jumped up and strode to the dresser, yanking open the top drawer and peering inside.

"We let her go home a couple of months ago," he said in that practiced, deceptively controlled voice. "She looks like hell. And she knows she looks like hell. I need socks, by the way. Socks. Dark ones."

He left the room before she could speak.

After Charles's confession about the woman whose face he had failed to make perfect, his bitterness increased steadily until he actually seemed to turn on his work. What had once been almost a religion soon became a matter for jeering and cruel humor. It was as though Charles had to make a strenuous effort against his own sorrow, or drown in it.

Charles stayed on at the hospital and the clinic, but he traveled more and more. The work he was doing with burn victims was gaining national attention and he was in demand as a speaker. For Mitzi and the children his new fame meant only that they saw even less of him.

"I get so depressed," she told Emily one morning. "I find myself sinking into this one role of housekeeper and mother, someone who's there to soothe the weary lord and master. And we don't talk anymore, only about the children and domestic things. Charles used to be so passionately political but now he doesn't want even to *talk* about things like that.

"He's becoming very conservative—sneering at civil-rights activists, that kind of thing."

Charles's bitterness about his work frightened her. The man who had once glowed with dedication now seethed with fury over the miracles he couldn't accomplish. He had turned against his work so early in his practice, becoming more and more a part of the social scene, drinking too much, making scathing remarks about do-gooders in the profession.

Emily said, gently, "I think it's time we got you out of the house, officially out. How about going back to college and getting your degree? There's a day-care center at the university and you could spend ten or twelve hours a week in class."

"I don't know that Charles would like that," Mitzi said.

CASTLES

"To hell with Charles," Emily said. "You can't do anything about the changes in him. But you can make a life for yourself, Mitzi, and you'd better never mind what Charles thinks. Just go on and do it."

Chapter Five _____

THE CAMPUS MITZI RETURNED TO IN 1967 WAS VERY different from the one she had left five years earlier. There was rage and frustration among the students, much of it because the war in Asia was escalating with, it seemed, the total support of the nation's leaders. At first the students' passion scared Mitzi.

"I didn't realize how much five years could change everything," she told Charles. "I feel like a stranger among them."

"So you should," he said, settling back against the sofa. "You're a wife and mother now and college is just a hobby for you. All those freaks on campus have nothing to do with you, thank God. They've got all the privileges—including draft deferments—and all they want to do is spit in the eye of the society that gives them those privileges."

"You didn't used to think like that, Charles," she argued. "There was a time when you were as committed as any one of them. And you're still committed to your work."

"That was different," he said. "Then we were willing to accept the rules, work within them. These little anarchists—"

"No!" she protested. "Underneath they're still striving for the things we wanted!"

"They sure look different," Charles said, sneering. "For that matter, so do you. I've been wanting to raise this with you, Mitzi. I let you go back to college only because it seemed like it might help you over this discontent of yours. I don't know why you should be discontented," he added, covering bewilderment with anger. "You've got everything—a fine house, children. Anyway, I wish you'd start to dress your age. I'm sick of seeing you in jeans all the time. You're my wife, and I'd like you to dress and act it. OK?"

"I'm sorry, Charles," she sighed. "I guess I have been letting myself go lately. There just doesn't seem to be time for dressing up, what with the house and the children and school."

He'd been waiting for just that opening. "So give up school," he said. "Even if you do get a degree, you're not going to use it. You know I'm not going to have you working."

"Please, Charles," she said. "I'll try harder around the house, and I'll make sure I'm always in a dress when you get home. But don't make me quit college again. I'm learning a lot and it's going to make me a better person. Better for you and the children, I hope."

By the end of her second semester Mitzi was leading a double life. She had joined SDS and, while careful not to be at the forefront of the group's activities, worked hard for them, raising money and organizing. She found she fit in easily with the radicals, sharing their anger at what they saw as betrayal by the nation's leaders. If she couldn't join the marches and sit-ins, her SDS fellows understood. She could share a little grass with them but they understood that she wasn't sexually available. She could spend long afternoons rapping with them but she couldn't stay for the all-night sessions. They understood and accepted her easily, much more easily, she thought, than Charles did. Perhaps ever more important was that she felt more at home with them than she did with Charles.

The children didn't seem to miss her. They loved their father and looked forward to being with him in the evenings—when he wasn't out on the lecture circuit. Mitzi herself was so often tired or preoccupied when she was with Dane and Shana. Mitzi understood why they would prefer the company of their father. He didn't have to live with them, so he was seldom angry or impatient with them.

One afternoon when Dane was in kindergarten and Shana in nursery school in the same building, Mitzi picked the two children up, as usual, settling them in the back seat of the station wagon, strapping them securely into their seat belts, a task she'd learned to manage despite their wriggling. Dane, especially, was strong and never sat still. As she walked around the car to the driver's seat, she smiled at herself. Mitzi Christgau, only child, shy little girl with only her father for a playmate, was now a mother with two sturdy children who always knew exactly what they wanted—or didn't want. What would her father think of frowning, somber Dane? Of chattering, bossy Shana?

As she drove home to the sound of their loud, arguing voices, she began to wonder just how her children could be so little like her and so much like Charles. After all, they spent most of every day with her and saw their father only a little. Sometimes he didn't even get home before they were asleep. But Dane's manner, his certainty about nearly everything, mirrored his father's personality. And Shana was nearly as direct and as sure of herself as her brother was. Mitzi supposed it was good. Neither child hung back, as she always had, and neither seemed to have a moment's hesitancy. Still, she thought wistfully, it would be nice . . . well . . . nice to see *some*thing of herself in her own children, for heaven's sake.

Charles wouldn't admit it, but Mitzi knew that her campus life really suited him just fine. He felt free to travel and, when he was at home, to be out many evenings. They were seeing less and less of each other and there was an unspoken truce between them that they would not make many demands on one another.

"It's funny," she told Emily one sunny afternoon in the Oak Brook garden, "but the pressures on our time seem to have helped us. We're no closer, but when we are together we treat each other with more respect. I don't think that's the way a marriage is supposed to work, but it does for us."

"I can see that," Emily said. "With a man like Charles you've got two choices: total subservience or total independence. I just hope he doesn't suddenly change the rules and rein you in.

"You've really blossomed since you went back to college. You're more alert, and you look much better. You were beginning to look almost mousy, you know, in your home prison, and you seemed to be sleepwalking."

Mitzi knew her mother-in-law was right. It was

as though Mitzi had awakened after more than a year asleep.

Charles was to be in Los Angeles for ten days. His absence would coincide with the Democratic National Convention, for which all Chicago was gearing up and which was making her college friends hysterical already. Like her friends, Mitzi was gleefully looking forward to the Confrontation, as they called it. Among other things, it would be their strongest demonstration so far.

She saw him off at O'Hare, feeling a surge of guilt that she was so happy at his going. She hugged him.

"I do love you, Charles," she said. He kissed her again, picked up his bag, and moved through the departure gate.

"Won't it be nice at Grandma's house?" she exclaimed to the children as she drove away from the airport and turned toward Emily's house. Mitzi had explained to the children that she wanted to study for her finals and that this was a great chance while Daddy was away. Dane and Shana happily accepted the idea: Their grandmother spoiled them and they were looking forward to the visit.

She was thanking Emily for having the children when Emily took her hand.

"I don't know what you're planning for your little escapade, dear," Emily said, "but I'm sure you're planning one. Do be careful." And she winked at Mitzi, who should have protested her innocence, but didn't. Why bother? Emily knew her very well . . . and encouraged her.

SDS headquarters was a command post. Posters

were drying against the walls, and earnest young people were working the phones, soliciting money for the bail they knew they would need, lining up paramedics to cope with the injuries the more seasoned of them knew they would suffer. There were rosters showing where demonstrators should be and when, lists of crash pads, duty sheets for manning the kitchens that would serve the protesters who were arriving from around the country. Mitzi loved every minute of it. It seemed like a great game, of course, but it was more than fun. The whole world would be watching them here in Chicago and they were going to get their message across no matter what.

Mitzi was a marshal assigned to the northeastern sector of the park across from the convention hall. Her assistant was a boy from the University of Wisconsin. Gary Hoolihan was a skinny, intense, bespectacled, nice-looking nineteen-year-old. Mitzi was amused at the deference with which he treated her.

"I hope I won't let you down," Gary said shyly. "This is my first big protest. I guess you've been through dozens of them."

"Enough," Mitzi said loftily, glad he didn't know she was as green as he. "All we have to do is keep calm and stay within the law. No one's going to do anything to us. Not in front of network television, anyway. Keep those cameras on you and you'll be safe."

He might have been, too, if he had stuck with her, if only because on that first night her sector was left alone by the police. The violence was directed against those farthest from the television lights. She heard the screams and the running feet but didn't realize the extent of the battle until, sometime before midnight, Gary found her at her post. He was covered with blood and nearly naked, and his left arm hung loosely at his side. She gasped when she saw him.

"What happened?" she demanded.

He could hardly speak. His mouth was a bloody mess.

"They jumped us in the south end of the park," he choked. "Undercover cops. They just moved in among us, pulled out rubber hoses, and went to work on us. There're kids all over the place, bleeding on the grass. The wagons are there now, carting them off to jail. I split."

"Let's get you to a hospital," Mitzi said. "It looks bad."

"No," he said. "The others told me to keep away from the hospitals. They've all been staked out by the cops and they're arresting anyone who comes in injured."

She made up her mind quickly. "My car's a few blocks from here. I'll take you home and get you patched up."

Gary sank to the ground, against a tree, as Mitzi hurried off through the dwindling crowd. She slipped past the convention hall, where there were still a few delegates milling around, red-faced drunks in funny hats, tooting horns and waving streamers. One of them, a grotesquely fat man with a donkey's tail protruding from his pants, made a grab at her as she edged by.

"Hey, hippie!" he yelled. "Let's make love, not war. Come suck my tail."

"You fascist asshole," she shouted at him, surprising herself. She broke into a run and rounded three corners before she slowed down. The car was where she had left it and she drove slowly back to the park. Gary was also where she had left him but two men were standing over him, prodding him with billy clubs. She got out of the car and advanced on them. The two men turned as she came up to them.

"What have we got here? A live one," one of them said. "Pretty little thing for a hippie. Shame to bust up that nice face."

"Please," she said meekly, taking confidence from her age and innocent face, "this is my brother. We weren't part of that awful fighting. We just came over to see the convention. It was so exciting. I even got close to Walter Cronkite! And then suddenly a mob of people surrounded us and started pushing us along with them. Someone started beating Billy. I just want to get him home. *Please*," she whined.

They studied her for a few moments.

"OK, we'll help you put him in the car," the silent one said. "But learn something from this: Don't hang around trouble." She nodded enthusiastically.

The older of the two cops managed to grope Mitzi as she was struggling to place Gary in the car, but she ignored it. She just wanted to get away, to get home to safety. Anger would come later; now she needed a refuge.

Gary recovered a little once they were on their way. He managed to sit up in the passenger seat and, blinking without the glasses that had been lost in the assault, looked around as they sped down the road.

Thank God she'd sent the kids away, she thought. This wild-haired, bloody boy, clad in ripped jeans and nothing else, would have scared them to death.

She helped him into the house and steered him straight into the downstairs bathroom. He looked so scared and young and vulnerable sitting slumped on the toilet. She began to run a bath.

"Just get out of your pants and soak in the tub for a while," she said. "Then we'll be able to see what needs bandaging."

He looked at the door, embarrassed.

"I . . . I don't think I can get out of my pants," he said. "My arm . . ."

She laughed nervously.

"Stand up. I'll do it for you."

He struggled up and Mitzi managed to undo the thick leather belt. She pulled down his jeans and supported him as he raised one leg, then the other. His shorts—gray and holey—came off then and Gary was naked before her. He covered himself with his good hand and she assisted him into the steaming water, making a show of not looking at him. She left him there and went to the kitchen to make strong coffee and hot soup.

Well, she thought as she measured out the coffee, was she doing the wrong thing in not insisting on the hospital? His arm might be badly hurt, even broken. She decided to find out how badly he was hurt and to force him into the emergency room if there was much pain. If there wasn't, she would let him handle it himself, his way. After all, he was nineteen and not a child.

Plugging in the coffee pot and leaving the soup to simmer, she went to the linen closet and took three sheets, one to rip up for bandages, the others to make up the bed in the guest room.

She tapped on the bathroom door, looking in with trepidation.

"You look a lot better already," she said. He was

lying back in the water. The steam had dampened his long, ash-blond hair. Most of the blood was gone.

"I wasn't cut badly," Gary said. "It's mostly bruises. The arm doesn't hurt, but I can't use it."

"Well, drink this," she said, holding out a cup of soup to him. "Then the coffee and we'll get you upstairs and into bed for the night. You can decide about the arm in the morning."

He drank the liquids and then it was time for him to get out of the bath. They were both shy. She held out a big fluffy towel for him to cover himself with but it fell away as he rose dripping from the water. He blushed scarlet as she saw his erection.

Mitzi was flustered but determined not to let it show. Wasn't she the veteran demonstrator? The experienced woman activist?

She took his good arm and led him up the narrow stairs to the tiny bedroom. He stood beside the bed, the towel around his waist.

"We'll just get you dry," she said, "then put some ointment on those cuts." He was still blushing. "Just relax," Mitzi said. "You can't cope on your own. I'm going to have to do it for you."

Really, it was just like drying off one of the kids. She gently patted him dry as he stood before her. He was still aroused but they both pretended to ignore it.

"Now lie down on the bed," she said. "I'll smooth some ointment into those cuts."

None of the wounds looked like it would need stitches. There was a long cut across his left shoulder, but it was already closing. A couple of scratch marks around his ribs oozed blood and she taped a length of sheet there.

"There's nothing I can do for your arm," Mitzi said. "Maybe we should put a pillow under it to keep it straight."

She made him as comfortable as possible, then gently covered him with a light blanket. He was silent until she turned to go. Then he spoke huskily, his brown eyes appealing. "Please, would you stay with me?"

She knew she should go to the safety of her own room, to the bed she shared with Charles. But Gary looked so afraid, so lost lying there. There could be no harm in staying.

She snapped off the light and quickly slipped off her shirt and jeans and slid into the bed beside him. They lay there in silence until she felt him trembling beside her.

"You may have a slight concussion," Mitzi said. She reached out and touched his forehead. "I think you're running a temperature."

He touched her face with his good hand.

"You've been so wonderful to me," he whispered, moving her hand down his skinny young body. It felt like electricity running through her when she touched him there. He groaned and she knew it was not from pain. She wanted him so much, but everything was holding her back—being here in this house, especially.

"Please," he whispered.

"I can't," she whispered back.

He was moving against her, thrusting against the hand which rested lightly on him.

She raised herself on her elbow and put her lips next to his.

"Just lie back and relax," she said. She began to work her hand on him, stroking gently but firmly.

He was so tense, straining. He moved with her, faster and faster, until, with a cry, he fell back. Slowly she moved her hand away.

"You'll be all right now," she said. A shaft of moonlight was spilling across the bed. His eyes were closed and his damp hair spilled down his forehead and she saw that he looked nothing like Charles, who had never looked vulnerable. A little later, when she slipped out of the bed, Gary did not stir.

Mitzi moved silently back to her own bedroom and lay there for hours. There was a yearning inside her, but satisfaction, too. She hadn't let Charles down. She hadn't given in. And yet she had done something she wanted to do.

She made herself act brisk and businesslike in the morning, fixing juice and coffee and scrambling the eggs so that Gary would be able to eat them one-handed. He came into the kitchen shyly, wrapped in a blanket, not meeting her eyes.

"Here," she said, handing him a red-checked shirt. "You'll need this. It's an old one of my husband's," she added without emphasis.

He mumbled his thanks and struggled with the shirt while she turned away from him.

"About last night," he said, "I'm sorry."

"Let's not talk about it, Gary," Mitzi said softly. "How's your arm?"

"A bit swollen," he said as he sat down at the table. "And it hurts some."

"Finish breakfast and I'll drive you over to the hospital."

She dropped him outside the emergency room.

"I don't know if I'll see you at the demonstration," he said. "With an arm in a sling I'd be too much of a target. I think I've been sidelined."

"You're very wise," she smiled at him. "Do you want me to wait for you and drive you back to the city?"

"No, no," he said. "I'm sure you've got other things you have to be doing. I'll make it back okay on my own."

"Have you any money?"

"Some," he said. "A couple of bucks somewhere. But I'll be able to hitch a ride."

She reached in her purse and found two twenty-dollar bills. "Take them," she said. "No one's giving rides to hippies, not in Chicago."

He took the money and began to thank her but she waved and drove away.

Headquarters that day was a field dressing station. The youngsters wore their bandages proudly. The phones rang continually with casualty reports and arrest statistics. There was a mood of ecstatic high adventure. Mitzi was immediately caught up in the elation. She felt as if she really belonged. Here were the good guys; the forces of evil were massing outside for another confrontation.

The big names were all there. Abbie Hoffman smiled at her. Jerry Rubin bummed a cigarette from her. She told anyone who would listen about rescuing her deputy marshal from the police. She didn't mention taking him home.

They passed the day quickly that way, swapping experiences and girding themselves for the night. It was six o'clock before she remembered to call Emily and ask about the children.

She was assigned the same park territory for the evening and, at first, it was quiet. It was only after dark, when the delegates were safely inside the hall, that she felt true menace in the air. At first it was just shadows flitting among the trees and over the grass, figures sensed on the periphery of their crowd.

The demonstrators huddled together. There was music, and pot, and jugs of wine were passed around. It might have been a party except for the sense that something terrible was about to happen to them.

She had just glanced at her watch when they came. It was ten o'clock. There were twenty of them, outnumbered easily by her group of fifty, but the smaller group came with such force and suddenness and with such intense brutality that the protesters had no chance.

"The pigs! The pigs!" She heard the shouts and then a sound she would never, ever forget, the deadly cracking of billy clubs against human bones. The marauders had her group encircled and were advancing to its center, beating indiscriminately as they went. Two boys and a girl just feet away from her went down, one of the boys screaming as blood spurted from a wide, deep wound over his eye. As they fell they were kicked savagely, the girl no less than the boys.

It was time to run and Mitzi began to step back, looking for a way out. Two policemen blocked her way. The taller of them raised his club and swung at her. She was lucky. The other man kicked her at the same time and she began to fall, so the club struck her only a glancing blow on the shoulder.

She lay there terrified, her face pressed in the bare earth, waiting for it to end, for the raiders to go away and leave them in peace. Instead she heard motors approaching, and suddenly headlights glared over their section of the park.

Rough hands grabbed her and she was dragged to a waiting wagon and flung inside with the others onto the hard steel floor. They were being jammed on top of each other into wagons. There was blood everywhere. People were crying or moaning as the wagons lurched off into the night.

It was dawn before they were bailed out. The cells hadn't been too bad except for those who were seriously injured, and through the night they had kept their spirits up by singing protest songs and loudly cheering the arrival of more of their fellows. But by the time she was released from the cell Mitzi was near the breaking point. As she stepped into the daylight, she knew she looked awful. Her shirt was ripped open and she could not hold it together because her shoulder ached so badly. At least she was wearing a bra.

Jerry Rubin was being bailed at the same time. "I'll help you out of here," he said. "Someone sent a car for me. I can drop you somewhere."

Rubin had his arm around her, supporting her, as they moved down the steps of the city jail. The morning light was so bright, she thought. Then she realized the blinding flashes were coming from press photographers, and she knew she was in deep trouble.

The *Sun Times* identified only Rubin in its caption, but the *Trib* had done its homework:

Yippie leader Jerry Rubin helps Mitzi Engers, wife of Chicago's prominent surgeon, Dr. Charles Engers, away from city jail after both were bailed following riots at Democratic convention.

* * *

It would have been better if he had yelled at her. Instead Charles was icily calm, almost patronizing, the way he sometimes was when he spoke to the children.

"You have caused me and my family the gravest embarrassment," he said. "I don't want to know what you were doing with those creeps because I don't want to hear about it. I could put up with your stupidity, your letting yourself be used, if only you had been discreet. I got nine calls in Los Angeles from colleagues, *respected colleagues*, suggesting I fly home to rescue my addlebrained wife. I could stand their pity, but the worst part was that I knew they were laughing at me.

"I tell you, Mitzi, if it were just you and me I would have stayed in Los Angeles. But there are the children. You've let us all down. I'm disgusted with you."

She knew better than to try to tell her side of it. And what *was* her side, anyway? It had once been Charles's side. Now there was no way of telling him that.

He seemed to get over it, gradually, but for a long time Mitzi felt as if she were on some kind of probation. She sensed that Charles was cooking up something and, sure enough, two months after the convention, she learned what it was.

"We're moving to Los Angeles," he announced. "When I was out there last I was offered a share in a thriving practice in Beverly Hills. It's where the money is. It's going to be a whole new life for us."

She was stunned.

"But . . . but what about me? And the children? It will mean leaving everything, everyone we know, your parents ... taking the kids out of school. Me dropping out of college—again."

"That's one more reason to go," he said blandly. "To get you away from the influence of those damn radicals. I've been very patient with you, Mitzi. I haven't been at all happy with the way you've been carrying on. It's setting a terrible example for Shana and Dane, and irrational behavior is certainly not what I expect from my wife. No," he said with a smile, "I think a fresh start is what we all need."

Why, for heaven's sake, didn't she say no? What paralyzed her? Was she forever going to be mousy Mitzi, doing as she was told? Sure, she still felt guilty about the notoriety she had exposed herself to, but Charles was talking about moving them all across the country, and he didn't seem at all concerned with whether she wanted to go. He *wasn't* concerned—that was the truth.

She astonished herself as, day after day, she failed to say no. She failed to say anything at all. Wasn't it, she accused herself furiously, simply easier to go along than to be something other than what Charles expected? She could hardly say, "I'm different, now, Charles." Worse, she wasn't at all sure it was true.

The only thing she did insist on was that they keep the house. They would rent it out, but they would not sell it.

"I want it always to be there for us, to retreat to if anything goes wrong," she told Emily.

Charles went along with that. With prices still soaring and money plentiful he arranged a second mortgage so they could manage the down payment on a new house in Los Angeles. His share of the practice was to be earned, no money down. That was how anxious his new partners were to employ the skills of the most promising young plastic surgeon in the nation.

"It's just as Patingay said," Charles told Mitzi. "I can use my talents to make money and attract supporters. A couple of hours a day at the burn clinic and the rest of the time patching up faded stars. We get the best of both worlds."

Another puzzlement to Mitzi was the children: Neither seemed hers anymore. If they were anyone's, they were Charles's. There was a steady communication between Dane and his father, a natural grace between them that was honestly never forced. Dane appeared to have none of the resentments Mitzi had supposed all boys had with their fathers. She guessed she was glad, but she wondered why. More than that—much more than that—she was shocked by the way the boy treated her. He caused little trouble, but he didn't seem comfortable with her, not unless she was catering to him. It was as though Dane considered her a guest in his house.

How had this happened? And when had it begun? she asked herself more than a few times. When had her first baby become a usually polite stranger?

If that puzzled her, then Shana's frankly distant attitude hurt her deeply. By the age of five, Shana had divorced herself from her mother entirely, suffering her along on trips to buy the child's clothing and tolerating her in the house, but only just. Neither child seemed to *feel* anything for their mother. Mitzi tried being as brutally honest with herself as she could be, but she couldn't understand it. If they'd all been strangers, people who met once every ten years at family reunions . . . but they *lived* together.

"I know it seems outrageous," Emily said sympathetically. "And nobody ever talks about it, but some children belong to one parent and have nothing in common with the other. It's not your fault," she hastened to say. "It's the way it is sometimes. Charles paid not the slightest attention to me until puberty, when he and his father clashed. Then he turned to me, but I often think it was only because he had to choose one of only two. It never made me feel close to Charles to know that he began loving me—if that's what it was—only when his father started criticizing him so much.

"No, it's not your fault, dear. It has nothing to do with you, really."

"But," Mitzi cried, "that makes me feel even worse!" And she cried as they drove away from their home, but neither Charles nor the children noticed.

Chapter Six _____

THE APARTMENT WAS HIGH IN THE HOLLYWOOD hills, in a building that was fancier than its neighborhood. It was comfortable, anonymous, and efficient, and it suited Moira Johnson fine. Moira got an acting job perhaps twice a year. She would be the fourth or fifth lead in a film, the second or third in a made-for-TV movie, occasionally the lead in a Los Angeles production of a Broadway play. Between those times, Moira had dates.

Charles Engers was her date tonight, and Moira had made her usual careful preparations. There was a bottle of Chivas on the red leather bar and two grams of cocaine beside it in a little glass ashtray that said, "Souvenir of Venice, Cal."

Moira checked her appearance in the mirrored wall of the living room. Her dark brown hair was piled up high and she wore only a touch of lipstick. The blue silk dress was tight, but not too tight, across her handsome breasts and flared from the hips to show off her long, slim legs when she moved. Moira was thirty-two but still passing, easily, for twenty-seven.

Moira went along with things. That was her special grace. She earned enough from acting to live comfortably and she had never taken a cent in alimony from her ex-husband, a playwright. Anything major she needed—a film role or a fur coat—was provided by one or another of her friends. She was, for example, going to need a fanny tuck one of these years and she knew Charles would be pleased to do the operation for her.

The arrangements worked very well for all concerned. Moira liked company, and her friends liked to have her there to visit. Sometimes she thought they came as much to relax as for the sex. She was funny, outrageous, and unafraid in a town where all those qualities were sadly lacking. But she didn't bother examining her friends' motives.

The door chimes rang out the first bars of "Moon over Miami" and she grinned. This place was so tacky that it was almost in style again. She crossed the white shag carpet and opened the door.

"Am I late?" Charles asked, coming in and kissing her on the cheek. "That awful Bender woman has been sitting in my office debating nose styles for the past hour. I don't know why she bothers. She's still going to look like a pig."

She took his raincoat.

"You're on time, Charles," she said. "We're not going out anyway."

"That's good," he said, flopping onto the white suede couch. "I was afraid you might have had a party in mind. I'm really bushed tonight. Thanks," he said, taking the drink.

"How late can you stay?" she asked. "I mean, have we got time for talk, or do you want to head straight for the sack?"

He grinned. "Straight for the sack, please. But there's no big rush to get home tonight. My mother's here to dodge the Chicago winter, so Mitzi has company."

She took his hand and led him into the bedroom, briskly helping him out of his clothes. She pushed him down on the circular bed, then took more time getting out of her own clothes, knowing that Charles, like most of her visitors, enjoyed watching her strip. She had dressed for that, of course. She carefully removed the blue dress to reveal herself in a white lacy bra and matching panties, white garter belt, and pale stockings. She took off everything but the garter belt and stockings and lay down beside Charles.

He moved to kiss her but she shook her head.

"You just lie back and let me do all the work, darling," she murmured and began to run her hands over his body. He was hard already and she wasted little time. She slid down the bed and placed her lips on his belly, leaving the faintest impression of her lipstick there. He was pushing up against her now and she teased him for an instant, moving her lips swiftly over his thighs and working downward from there. When she could feel the frustration mounting she quickly took him in her mouth and began to work up and down, swirling him around in her mouth, her tongue performing a separate massage of its own. He came very quickly, shuddered, and fell back against the pillows.

"There now, that's better," she whispered as she drew herself up alongside him. His eyes were shut and he was breathing heavily. She let her hands wander over his arms and through the dark hairs on his chest. She gently tweaked his nipples and he opened his eyes.

"I'll get your robe and we'll go sit outside and drink and do a little coke," she said. He nodded and smiled and watched as, gloriously naked, she crossed to the walk-in closet, tossed him a toweling robe, and wrapped herself in a sheer white gown.

In the living room she took the cocaine and bent over a glass-topped coffee table, dividing the powder into neat white lines. He made a Scotch with ice and sat by the table.

"You first," she said and handed him a slim silver straw. He closed one nostril with his finger and snorted up a line through the other, then snorted through the other nostril, his thick brown hair falling over his forehead.

"What are you laughing at?" he said when he glanced up at her.

"I was just thinking how much business the coke habit brings to you plastic surgeons," Moira said. "All those nose reconstructions. I'd have thought it would have scared you away from the stuff."

"I don't do much," he protested, frowning. "Only here, and parties every once in a while. Never at home. Mitzi would flip out if she knew."

Moira was down on her knees sniffing up two lines. She finished and looked at him across the table.

"You're a funny guy, Charles," she said. "You talk so much about Mitzi and you seem to defer to her on a lot of things. I think you two must be in love."

Charles could feel the hit relaxing him, distancing him.

"I am," he said gravely. "I love her very much. But I sure as hell don't understand what's going on with her. She seems so . . . so restless. She keeps talking about taking a job."

"Well, why shouldn't she?"

"It wouldn't look right," he said. "She's my wife and her job is to take care of me, the children, and the house. I want her there when I come home at night."

"*When* you come home at night," she laughed. "Half the time you work into the evenings, or you're at some party, or you're over here with me. And she's supposed to just sit around home waiting for you?"

"Yes, she is," he said emphatically. "That's what marriage is. The husband provides shelter, and the wife looks after it."

"Jesus, Charles, you're prehistoric," Moira said. "Women don't have to be housebound anymore—and they don't have to be one-man women, either. Look at *you*. You play around a lot. And not just with me, either."

"This doesn't mean anything," he said.

"Well, gee, thanks a lot," she said with a laugh.

"No, I mean it's different for a man," he said. The coke had hold of him now and suddenly he found it easier to talk.

"Look, I love my wife but sometimes it seems like I've been married forever," he said. "I look around me and I see glorious women everywhere and I start to wonder if I'm still attractive to them. Youngsters have so much freedom. I'm envious."

"I understand that," she said. "Most of the guys I know are moping around, regretting the choices they made, or not being married at all. But where does that leave Mitzi? What about *her* doubts, *her* regrets—*her* boredom?"

"That's different," he protested. "You have to give up *something* if you expect to be taken care of. Women have it so easy. They don't realize that—"

"That it's a jungle out there?" She was laughing at him. "Charles, guys like you really infuriate me. Here you are, drinking and doping and fucking around, and you expect your wife to be happy with the very life you can't stand?"

"Could I have another drink, please?" he said. "I didn't intend to get into a feminist debate tonight."

"This isn't about feminism. It's about people expecting of others what they won't do themselves," she said over her shoulder as she moved to the bar. "You've got to treat people the way you expect to be treated. If you're bored, how bored do you think your wife is? You should encourage her to get a job."

He shrugged. "There's nothing she could do, anyway. Nothing she's trained for, that is. Even if I'd let her."

"And whose fault is that?" Moira demanded. "You're the one who told her to forget about finishing college, you're the one who stuck her in the rose-covered cottage and got her pregnant as fast as possible. Jesus! Men! I bet you're not even a good lover to her anymore."

Charles was stunned.

"We have a wonderful sex life, if it's any business of yours," he snapped.

"Oh?" she laughed. "Then what are you doing over here every week? And you drink too much, Charlie. That's got to be screwing up your love life."

He considered storming out but decided on another couple of lines of coke.

"You're being very unfair, Moira," he said. "You don't understand the situation."

"Sure, Charlie," she smiled. "It's none of my business. And I'm sure your wife is going to learn to take care of herself. Come on," she said, standing, "back to the bedroom for round two. You're such a great lover, you can do the work this time."

Emily Engers smiled at her daughter-in-law and patted the couch beside her.

"Come sit here, Mitzi," she said. "I know you're surprised to hear me say it, but I do understand."

"So little seems to happen," Mitzi said. "The children grow up a little every month. Charles gets busier. Me . . . sometimes I don't see myself at all, just them."

"I understand what you're saying," Emily said with a nod. "It's awfully hard being married to successful men. I'm sure I wouldn't want to be poor, but . . . I know I got damned tired of always being the gracious wife and homemaker for Henry. If I ever complained about how meaningless my life seemed, he'd just point out all the comforts he provided for me. He never understood. He never tried to."

Mitzi was surprised. She looked at the gentle, white-haired woman and realized that she didn't really know very much about her life. They had been good friends ever since she and Charles had married, but when his father died, Emily took to traveling. Now Emily saw her son and Mitzi only once a year.

"I always thought you and Henry were happy," Mitzi said now. "You seemed to be such good friends, apart from being husband and wife."

"As marriages go, I guess it was about as much as you could expect," Emily said. "But then, that's not very much, is it? The big problem is that men are so damned self-important. Give them a little bit of success and they're unbearable. Their wives are expected to be undemanding, dutiful, and . . . grateful."

"But you seemed to have everything," Mitzi protested.

"Oh?" Emily said, looking at her closely. "*You* seem to have everything. I can see how happy it's making you, too.

"Why don't you get a job?" Emily asked, not for the first time.

"Charles won't hear of it," Mitzi said with a laugh.

"He's his father's son," Emily said. "I went through the same thing with Henry, and in the end I just gave up the battle. By the time I realized what a terrible mistake I'd made, it was too late. That was when Henry told me he wanted a divorce."

"Emily," Mitzi said with shock, "what do you mean, a divorce?"

"Henry decided he was in love with a woman doctor. He told me all about it, expecting me to sympathize. According to Henry, he and the doctor had so much in common. The implication was that I was too dull, too housebound, and had no work in common with Henry. He was right: I didn't."

"What did you do?"

"I just hung in and tried to keep things together. It turned out the doctor wasn't the first. There's been a string of women, almost all of them businesswomen, *professionals*. The affairs each lasted a few weeks or a few months, and then the good Dr. Engers would decide it was time to devote himself to his wife and family again. He told me all about them, very tearful and contrite, to try to convince me that this time he was really in love and that I should let him go. Before we ever resolved it he got sick, as you know. He was dead within six months. I like to think he appreciated the care I took of him but I don't think he did. Sometimes I'd see him staring off into space and I just knew he was thinking about her and what might have been. Thirty-eight years of marriage to end like that—Henry wishing he was with someone else, me wishing I'd never allowed myself to be trampled down like I had. Both of us giving in to something we didn't want to give in to."

"I'm so sorry," Mitzi said. "I never realized. I always thought you were just about the perfect couple. So did Charles. He holds you two up to me as an example. Says you never complained about being 'just a wife and mother.' It's how he ends all our arguments about my getting a job."

"As I said, he's his father's son," Emily said with a smile. "I tried not to spoil him as a child but I see so many of Henry's traits in him. It's not that either of them are, or were, bad people," she added. "It's just that they are rather selfish, quite short-sighted—and damned immature. I certainly didn't know how to handle Henry until it was too late for me. I don't want the same thing to happen to you," she said earnestly.

"What would you suggest I do?" Mitzi asked. "I've built my whole life around our marriage, and whenever I think of other things I feel so helpless."

"Well, you could have an affair," Emily said, smiling as she saw the shock register on Mitzi's face. "How *is* your love life, by the way?"

Mitzi was flustered. "Gee, I don't know. Compared to what? Charles is the only experience I've had in the past ten years. We . . . do it . . . once a week most times and it's OK, I suppose. It's just not very important anymore. I mean, you don't stay newlyweds forever, do you?"

"No, more's the pity," Emily said. "That's one of the biggest problems of marriage. One or both of you stop trying as hard." She smiled again. "Maybe an affair's not the answer for you. It'll have to be a job—something to get you out of the house and give you a sense of yourself as a whole person, rather than just an appendage of Charles. You've got to do it, Mitzi."

"He won't hear of it," she repeated miserably. "And even if I ignore him, what could I do? I'm not trained for anything except running a house. And I'm even redundant at that now, with Mrs. Truman taking care of everything."

Emily was pacing. "Why don't you try real estate?" she asked. "It's ideal for women. Equal pay, equal opportunity, and women even have an advantage. They have a better feel for houses, for what makes one place desirable to a particular buyer. Our last two houses were handled by women realtors. And you know housing, Mitzi. What about the great deal you made on the Oak Brook place? You have a talent for it."

"That was different," she protested. "In that case I was looking for a place for *us*. It doesn't mean I can sell to strangers."

"Nonsense. You're living in the hottest real-estate market in the world. You're bright. And you're bored," Emily said. "It's just the thing for you." She moved to the telephone table and picked up the Yellow Pages. "Here we are. 'Real-estate Schools.' Dozens of 'em. We'll enroll you in one of these, get you your license, and you're on your way.

I'll stay here for a couple of months so I can oversee the housekeeper, or whatever else you do all day, while you go to classes."

"But what about Charles?"

"What Charles doesn't know won't hurt him," Emily said with a chuckle. "Come sit here and we'll pick out a school now so you can register tomorrow."

They were still going through the listings when Charles returned home soon after eleven o'clock. He kissed them both and went to the living-room bar to fix himself a drink.

"What's with the Yellow Pages?" he asked idly as he put ice in an old-fashioned glass. "Still looking for new draperies?"

"Something like that," Emily muttered before Mitzi could say anything. He took a long pull at his drink before sitting down across from them.

"It's really great to have you here, Mother," he said. "I know Mitzi loves it, too. You two get along so well together."

"Yes, don't we?" Emily said. "But then, we're both women, Charles, so we have a lot in common. And of course we both think *you're* nothing short of *wonderful*."

Charles scowled. "I've had a rotten day."

Mitzi jumped up and moved to his side. "Poor Charles," she said. "You work so hard. What was it tonight?"

"That damned convention," he said, sighing. "I don't know why I ever let myself be drafted onto the hospitality committee. No one can agree on anything. Disneyland or a Dodgers game, a studio tour or a golf day? It's like trying to get a bunch of children or women to agree on something." He stretched and stood up, draining his glass. "I'm going to call it a night. You two sit and talk. Don't let me break it up."

Mitzi followed him. "No," she said, "I'll come to bed too. I know Emily must be tired."

Mitzi was feeling guilty, disloyal, and sorry for Charles. Charles could be annoying and unthinking, but he did work so hard for them all and he was a kind and decent man who loved her.

She undressed quickly in her bathroom, brushed her teeth, and dabbed on a light perfume. They would make love tonight and everything would be all right. She moved swiftly back to the bedroom, naked, and saw that Charles was already in bed. She slid in beside him and kissed him on his bare shoulder. She placed her hand on his hip and moved it gently over him.

"Not now, Mitzi," he said roughly, shoving her hand away and turning his back. "I'm really bushed." He appeared to fall asleep immediately.

Mitzi picked up a book and tried to read. But the words swam before her.

The next morning she was accepted by the West Hollywood School of Realty.

Chapter Seven _____

THE WEST HOLLYWOOD SCHOOL OF REALTY WAS conducted in Mrs. Iris Scanlon's living room. The house itself would have provided a challenge for the most brilliant of Mrs. Scanlon's graduates. It was grimy mock-Spanish, sitting in a row of similar houses all twenty feet apart in a treeless street of no character whatsoever. An empty, cracked birdbath decorated the bare backyard, a toppled iron flamingo the front yard. Mrs. Scanlon had the same beaten look about her.

There were nine other students in the room the afternoon Mitzi arrived. The air conditioner was broken, the room smelled of stale cabbage, and the folding chairs were small and wobbly.

But from the first, Mitzi loved it.

"This course," Mrs. Scanlon explained to the class, "will require sixteen hours and will result in your receiving your California real-estate license. That I guarantee. I have never had a student fail the test.

"During the course, I will teach you all I know, and all you will need to know, about getting that license. I will also teach, for those of you who care to take it in, some of the principles of selling. In this market, you don't really need to know much of anything, but you've all paid your two hundred and fifty dollars so you might as well listen."

Mitzi looked around the room. Seven of her fellow students were women, most of them older than Mitzi. There were two men in their early twenties. Everyone had a beaten, desperate look, as if this course in this depressing little house was their last chance. Did she appear that way to other people?

"The main thing you must always do," Mrs. Scanlon was saying, "is match up your house and your buyer. There's no point in showing a ninety-thousand-dollar place to someone on a sixteen-thousand income. They won't get financing and you'll have wasted your time. So before you take anyone to a home, check them out carefully. Know what they can afford and don't show them anything more than 20 percent above that price."

The woman in the next row, two seats away from Mitzi, was Mitzi's age, maybe a year or two younger. She was wearing a ridiculously colorful muumuu. She was a big-boned woman, vibrant-looking with a mass of dark hair, deeply tanned skin and, when she glanced around, large sparkling brown eyes. She winked at Mitzi and Mitzi smiled back.

"The next thing you must do, and this is still before you let any prospect near a house you're selling," Mrs. Scanlon was saying, "is learn what it is the prospect is looking for in a house. Then you adjust your properties to suit that image. If, for example, the client has three children and the house has only two bedrooms, you are going to have to create the illusion of that other room. If there's a basement, you're home free, or a garage that will turn into a guest suite, or a family room that becomes a convertible bedroom. It's easier the other way around, with a big house for a small family. All those unneeded bedrooms you describe as the study and the sewing room and the breakfast room. Never say there are three extra bedrooms!

"But whatever the house you're selling, remember it's not four walls and a roof. It's a concept," she said.

One of the young men raised his hand.

"When," he asked, "do we get to study the test forms?"

Mrs. Scanlon looked annoyed.

"You'll have plenty of time for that," she said. "It's as easy as a driver's test. What I'm trying to pass on to you now is the philosophy of selling real estate."

The young man shrugged and settled back into his chair, took out a pocket calculator, and appeared to take no further interest in the class.

Mrs. Scanlon continued on for another hour and the room got more oppressively hot until even Mitzi was finding it hard to concentrate. She was relieved when Mrs. Scanlon announced the end of class, but Mitzi knew she would be eager again the next day.

Mitzi remained standing on the baking sidewalk for a moment, trying to decide what to do. She could go home, but it was still quite early in the afternoon and she wasn't really needed at home. And she wanted to spin out the experience of doing something on her own before it was swallowed up by home and family, and swallowed up it would be.

"I don't suppose you could give me a lift. I'm never going to get a cab."

Mitzi turned and saw the young woman she had smiled at.

"I'd be happy to," she said, glad of the company. "My name's Mitzi Engers."

"I'm Meredith Jackman," the woman said with a smile. She was six feet tall, vivacious, out of place on this depressing street.

Mitzi's red Pinto was like a furnace and they hastily wound down all the windows before starting down to Beverly Hills.

"What did you think of the class?" Mitzi asked.

"It's as good a way as any to get a license," Meredith said in her low, husky voice. "Mrs. Scanlon makes it sound just like selling used cars. What do I know? Maybe it is. Still," she said thoughtfully, "if the lady knew what she was talking about, wouldn't she be out selling instead of teaching a desperate bunch like us?"

Mitzi laughed. "I guess she wasn't terribly inspiring, but I loved it. Where can I let you off? I'm going to Beverly Hills."

"Anywhere there that I can pick up a cab," she said.

"Look, I feel like a drink to celebrate," Mitzi said impulsively. She already liked Meredith. "Will you join me?"

"That'd be nice," Meredith said. "You pick the place. I don't get around very much."

Meredith gave Mitzi a sidelong glance when she turned the Pinto into the drive of the Beverly Hills Hotel. Meredith was silent as a smiling valet took the car and drove it off to park with the Rollses and Mercedes and Cadillacs. She said nothing as she followed Mitzi through the glittering lobby to the entrance of the Polo Lounge. Then she spoke.

"Mitzi? Are you sure . . . ?"

"Ah, Mrs. Engers," the maître d' said with a smile. "How many? Two. This way, please." And he led them to a table in an alcove where they could see everyone coming and going.

A waiter appeared immediately. They both ordered a Tom Collins.

"What's the game?" Meredith hissed when he had gone. "What are you doing enrolling in a rinky-dink place like Madame Scanlon's when you're Queen of the Polo Lounge?"

Mitzi blushed. "No one knows *me*," she said. "It's my husband. He's a plastic surgeon, so he has to socialize a lot and sometimes I get dragged along. It's got nothing to do with me."

"If he's a plastic surgeon in *this* town," Meredith said, the brown eyes bright, "that means you're rich. So again, why the Scanlon School of Schlock?"

"Charles doesn't want me to work," she confessed. "So I figured I'd get my license through the most obscure place I could find, with no chance that one of his friends would see me and tell him what I'm doing. Why did you choose the school?"

Meredith was laughing now. "This is rich!" she said. "I chose it because it's the cheapest course in town. Here we are, you hiding from a wealthy husband and me having to support my husband."

Meredith explained. She had been a librarian in Minneapolis. Her husband, Frank, was a newspaper reporter. Frank wanted to be a screenwriter and they had come to Los Angeles the year before.

"He's got a very iffy job in Paramount's publicity department," Meredith said. "We have this little apartment in Century City and it's a hell of a struggle to get by each week. We both want to have babies as soon as possible—I'm thirty—but we

83

can't afford it until Frank gets his break. There's no demand for librarians out here, so I thought I'd try real estate. I mean, it's the only thing anybody is talking about. But"—and she was serious now— "just as soon as Frank makes it I'm settling down to be a wife and mother. That's everything I want from life."

Now it was Mitzi's turn to laugh. "I need a job to get me *out* of the house," she said. "I've been wife and mother for ten years now and I feel as if I don't exist at all. I have everything you want but no sense of who I am."

"I don't see why taking a job should be a problem," Meredith said. "Why should your husband object? Frank wouldn't care."

They ordered two more drinks.

"This is fun," Meredith said, beginning to like Mitzi very much.

Mitzi happened to glance over to the entrance just then. There was a pleasant shock of recognition. The tall man coming in was Charles. She rose and waved happily. He caught the movement and stared straight at her but instead of coming over to their table followed the maître d' to a banquette at the far side of the room. The slim brunette with him was beautiful in a tailored white linen suit. She looked vaguely familiar. Charles saw her seated comfortably, said something to her, then started toward Mitzi.

"Here's my husband," Mitzi said. "What a lovely coincidence. I did want you to meet him."

Charles was standing over them and she stood up to kiss him but he did not bend his head and she ended up holding his arm.

"Meredith Jackman," she said, "I'd like you to meet my husband, Charles."

He nodded briefly at Meredith, then turned to Mitzi.

"What are you doing here?" he asked, his voice low. "I expected you to be home with the children."

"Well, with your mother here . . ." she began, but Charles really wasn't waiting for an answer.

"You should be there when they get out of school," he said. "I've got business to attend to. I'll talk to you when I get home." He turned and walked away.

"I'm sorry, Meredith," she said, confused by Charles's brusqueness. "He's not usually rude like that. I guess he got a surprise seeing me here."

"I guess he did," she replied. "Wow! That's a very handsome man, your husband. And the woman with him doesn't look like she needs a face-lift. I've seen her in the papers—one of L.A.'s bright young socialites."

"Oh, he has to deal with all kinds of people," Mitzi said. "He's always complaining that he has to spend more time socializing than actually performing surgery." She looked across the room. "She is pretty, isn't she? That's the way I always wish I could look—so cool and elegant, like she belongs in places like this. Me, I look at home in the Laundromat."

Meredith was looking at her quizzically.

"You really believe that, don't you," Meredith said. "You're not just fishing for a compliment."

"I know what I look like," Mitzi said. "Plain, wholesome, dependable . . . all the things that hurt when you're a girl but don't matter anymore when you've grown up."

"I know you won't take my word for it, Mitzi," she said, "but you are a very good-looking woman. Blond, built, great skin, yes—you'd have given

June Allyson a run for her money. And you've got that glow of excitement about you that most of the women out here lost long ago."

Mitzi was embarrassed. "I'm very used to the way I am. Sometimes"—and she was almost whispering now— "it scares me. I wonder how I ever got a person like Charles to love me. He was every girl's target when I was in college, but for some reason he picked me. It's always bothered me."

Meredith was shaking her head. "That must be why you let him talk to you like that. One of these days you'll find out the truth about yourself," she said. "I hope I'm around to watch the blossoming. Meanwhile," she said, glancing at her watch, "I have to get back to the apartment to prepare for the return of the budding Fitzgerald. Poor baby, he needs an awful lot of comforting to make up for the job he's got."

Graduating from Mrs. Scanlon's was easy—no one ever failed the course—but putting her real-estate license to work was not. Mitzi made the rounds of all the agencies but, with the boom already under way, they were all fully staffed. She wasn't offered anything, not even office work.

"The story of my life," she told Meredith.

They were sitting by the pool, the children at school and Charles at work. Meredith, who had also found no work, had taken to dropping by during the day. Without anything being said, she knew she had to leave before Charles got home.

"Cheer up, we're going to make it," Meredith said. "I was reading the *Times*'s real-estate section and there was a piece about a woman who made half a million in commissions her first year. They'll be writing about us soon."

Mitzi laughed. "That's what I love about you," she said. "You're so optimistic. At least it offsets Charles's attitude."

"He's still giving you a hard time?"

"Yes," Mitzi said. "He finally agreed to my trying to get into real estate. He has this attitude of 'Let her realize she's got no chance in the big world and she'll settle down and be grateful.' Every day that goes by that I don't get the chance to make a sale, he gets more superior. He hasn't said 'I told you so' yet but it's taken a great effort not to."

Charles stayed out late more and more frequently, sometimes not coming home all night. Mitzi tried not to be suspicious, reminding herself he had work, he consulted with other doctors, and that he had made commitments to several Los Angeles charities.

Then, suddenly, there came the time when she no longer fooled herself. He *was* busy. But he also was seeing other women. Of course he was. Charles had always been especially susceptible to flattery, though he took great pains to disguise that fact. He was tall, very good-looking, and had a warm, sympathetic air about him which must, she knew, attract women to him whether or not he was hunting for affairs.

The realization of Charles's infidelity, or possible infidelity, didn't stun Mitzi nearly as much as her response to it. In a way, a very persuasive way, she was glad to think of him having affairs. It took a pressure off her. She didn't know why, precisely. It had nothing to do with sex. She enjoyed their times together and was neither a prude nor especially lustful. But the idea that some woman, somewhere, had to work at pleasing Charles, pleased Mitzi. She knew damned well that this did her no credit.

If only she could get work, she thought, she would be reasonably content. In the end she decided to return to the only person who might help her—Mrs. Scanlon.

"It's just the first break that's hard to get, dear," she told Mitzi as they drank tea in the hot living room. "You're just going to have to make that break yourself."

"Great," Mitzi said. "Tell me how I do that."

"Steal other people's clients," Mrs. Scanlon said smoothly. "That's how it's done. Go into all the smaller agencies—avoid the big ones, they'll spot you right away—and pose as a house buyer. Ask to see modest properties, the kind you're going to have to start off selling. Once you know where the houses are, you contact the sellers and ask if you may handle their properties. They've got nothing to lose with multiple listing. It doesn't matter who they pay their 6 percent to."

"That doesn't sound very ethical," Mitzi said dubiously.

"It isn't," Mrs. Scanlon said cheerfully. "This is a tough business. Remember, there are three hundred thousand realtors in this state."

"Good idea," said Meredith when Mitzi told her Mrs. Scanlon's scheme. "But it needs a little refinement. One of us checks out the house, the other follows up with the seller. That way the agencies won't know."

Meredith was right.

They rounded up four properties that way and advertised them in the *Times*. At Meredith's suggestion they called themselves M and M realty and used Meredith's phone number.

"Shouldn't we register the company or something?" Mitzi asked.

"Time for that later, after we've made a sale," Meredith said. They were composing the ad on her kitchen table. "We'll throw in a few bogus properties, too," Meredith said. "They serve as come-ons. Lots of small agencies do that. People even expect it."

The response was slow and some of the people who did call almost certainly were playing the same game as Mitzi and Meredith. But finally it looked as if they had a prospect.

They were a young couple, newly arrived from Atlanta, who wanted to buy a condominium on Doheny. It was only seventy-five thousand dollars but there was so much wrong with it that it had been on the market with a dozen agencies for over a month. The Atlanta couple, however, were desperate. Mitzi had scouted the condominium so Meredith was the agent on it.

"The owner's a real creep," Meredith told her. "He kept hinting that, if I played with him, he'd drop the other agencies. I went back to see him a second time and gave him the full treatment—lots of leg, a good look down my dress. The things a girl has to do!"

Then, just when it looked as if they had a sale, two things happened. The Atlanta couple called to say they'd found something more suitable, and the man who owned the condominium called to say one of the other agencies had sold it.

They both went back to Mrs. Scanlon to tell her what had happened.

"Did you leave the buyer and seller alone for one instant?" she demanded.

"No," said Meredith, "but they did exchange telephone numbers."

The older woman laughed bitterly.

"You blew it," she said. "Never let them know anything about each other until you've got a signed contract. Even then, keep them as far apart as possible. It happens all the time: They get together and cut the realtor out. The seller drops the price by 3 percent and makes 3 percent more than he would have if he'd had to pay your commission."

"But that's unethical," Mitzi protested. "Can't we sue them?"

"You could," Mrs. Scanlon said. "But it would cost more than it was worth. Learn a lesson from it instead."

"Yes," said Meredith. "And our own ethics left a lot to be desired. But what makes me mad is that that creep didn't think my body was worth a lousy 3 percent of the price."

"Meredith!" Mitzi said, shocked. "You wouldn't really have . . . ?"

"No," she said, "but *he* didn't know that."

That night Mitzi spilled out the whole story to Charles. She expected him to laugh, but he was tender and compassionate.

"Poor baby," he said, hugging her close to him. "You tried so hard. Now you'll realize what a jungle it is out there."

"What am I going to do now, Charles?" she asked. "I hate just to give up."

"I'll make a deal with you," he said gently. "You know the Olsons? Well, Sam was asking me the other day whether you'd want to handle a little place they own up in Benedict Canyon. They bought it for their boy—it's just a bachelor pad— but he's gone off to New York to be a folk singer. I told Sam I'd talk to you about it."

"Charles, that's wonderful of you," she said. "I thought you were against this."

"I am," he said. "But I've come to see how much it means to you. So that's the deal I'm offering you. If you can sell the Benedict Canyon place, then maybe you've got a future in the business. If you can't, you quit and settle down at home as the very respectable wife of Dr. Engers."

"It's a deal," she said and kissed him.

The place in Benedict Canyon wasn't pretty. It hadn't been lived in for three years. Hidden among scraggy trees and overgrown bushes, the inside was even more depressing. There were dirt and dust and cobwebs over fading, peeling paint. Several windows were broken and there were dank, musty patches where it had rained in. The house itself was just one large room with a picture window opening onto a sundeck. In back were a tiny kitchen, bathroom, and bedroom.

Mitzi looked beneath the squalor. She remembered all her father had taught her about construction and she could see that the house was solidly built. And she remembered her gatehouse before its reconstruction. She spent two hours looking around the house and then she visited Sam Olson in his office. He was a big, gruff man, a millionaire many times over from the conglomerate he had built on the base of a plastics factory. They had met several times at dinners and parties but today Olson was all business.

"We just want to be rid of the damn place," he said. "Jeannie had me buy it for John about five years ago. She thought it would settle him down, having his own place, but not too far from home. He was enthusiastic at first, wanted to fix it up and everything, but then he just lost interest. He's on drugs, you know," Olson said casually. "He's not interested in anything else. It breaks his mother's heart. That's why I want the place disposed of. She sees it as a monument to our failure with John."

"What did you pay for it, Sam?" Mitzi asked.

"Forty thousand, I think," he said. "It seemed like a hell of a lot for a shack, but Jeannie wanted it badly."

"I think if we spent a little money wisely on it I would get you quite a bit more than that," Mitzi said. "Canyon property has gone crazy."

"Do what you like, spend what you like," Olson said. "Just get rid of it for us."

It took up all her time for the next two months. She hired an old Japanese gardener to devote his full time to the place, bringing back the existing trees and shrubs and planting new ones. She had contractors in to gut the old kitchen and bathroom and replace them with spanking modern fixtures. All the paint was stripped to reveal the good raw wood underneath, and the floors were stripped and sanded and buffed until they glowed, rich and dark. The kitchen garden was taken out and flagstones laid in place of it. In the middle she had a large hot tub installed. The Japanese gardener suggested the final touch for the tub: clumps of pine and elegant, cool bamboo all around it.

She bought a set of yellow canvas chairs and a low white wrought-iron table for the deck and planted geraniums in boxes all around the edge.

She was ready. The ad in the *Hollywood Re-*

porter was a gem. It featured a photograph taken from inside the house looking out over the deck to the view of the city below. The copy promised a rustic hideaway right in Benedict Canyon, a house designed for easy living. No price was mentioned.

There were more than two dozen calls the first day and it was hard for Mitzi to conceal her excitement. But she knew she had to play it cool. If she were too eager, prospective buyers would wonder what was wrong with the place. And she wanted to find just the right person for it. That would be the key to selling it.

Kay Royce seemed to fill the bill exactly. She was one of the hottest new young stars in Hollywood, something of a rebel, a woman who picked her roles carefully and was more interested in the right part than in the money. When she called, Mitzi managed to give the impression that she dealt with stars every day.

"Yes," she said, "I think the place would suit you very well, Miss Royce. It's small, just right for a busy person who wants somewhere to get away from it all while still being within easy distance of the studios. I'd like to show it to you in the evening because that's when you'll be spending the most time there." Then she laughed. "And that's when it looks best."

Kay Royce laughed, too, and they arranged to meet at the house at seven the following night.

Mitzi spent the day there, primping the house. She built a fire of pine logs in the grate and lit it and a scented candle an hour before the star was to arrive. A bottle of chablis was chilling in the new refrigerator; Mitzi had brought two of her own crystal wineglasses. The new track lighting, fitted with soft fifty-watt bulbs, combined with the fire's glow to cast a gentle warmth throughout the house.

Kay Royce walked in at seven sharp and strode straight to the center of the room. She turned around slowly, then moved to the deck. Mitzi hadn't even spoken yet.

"I'll take it," Kay Royce said. "It's beautiful. What's the price?"

Mitzi had to stall for time.

"You haven't seen the rest of it yet," she said. She was trying to decide what figure to put on the place.

"OK, show me," the star said. "But I want it."

They strolled through the other tiny rooms and then out the back, where the hot tub was lit up and the breeze moved through the bamboo.

"Better and better," Kay Royce said. "How much?"

"One hundred and seventy-five thousand," Mitzi said.

"That's high," Kay Royce said. "But what the hell. It's just the place for me. We've got a deal."

They went back to the deck. Mitzi got the wine and they sat in the twilight drinking and watching the lights come on below.

"You could probably make an offer, get them down a little," Mitzi said at one point. She was getting to like this woman and guiltily remembered that the Olsons didn't need the money, anyway.

"Christ, you're new to this game, aren't you?" Kay said. "I told you the price is OK. They pay me seven hundred and fifty thousand a picture and I know I'm not worth that. So what's the price matter on a house I love?"

Charles was in the library when she got home, and she ran into his arms.

"I did it! I did it!" she cried. "I just sold that house. I just made ten and a half thousand dollars' commission! Oh, Charles!"

"I'm very proud of you," he said. "And I'll keep my part of the bargain." She sensed something was wrong.

"I hope it's going to be all right for us, Mitzi," he said. "You know I'd rather you didn't work. I'll do my best to adjust to it but please be patient with me if sometimes I let you down."

"Of course, darling," she said. How could he let her down? How could anything spoil the happiness and pride? She hugged him to her. Everything was going to be wonderful from now on.

The next day she sat down with Sam Olson.

"I spent twenty-three thousand dollars on the house," she told him. "I've been sending the bills to your lawyer and they've all been paid."

"Yes," he said with a shrug. "He called me. It's worth it if it helps unload that shack."

"Well, Sam," she said, savoring her moment, "I've sold 'that shack' for . . . one hundred and seventy-five thousand dollars!"

"Oh Christ!" he said. "That's a hundred grand I'm going to have to pay capital gains tax on. Oh, fuck."

A week after her triumph Mitzi received a call at home. The voice on the other end was deep and smooth and assured.

"This is Jay Pressler," he said. "At Castles. Do you know about us?"

"Of course," Mitzi said. "The most important

firm in real estate. I don't know why you're calling me, though. I never tried to steal a client of yours. You're too big for me."

He laughed. "No. What I'm calling about is this. I spotted your ad for the Benedict Canyon place and I followed up and learned what you sold it for. Good lord! I checked that place out a year ago and decided it was too far gone to bother with. Sam Olson's an old friend of mine and he hinted that he'd like me to get rid of it for him but I wouldn't take it on. Now you've made me look like an idiot. I'm very impressed. What I'd like you to do is come have lunch with me and talk about your future. Anyone who can outsmart Castles should be working for us."

Chapter Eight _____

"MITZI, COULD YOU STOP BY MY OFFICE BEFORE you leave today?" Jay Pressler asked, looming over her desk. She started to get up, nervous, and banged her knee against an open drawer. One pair of pantyhose ruined.

"Sure. Of course," she stammered. It was the summons she had been dreading. Her three months' trial at Castles was up and Jay was going to give her the verdict. Mitzi thought she had done quite well, but she knew she wasn't in a class with the better-established agents. She hadn't made a single sale yet. Wistfully, she watched Jay go back into his office. At least it had been fun here, and she had learned a lot.

Just after five o'clock she tapped on his door. He was lying on a couch, his feet up, a drink in one hand and the *Hollywood Reporter* in the other. Somehow he looked even taller and thinner lying down. He waved her to the chair opposite him.

"Drink?" he asked. She shook her head and waited while he put down the paper, swung his legs around, and sat up. He was nearly as tall as Charles, with black hair and deep blue eyes.

"Three months," he said and smiled at her. "The time's flown. What do you think you've learned here?"

She started falteringly. "Well, this is a very . . . aggressive business," she said, "but the trick seems to be never to let the customer realize that. I've noticed the way you and your people sort of coax a prospect along to the point where *he* thinks buying a certain house was *his* idea. And that you don't overhype a house, just outline all the features, then let it sell itself. Lots of other things, too, technical things," she said, "but mostly I just think I've begun to understand the philosphy of Castles." It was inadequate but it was the best she could do. She crossed her legs, carefully trying to conceal the huge run in her stocking. She had blown it all.

"That's not bad for starters," Jay said. "I haven't been able to give you any help in the try-out period because it wouldn't be a fair test if I did. But I've been watching you and I think you're going to make it in this business. Except" —and he grinned at her— "you'd better remember always to keep a spare pair of pantyhose in your desk—the girls tell me selling real estate is hell on stockings. If you want it, as of tomorrow you're on staff. You'll start on two-fifty a week retainer. You keep half your 6 percent commission and the other half goes to Castles. Does that sound OK?"

She was smiling radiantly at him while trying to absorb what he had said. She'd gotten the job! She was going to be a full-fledged member of the hottest real-estate operation in town! She wanted to laugh or cry or jump up and down.

He seemed to understand that she was accepting. "Would you like that drink now?" he asked.

"Yes," she said. "Something to celebrate. You don't know how much this means to me."

He fixed her a gin and tonic, sat down, and began to ask her about herself.

"How is your family coping with your working?" he asked. "I recall that this is your first full-time job. It sometimes puts a big strain on a woman's domestic life."

She told him, frankly, about the situation at home, about Charles's early attempts to make her quit, about the resentment he still sometimes displayed toward her.

"But I'm sure Charles will learn to live with my working."

Jay was listening intently.

"I hope you're right," he said. "It's one thing to sell real estate in your spare time. It's another to work out of an office like this. This is a very demanding, high-pressure job. I should know.

"I started married life working as an insurance claims adjustor. I did it for five years and could never understand why I felt lousy all the time. It was the job, of course. I hated it. Anyway, one day I inspected this flood-damaged house. It looked a write-off. But I mentioned it to a young guy who knew how to use his hands and I put him together with the owner and they worked out a deal. That got me involved in real estate and a few months later I quit my job and started selling. The first couple of years were tough but I loved it, except that it took so much of my time that my wife became resentful. In the end she issued the ultimatum—back to my old, safe regular job or she was leaving.

"I chose my job," he said, draining his drink. "I've hardly ever regretted it. I tell you this because you may face the same choice someday." He glanced at his watch. "On that note, you'd better hurry home," he said. "You can always come and talk to me if the going gets rough. Remember, I've been through it."

The next three months at Castles were heaven. She threw herself into the work and, with Jay's guidance, she began to make real progress. Finally she made a sale, a modest one-hundred-ninety-thousand-dollar split-level in Brentwood. She and Jay had drinks in his office to celebrate. It was, she felt, one of the most wonderful moments of her life and she was disappointed when Jay began putting the glasses away.

"I've got this damned charity thing tonight," he apologized. "Otherwise I'd take you out to dinner and really celebrate. Come on. I'll walk you to your car."

In the parking lot it was dark and he took her arm to help her over the concrete markers that protected the spaces. Even so, she stumbled and fell against him. He laughed.

"That's what a couple of drinks do when you're exhilarated," he said. "You drive carefully, now. I wouldn't want to lose my most promising agent."

She smiled at him and, on impulse, stretched up and kissed him on the cheek.

"I'll never be able to thank you enough, Jay," she said. "You've opened a whole new life to me."

She sang along with the radio all the way home and was still singing when she turned into the drive. Charles's white Mercedes was sitting squarely outside the front door and she felt just a little annoyed. The damn thing cost so much, the least he could do was put it away in the garage. She turned into the garage, turned off the engine, and sat in the car for a moment. This was no time to let Charles's extravagances upset her. She wanted him to share her joy tonight.

She checked her watch as she entered the back doorway and headed for the kitchen. Seven-fifteen. Plenty of time to prepare the lamb chops—the family favorite—sit down with all of them and tell them about her wonderful day.

Suddenly she heard voices in the library. Damn! Company. Mitzi hurried from the kitchen, stopped by the hall mirror to pat her hair into shape, and went into the library.

Charles was pacing, glass in hand, and Simon and Jean Culver were sitting on the long red leather couch. They were all in evening dress and Mitzi knew at once that she had slipped up. She smiled as hard as she could.

Simon Culver rose as Charles spoke.

"At last!" he said, almost snarling, "the working wife is home to the hearth."

"Hello, darling," she said, crossing to him. "Simon, Jean. I hope I haven't kept you—"

Charles cut her off, clutching her arm and steering her out of the room. "We'll just be a moment," he called over his shoulder.

In the kitchen he shoved her, quite hard, against the wall.

"You bitch," he hissed. "The one night I ask you to do something for me." He moved closer to her. "I thought so, you've been drinking," he said. "You knew how important the Music Center benefit was to me. And the Culvers . . . Jesus Christ, the most prominent people we know. We should have been out of here thirty minutes ago but instead I've been in there, looking like a fool, pretending you were at the hairdresser.

"And then," he said, his anger mounting, "you stagger in from drinking with whomever, looking like some damned assistant saleswoman." He slapped her. "I'll tell them you're sick and we'll go without you. And we'll have this whole thing out in the morning." He stormed out of the kitchen, his rage not at all diminished.

She stayed leaning against the sunny yellow wall, touching her face, until she heard the front door close and the soft whine as the Mercedes started. Her cheek wasn't too bad, probably wouldn't bruise. Her tears were of anger, from the unfairness of it all. How many times had *he* failed to come home at all? Forgotten about guests, or left her waiting for him at parties?

But how could she have forgotten tonight's party? She couldn't have known about it. She was meticulous about things like that. Maybe he'd forgotten to tell her. Or maybe he was right, that the job at Castles was making her an unfit wife and mother. The kitchen door opened just then and she blinked to hide her tears from Mrs. Truman.

"Oh, I'm sorry, ma'am," the housekeeper said, startled. "I thought you and the doctor would be long gone to your party now. I just dropped off the children at their sleepovers and came back to see that everything was all right here for the weekend."

"I, uh, wasn't feeling well, Mrs. Truman," she said, worrying that her cheek showed where he had hit her. "I'm going up to bed."

She would just have to try harder. She would prove to Charles that she could cope with both the job and her responsibilities at home.

She sighed. Charles had given up all the work he'd been doing when they met, his disappoint-

ment in the powers of medicine having become
deeper and deeper in recent years. Now instead of
committee meetings and planning sessions it was
charity balls with other rich doctors and their rich
patients. Instead of Charles coming home filled
with enthusiasm over some new technique it was
always an out-of-sorts Charles who staggered in,
usually complaining. Were all the other plastic
surgeons in the world so defeated? Did all doctors
lose their faith so quickly?

Upstairs in the big master bedroom she undressed, dropping her clothes on the floor, and
went into her bathroom. She spent fifteen minutes
under the shower and when she emerged she was
feeling a little better. Back in the bedroom she
picked up the discarded clothes. Untidiness made
Charles angry. Poor Charles, she thought, as she
slid between the cool blue sheets. She'd make it all
up to him, starting first thing tomorrow. Or even
tonight. She would stay awake until he came home
from the party and then she'd tell him how sorry
she was and they would make wonderful, passionate love. She would do all those things he liked her
to do. Their love life had been lousy for months
now and she guessed a lot of it had to be her fault.
Tonight . . . she drifted off to sleep, still thinking of
the pleasure she would give Charles when he came
home.

It was the sound of birds, not Charles, that woke
her. He was there, though, on the other side of the
bed, his limbs flung out, thick brown hair di-
sheveled, breathing heavily through his mouth.
She sat up carefully and looked around the room.
His black silk jacket lay on the floor beside a chair.
His white ruffled shirt had missed a doorknob.
Pants, underwear, shoes, and socks laid a trail

from the door to the side of the bed. He must have been in some condition when he came in. Still, she would not have minded if he had woken her. She smiled and decided that, even if the night had been lost, she would make this morning a very special one. The light creeping around the heavy draperies promised another brilliant day, just right for a splendid brunch on the terrace, just the two of them.

Mitzi slipped out of bed and moved soundlessly to her bathroom. She showered as quietly as possible, patting herself dry with a big soft towel, then liberally applied a gentle, summer-scented perfume. In her dressing room she decided against her usual weekend wear of jeans and shirt and instead selected a romantic flowing print dress, one of his favorites. She opened her lingerie drawer and took out a white silk teddy, frivolous, fun, sexy. Wooden sandals in hand, Mitzi moved out through the bedroom with a final glance at Charles. He hadn't stirred and looked like he would sleep for hours. She had plenty of time to make her preparations.

Even the Pinto seemed in a good mood this morning. It started at the first touch and she eased it down the drive and into the light Saturday morning traffic on Mulholland. It wasn't nine-thirty yet and she had plenty of time to shop at the gourmet place and be home before Charles awoke.

The gleaming white store was already crowded, most of its patrons smart young matrons. Smiling, Mitzi took a basket and began working up and down the aisles, planning as she went. Belgian endive and cucumber dressing for his favorite salad; oranges to squeeze fresh for mimosas with the bottle of Tattinger she had already placed in the refrigerator; a dozen perfectly matched brown eggs; a crusty Italian loaf; delicately sliced salmon.

"Splurge! You deserve a treat," she heard over her shoulder. She turned. Grace Jensen, whose husband was something-or-other at Fox, was grinning at her.

"Hi, Grace," Mitzi said and managed a smile. "I'm shopping for Charles. He's still sleeping off last night and I wanted to wake him with something special."

Grace Jensen was looking at her in a funny way, a mixture of—what?—malice and sympathy, Mitzi thought.

"He should be fixing breakfast for *you* after last night's performance," Grace said.

"What do you mean?" she asked.

"Oh, you'll hear soon enough, dear," Grace said, moving her shopping cart away.

Mitzi moved quickly after her and placed her hand on the cart. "What did Charles do last night, Grace?" she demanded.

The other woman looked at her for a moment, then shrugged.

"I don't want to be the bearer of bad news but . . . at the Music Center last night, your husband was just about the main attraction. He really tied one on. Then late in the evening he ran into your boss, Jay Pressler. Well, Charles started shouting at Pressler, even tried to hit him. They had to drag him away. It was quite the high point of the evening."

Mitzi knew she had turned white. The mounting fear climbing up from the pit of her stomach and catching at her throat was surely visible to this horrible woman.

"You must tell me all of it, Grace," she said.

"Well, he was saying that you and Pressler were . . . having an affair. What he actually said was, 'Pressler, you've been fucking my wife.'"

The jar of caviar dropped from Mitzi's hand and shattered on the tiled floor, the precious blue-gray grains forming an obscene puddle. She felt other shoppers staring at her as she moved, dazed, down the aisle and out past the check-out. She heard someone behind the counter call to her but she just kept on moving out into the sunlight that had seemed so warm and gentle a few minutes before and that now was white and harsh and searing.

Somehow she made it to the parking lot and into the awful little car. She fumbled for her keys. It was burning hot inside the car and she began to panic when it refused to start. At the fifth attempt the engine grudgingly turned over and caught and she raced out of the parking lot in a shower of gravel.

Mitzi drove aimlessly for the next half hour. Her mind had gone into some neutral place and she wanted to keep it like that for as long as possible. She knew pain was waiting.

Eventually she found herself in a park high in Beverly Hills, and she carefully stopped the car beside a low stone wall. A tourist bus stood about a hundred yards away and its occupants were spilled around it, photographing each other and the magnificent views. She moved to the fence and looked over. It wasn't much of a drop; more just a gentle slope. There was no refuge there.

She needed a cigarette and returned to the car. The shopping basket, with its lush contents, was on the front seat. She had run out of the store without paying, but being a shoplifter was the least of her troubles. She found her cigarettes, lit one, and went back to the wall. Pain, humiliation, and anger flooded over her. What was she going to do? She would have to leave town, that was for sure. She could go back to Chicago, or better still, go and hide in her father's house in the woods outside Pittsburgh until the laughter had died down.

First, though, she owed Jay an apology and an explanation. Mitzi ground out the cigarette. She dreaded this, the shame of going before someone she so admired. He would be in his Malibu place because it was Saturday. She could just telephone, but that was the coward's way out. No, she would drive down to the beach now. She sighed, returned to the car, and winced as the burning vinyl touched her bare legs.

She wasn't sure she would recognize Jay's Malibu place. She hadn't been there and had only the vaguest description of it from him: "a comfortable little place I picked up before Malibu was chic." In fact, if it hadn't been for the white Rolls Corniche in the carport, she would have missed it.

The house was hidden from the road by scrubby, windblown trees and there was a steep climb to it up weather-beaten gray wood stairs. She made the ascent slowly, the heels of her sandals threatening to trip her. There was a landing at the top and she saw the house itself, cantilevered out over the beach. A screen door faced her and she pressed the bell. Chimes echoed softly somewhere within the house but there was no reply. Then she heard a voice, sounding annoyed at the intrusion.

"Around here," she heard Jay call. "On the deck."

The wooden sandals made a loud clatter on the

deck as Mitzi moved down the side of the house to the front. As she turned the corner she saw Jay sprawled in a deck chair, a tall glass in hand, gazing out to sea. He did not look up as she approached. He had relaxed his office role. Now he was wearing a white muslin shirt and drawstring pants; his long hair flopped over his face, and his bare arms were deeply tanned.

"Jay," she said softly, "I had to come. I feel so sick and awful about what happened last night."

Then he was unfolding himself from the chair, stretching to his full height, and moving to her.

"Hey, what a great surprise," he said. "I've been sitting here wasting this glorious day on my hangover and wishing for some pleasant company . . . and suddenly you appear. And I thought you were the delivery boy!"

Amazingly, he sounded truly pleased to see her.

"Sit down. Let me get you a drink," he said, towering over her and smiling. "I'm having a Bullshot. Does it interest you?"

She nodded, pleased to put off the moment of confrontation for a little while, and watched him slide the glass door open and vanish into the cool dark of the house. Then he was back, handing her the drink. She took a swallow and the bouillon gave her strength. She put the glass down on the deck and sat up straight in the chair.

"Jay," she said, speaking quickly, "I came here almost as soon as I heard what happened last night. I'm so ashamed for you, and for me . . . even for Charles. Of course, I'm resigning immediately, and I'm going away. I wanted you to know that the months I've spent at Castles have been just about the happiest of my life. You've taught me so much and, more important, you've been a truly wonderful friend to me. I feel sick that that friendship should have been turned into something evil by Charles."

He raised his hand almost wearily. "Mitzi, please don't—"

She cut him off. "No, Jay, I've got to say all this. What Charles did was inexcusable, but he has been under a terrible strain lately. He's always resented my working, but I thought I could make it all right. Well, I didn't." Taking another long drink and pushing herself up out of the deck chair, she said, "I came to say good-bye, thank you, and I'm sorry."

That was when the tears started and there was nothing she could do to stop them. The next thing she knew she was sitting down again and Jay's arm was draped around her shoulder. He was murmuring soothing sounds in her ear and while she didn't quite know what he was saying, she knew enough to let everything pour out.

"I just went on pretending for months, for years, that it was all right between Charles and me," she said, sobbing. "The stupid fights, the accusations, the times when he didn't come home, the nasty things he said when I took this job ... even our love life. I tried to please him by being as damn near perfect a housewife as I could be, but he just seemed *bored*. Even the children treat me like an unwelcome guest in my own house. I thought the job would make it better, that they'd all be proud of me for getting out and doing something. But they all treat me like an imposition. Last night, that hideous scene ... oh, Jay, I want to die."

He continued to hold her, gently patting her back and murmuring.

She didn't know how long before the flood of

tears stopped but finally it did. She felt exhausted, drained, but somehow better. Still not looking at Jay, she took a little more of her drink. Then he started to speak.

"If you weren't feeling so tragic," he said, "I'd laugh. Really, this is a hell of a funny scene. Your husband gets a load on and accuses me of having an affair with you. I'm not embarrassed! I'm flattered as hell to think that I could attract a beautiful and vibrant young woman like you. I know it's ridiculous and you know it's ridiculous but half of Los Angeles now believes I'm a lady-killer. I feel twenty years younger!"

She finally looked at him. "You mean . . . you mean you're not disgusted?" she asked, doubting.

"Of course not," he laughed. "Look, back in Oak Brook, or wherever, they may still fight duels over accusations like that, but out here, hell, adultery is almost *de rigueur*. Also making scenes at charity parties. It's always more fun than the floor show."

He was silent for a moment, then said gently, "Mitzi, dear, I know how you must be feeling, really. But this incident will pass. Forget about it. What you do have to consider is how bad things are at home and what you want to do about them. Quitting your job doesn't seem to me to be the answer, but I don't know much about your situation with Charles. It does look as if he's a rather troubled man, perhaps, as you say, resentful and possessive of you. But I've got a pretty strong idea that he loves you. What you have to decide is whether the love is worth the hassle that goes with it. I decided years ago that it wasn't, but don't use me as an example. I'm now just a rich, lonely old man whose only excitement is being accosted by wrongly jealous husbands."

"But," she said, confused, "but you're saying I could just go on at Castles as if nothing had happened."

"Yes, if that's what you want to do," Jay said. "It's certainly what I want you to do. You've got a big, big future in this business and, hell, I like having you around the place." He was watching her carefully. "Hey, don't start crying again. Enough for one morning. Come on," he said, rising and taking her hand and tugging her out of the chair, "we'll take an amble along the beach and look at all the stars trying to enjoy their overpriced beach shacks."

Meekly she followed him down the steps to the beach and together, not speaking at first, they started walking north through the clean white sand, Mitzi carrying her sandals, Jay loping ahead a little.

After a while Jay began to talk about some of the beachfront properties they were passing.

"When I first moved out here, you could buy most of this stuff for sixty, eighty thousand," he said. "Now it starts around six hundred thousand. That place up there"—he pointed to an unspectacular low, white clapboard—"I sold for three quarters of a million a year ago. Actually," he said with a laugh, "I've sold that house nine times over the years. McQueen had it for a while, then a string of writers, now Del Cannon lives there. So I've had 54 percent of its value in commissions over the years. That's the great thing about this business. If you do right by your customers they always return to you.

"You've got to know what's happening, too. Who's marrying or, more often, getting a divorce. A couple splitting up are going to want to dump their mansion in Bel Air. A couple getting married with maybe five kids existing between them are going to need a big place. So you have to listen to industry gossip. If a Donahue or a Carson is moving his show to the Coast, he's going to need a home, and chances are the first reputable agent who contacts him will get the business. So I hang out at the Polo Lounge. I know all the columnists and I get the inside track on the industry moves." He laughed again. "And it's not just for business, either. I love it. I'm a groupie for this business."

They were retracing their steps now, back toward Jay's. The sun was directly above them, and Mitzi could feel its heat beating on her bare shoulders. She felt easy and fluid, far away from the tensions of home. She glanced at Jay. He, too, was looser than she had ever seen him, striding along the sand, tall and handsome. There was a light offshore breeze now and it ruffled his hair. He was, she thought, so unlike the debonair Jay Pressler she saw every day in the office. They reached the house and both were out of breath after they climbed the steps to the deck.

"It's going to be too hot out here from now on," Jay said. "I suggest we move inside and slip into a cool drink. I might even drum up some lunch. That is"—he looked at her, one eyebrow raised—"if you can stay for lunch."

"Oh, sure," she said. "I've got nothing pressing. Just so long as I'm not messing up your plans."

"I never plan the weekends, my dear," he said. "I always leave them open, confident that something absolutely wonderful is going to happen. Of course, it never does, but the expectation is fun."

They were in the living room, cool and dim, washed with a dark green light that was the sun reflecting off the sea and sand. She sat on a rattan couch upholstered in a bright green-and-white flower pattern. The whole room was decorated in the same theme, all of it casual and summery, masculine but soft. Jay was standing behind a bamboo-fronted bar at the rear of the room.

"What'll it be?" he asked.

"What I had before would be great, thanks. I still haven't had breakfast."

"I'm sorry," he said with a laugh. "I forgot that you've had a disrupted morning. One more Bullshot, and then I'll see what I can rustle up in the kitchen."

He gave her the frosted glass and vanished into the rear of the house. Mitzi eased herself back on the couch and sipped her drink. She felt so safe and peaceful here in the beach house, the only sounds filtering in those of the sea and the gulls. She suddenly realized that she was not thinking at all of Charles and their problems—and she felt no guilt.

"It's only a snack, I'm afraid," Jay said as he came back into the room bearing a wooden tray and setting it down on a glass table in the center of the room. "I live very simply on weekends. A steak on the barbecue at night is about the extent of my cooking."

He carefully laid out a side of smoked salmon and a platter of Westphalian ham, a pâté, a wheel of Brie, and a salad of raw broccoli and cucumber. He made one more trip to the kitchen, returning with a long Italian loaf tucked under one arm, a bottle of chilled white wine under the other, and two wineglasses in his hands.

"I love your idea of a snack, Jay," she said. "I think you do very well for yourself down here."

"Well," he said with a grin, "one advantage of living alone is that you have to please only yourself. Some nights it's a frozen pizza eaten in bed with the television on. I do pretty much as I please."

She took some pâté and *cornichon*. Suddenly she felt nervous . . . girlish . . . and she giggled.

"What's so funny?" he asked, the eyebrow raised again.

"I don't know. This . . . sitting here picnicking on a Saturday as if the rest of the world didn't exist," she said. "I feel as if someone's going to walk in any minute and shout 'Out!' and send me home."

"Not if you don't want them to, they won't," he said. "Wine?"

She nodded and he filled her glass. The wine was delightfully soft and cool and she felt her confidence returning. She carefully sliced some of the pink salmon. It was delicious.

"You like that?" he asked. "It's Norwegian. A friend caught that fellow on Tuesday and shipped it to me the day after. I'm just a spoiled old man."

She raised her glass and looked at him over it.

"Jay," she said, "I don't know anyone who more deserves a little spoiling than you." And then, unaccountably, she was crying again.

At first he was uncomfortable, embarrassed. But finally he got up and came and stood beside her, his large gentle hands on her shoulders, gently massaging her.

She reached back and placed one of her hands on his.

"I'm sorry," she said. "I'm all right now. I just suddenly felt so grateful to you for all you've done for me. I don't know what would have happened to me without you and Castles."

She stood up from the table and turned to him and it was the most natural thing that she moved into his arms and they kissed, long and warmly. After a minute he made to move away from her but she held him. She could feel his chin on the top of her head.

"Jay," she said softly, "would you . . . do you want to . . . ?"

She felt him nod and he took her hand and led her across the living room and into an even darker bedroom. He released her hand and she slowly undid the straps of her dress and let it fall in a soft pile around her ankles. She heard Jay draw in his breath sharply.

"You're so beautiful," he said softly.

She looked down at herself then and saw, with a shock of pleasure, that she was, indeed, beautiful. The nervousness was gone and she felt proud and strong and eager. She leaned her head against Jay's chest and calmly, as if it were the most natural thing to do, unbuttoned his shirt and pushed down his pants. When he was naked he moved slowly back onto the bed and lay there watching her. She gazed back at him, unblinking, and removed her flimsy white teddy.

"You look like a dream," he said. "I'm so glad you're not."

They lay together on the bed and their hands began to explore gently. It was slow and leisurely lovemaking, as if they had known each other's body for a long time. When he entered her they found a shared rhythm and moved together, building slowly toward their climax. When it came it was the most complete, fulfilling sensation she had ever known.

They lay there after it, saying nothing, their bodies touching and the breeze washing over them from the shaded window. At one point Jay slipped out of the bed and padded off to the kitchen, returning with a fresh bottle of wine and glasses. She spilled a little of the cold wine on her breasts as she tried to drink lying down, and they laughed together. Outside the wind was building and it began to grow dark.

"What time is it, Jay?" she asked, sitting up.

He found his watch on the bedside table. "Only three forty-five, but it's so black out there," he said. "There must be a storm coming." He jumped up from the bed. "Come on out to the deck. These summer storms look great from there."

She followed him as he gathered up the wine and the glasses and moved through the house, taking pleasure in their nakedness.

He slid the glass doors open and she felt the wind against her. The beach before them was deserted under the black sky. The sea was rising ahead of the gale. She stood on the deck beside Jay, and the first lightning bolt hit somewhere up the beach, illuminating the two of them. They moved back to a deck chair and huddled in it as the storm raged.

This time their lovemaking was like the storm, swift and savage, and they didn't notice the rain that was drenching them. Mitzi could hear herself crying out over the noise of the storm, wild words she had never used before. Finally, shivering and soaked, they came apart and Jay pulled her from the chair and hurried her back inside.

"Get yourself into a long, hot shower," he ordered. He led her to the bathroom and turned on the water, testing it before helping her into the shower. She stayed there for a long time, then wrapped herself in a big towel and went into the living room, where he was sitting draped in an old red terry-cloth robe and smoking a pipe.

"Come sit here," he said. "Would you like anything? A brandy?"

She shook her head. All she wanted was to be there, with his arm around her shoulder, watching the storm subside outside the windows. "I don't want to leave," she said, "but I have to go home now."

"I want to talk to you about that," Jay said. "Going home. How do you feel now, after today, about Charles and everything?"

"I'm not sure," she said. "The anger has gone. I kind of pity him. And I think I love you. Is that silly of me?"

"No," he said, smiling. "What we feel for each other is very special, founded on friendship and respect and maybe it's more lasting than love."

Mitzi was silent. She knew he was talking sense but something inside her had wanted him to speak only of love, of running away, of being together always. But he was right.

"I understand, Jay," she said. "Thanks for being a very dear friend and a wonderful lover. Now"—she stood and stretched—"I have to get back in my clothes, resume the role of mild-mannered suburban mother, and speed back to Beverly Hills."

He saw her to the door and placed a hand softly on her shoulder before she started down the steps.

"It was a lovely day despite the rain," he said. "I'll see you in the office Monday."

The rain had stopped but she drove carefully.

The roads were still soaked. She was singing something or other and once she glanced in the rearview mirror and smiled broadly at herself.

It was dusk when she turned into the driveway of their home, and all the outside lights were on. Charles came out the front doorway when she stopped the car to open the garage.

"Where the hell have you been?" he demanded, keeping pace with her and speaking through the window as she carefully steered the car into its space. "I've been so worried about you. No note, no phone call."

They were in the garage now and he had to step back as she swung open the Pinto's door. She slid out of the car, remembering to take the unpaid-for groceries with her.

She leaned back against the car and studied her husband in the dim light.

"Can't you figure out where I've been, Charles?" she asked. "All you have to do is think about which story is the funniest being told about last night's party and you'll work it out."

He looked blank.

"Charles," she said, "I had to go apologize to Jay Pressler for your drunken outburst. He was very understanding but I think you should call him and explain that you were just drunk."

"Mitzi, Mitzi," he said, his head hanging, "I don't know what came over me last night. I was angry and jealous of the time that damned job of yours takes. Of course I know you aren't having an affair with that man. I just wanted to strike out and hurt someone."

"Well, Charles, if we're going to go on living together, you're going to have to grow up and learn to control yourself," she said briskly. "And you're going to have to cope with my working at Castles because it's what I want to do and I intend to be damned good at it."

He was staring at her. "You mean . . . you're going back to Castles after what happened last night?"

"You bet," she said and turned and headed for the house.

During that terrible, dreary up-and-down time with Charles, she had one glorious week. She and Jay stole an afternoon away from the office and spent it in his bed, with champagne and nothing to eat. They made noises about going out onto the sundeck because it was such a lovely day, but they stayed where they were. The next day, they stole another afternoon and explored the hills above Hollywood, lingering until the lights came on in the city below.

Mitzi wondered why she felt so thoroughly at ease about her affair with Jay, and she thought it was Jay himself. While she often felt guilty about neglecting Charles's social schedule, not being there for all the charity balls and dinner parties, she never felt that her love for Jay cheated Charles of anything. They were separate loves, and neither encroached upon the other.

Chapter Nine_____

IT WAS ELEVEN O'CLOCK ON A TUESDAY MORNING
several months later and Jay still hadn't put in an
appearance at the office. Mitzi was worried. He
was fastidiously punctual and, if he was going to
be delayed, he would phone. The ten other agents
in the Castles office were out just then. Apart from
the three secretaries, she was the only person in
the office. Finally he telephoned and she thought
something might be wrong. He sounded faint and
tired.

"Mitzi," he said, "I'm sorry to do this to you, but I
can't come in today and this is important," he said.
"At one o'clock I'm supposed to be going up to
Conrad Oaks's place to see if the old bastard
considers Castles the proper agency to handle it.
It's probably a wild-goose chase. He's had half a
dozen agents up there already and found fault
with every one of them. But that place will go for a
million dollars and we could do with the commission right now.

"I want you to go in my place," Jay said. "You're
ready—you can handle it."

A million-dollar deal was beyond her. Just leaving a favorable impression with the legendary
producer, Conrad Oaks, seemed too great a challenge. But Jay was going on, giving her details of

the property and, more importantly, of its demanding owner.

"He's the last of the dinosaurs," Jay said. "They kicked him out of Universal General last year in a boardroom coup. But he refuses to believe that he's not still all-powerful. The way I hear it, he wants out of the Bel Air place because it's too big now that his wife's dead. I think he probably needs the cash, too. Whoever gets the business will also get the job of finding him a new place, something cozy around the three- or four-hundred-thousand mark. So there's a lot of commission involved. The Bel Air place is as good as anything that will come on the market this year and I'd love Castles to handle it. But, as I said, it's probably a waste of time. Oaks is one of the worst sons-of-bitches in this town. He likes making people jump through hoops for him, then abandoning them when they've given him their best. But there's nothing to lose by trying. He may even like you."

"But what do I say to him?" she almost wailed. "Jay, I'm not up to impressing a man like that. Can't you do it?"

"Yes you are and no I can't," he said, laughing. "If Conrad Oaks is capable of liking anyone, you're the one. Just try, for me. By the way," he added, very casually, "what are you wearing?"

"Slacks, blazer. I look perfectly respectable, if that's what you mean."

"It might help," Jay said carefully, "if you trotted home and put on something a little more . . . feminine. A nice skirt and blouse, with a bit of cleavage showing. Oaks is a lecherous old bastard, though at his age it's probably all wishful thinking."

She didn't know whether to be angry or amused.

"You want me to play the femme fatale for a famous Hollywood producer, a veteran of the casting couch?" she said. "Come on, Jay, I'm not the type. Anyway, I resent the whole idea of playing on my sex."

She heard Jay sigh. "Mitzi, in this business we all have to whore a little. Just a little. Pretend you're auditioning for a role—which in fact you are. Just do it for me, will you?"

"OK," she said, laughing. "It's miscasting, but I'll rush home and get into my sexiest outfit and go up to Bel Air and try to make an old man very happy. Hell, they never taught this at real-estate school."

"That's why most of their graduates are still selling east of Doheny," Jay said. "You'll be OK. Take my limo and driver, too. I don't want you turning up in that junk heap of yours."

So, just before one, Mitzi found herself reclining in the huge limousine, being whisked silently up through the winding roads of Bel Air, past the beautiful homes that nestled among the flowering trees, above the smog and noise of the city. There was an order, a charm to Bel Air that to Mitzi's mind made it the most desirable section of the most desirable stretch of real estate in the world. She smoothed the lap of her gray silk dress and smiled.

The car pulled left and stopped at a wrought-iron gate set in a high stone wall. A door in the gate's left portal opened and a tall, dark man in a black chauffeur's uniform stepped out and walked to the driver's window. She heard her driver identify them as the Castles people, and a moment later the gates swung open. The car nosed its way down a wide graveled drive, through formal lawns and stands of exotic trees. Through the trees Mitzi could see the extension of the stone fence several hundred yards away. The property, she knew, was only a little over four acres, but the fact that it was surrounded by the country club on three sides made it seem larger. She could see the house now, a vast Mediterranean-style place with tall poplars flanking the main entrance. She was extremely nervous as she pressed the bronze bell set in the oak front door.

The door opened silently—everything was silent in Bel Air, she thought—and she was looking at an old and portly butler in full regalia.

"I'm Mrs. Engers, from Castles," she said.

He looked puzzled. "The master, I believe, was expecting a gentleman, Mr. Pressler," he said, and she feared for a moment that he would close the door on her.

"I know," she said. "I came in his place. He was not available. Would you please tell Mr. Oaks I'm here?"

"Certainly, madam," he said. "If you'll come in and wait a moment, please."

She was ushered into a broad entrance hall lined with gold brocade draperies. The floor was of white marble, etched with gold flowers, and she tried not to make a clatter with her heels as she moved across it. There was an ornate mirror on one side of the hall and she quickly checked her hair and makeup as she waited for the summons to attend the great man. She glanced around and smoothed her pantyhose over her thighs. She had been waiting five minutes when she had the feeling she was being watched. Then she spotted him, a tiny bald man standing on a gallery that was almost hidden by the draperies. She started and heard his laugh, almost evil. The man stepped back behind the draperies and a moment later appeared in the hall.

"I was told there was a fellow coming," he said. "I don't like people altering their arrangements with me."

She couldn't help but stare at him. He was shorter than she was, only about five feet, completely bald, and dressed all in black—long black riding boots, black jodhpurs, and a black turtleneck sweater. He would have been a caricature of the old-time directors except that there was nothing comical in his manner. His eyes were vivid blue, hard and demanding, the eyes of a man who always got his way.

"I wouldn't have agreed to see you, in fact," he said, a smile on his thin lips, "except that you do have very nice legs."

Mitzi blushed. This rotten little man had been spying on her.

"I've always been famous for my eye for beautiful women," he said. "That is the secret of my success. Anyway, we've wasted enough time. Follow me."

She trailed after him down the hall and into a high-ceilinged room with full-length glass doors opening onto a formal garden where a marble fountain played. Oaks seated himself in a carved mahogany chair which had been skillfully scaled down so that his feet could rest on the floor. He waved her into a seat directly opposite him, a soft overstuffed chair that was tilted back in such a way that she had difficulty sitting without exposing too much leg. Determined not to satisfy his lechery, she tugged her skirt down and saw that he was smiling at her.

"It's all a game," he said. "Now let's get down to

it. Why should I entrust Castles with my estate? I should tell you that I've reviewed many other realtors and found them all lacking. There was one fellow I liked, but then I learned he has a press agent and keeps a goddamned pet ape in his office. That's show business. Handling my estate is business business, and I don't want any gimmicks."

"Then Castles is right for you, Mr. Oaks," she said smoothly, determined not to be nervous. "We have the most professional staff in California, we handle only the most exclusive properties, and we have a discreet list of buyers whom we try to fit with those properties. We pride ourselves on bringing a little dignity to what may seem to some like an insane field."

"Bullshit," he snorted. "Next you'll be telling me you don't take a commission like the rest of them. Whoever I hire is going to make sixty thousand dollars out of the deal for doing very little. This house will sell itself. A million's cheap."

She looked at him squarely.

"You're right to a large extent," she said. "From what I know of its location, a million is a reasonable price. But times have changed. There aren't that many buyers for the great estates now. The new stars aren't like the old ones. Many of the new people are content to live in apartments and do their entertaining at Chasen's. All the foreign location work means they're not spending as much time in Hollywood, and that affects demand for places like this. So, yes, the price is fair and it will probably look like a ridiculous bargain if and when the film industry bounces back. But right now it will take a lot of hard selling."

He was smiling at her again, benignly now.

"I see you've done your homework," he said. "I like that in someone I'm doing business with, Mrs. . . . ?"

"Engers," she said. "Mitzi Engers."

"Well, you've got off to a better start than the others, I'll admit that." He stood up and began to pace.

"It's important to me what happens to this house," he said. "I've owned it for more than thirty years and my whole history is in these walls. Lombard sat where you're sitting. Flynn took his clothes off and jumped in that fountain out there. Garland sang to one hundred and fifty people in the ballroom. Then we were kings and we ran the industry the way it should be run. Films came in on time and on budget and the people lined up around the block every week to see them. We were selling romance and beauty and escape. Now"—he looked as if he were going to spit on the carpet—"now these scruffy kids out of New York acting schools are slouching and slurring their way across the screen and calling it art. Well, it's certainly not entertainment and the public knows it. That's why they're staying away and that's why the big studios are going bust. They've all forgotten the rules of the game. There is only one rule: Give the public what it wants, not what some bunch of Communist hippies thinks it should have.

"It's all so different now, so tacky," he said, shaking his head. "Nobody has any class. That's why it's important who this house is sold to. I have no use for it now, with all my friends gone. But I want it to go to someone who will keep it up. I know there are people around who would buy this and subdivide it, and I don't want that happening."

"I don't think it could be sold with a covenant

prohibiting subdivision," Mitzi said carefully. "But we would do everything in our power to respect your wishes. Anyway, it's such a beautiful estate that I can't imagine anyone breaking it up."

"I should hope not," he said. "Now I suppose you want a tour of the place. You'll need to know what you're selling—if you get the job, that is."

She followed him eagerly through the grand downstairs rooms. There was a formal, walnut-paneled dining room with a main table that would seat thirty, and smaller tables lining the walls. The floor was polished cedar and it reflected the glow of the rich red velvet draperies. A massive marble fireplace dominated one wall. Oaks was fiddling with some buttons behind one of the draperies.

"Watch this," he said proudly. He pointed to the end wall, and the panels slid back to reveal a full-scale projection system. Another button made the panels on the opposite wall slide apart to uncover a massive screen.

"I always thought it ostentatious having a separate projection room in your home," Oaks explained. "This served us very well."

The ballroom ran all the way down one side of the house. In daytime it doubled as a massive solarium, and just then sunlight was streaming onto a gleaming dance floor edged with marble pillars and greenery. For a moment Oaks seemed to have forgotten she was there. He stood in the center of the dance floor and slowly turned around, examining the room.

"They all came, the greatest of them," he said at last. "There would be a ten-piece orchestra playing on the bandstand and we'd dance and laugh the night away. The younger ones would go dashing off into the pool and when the sun came up battle each other on the tennis courts. We knew how to live then. Nowadays it's cocaine and rock music in some shack in Malibu."

She followed him out of the ballroom onto the lawns beyond it. The swimming pool was shielded from the house by a grove of orange trees. It was an enormous pool, more than forty feet long, and blossoms from the overhanging trees drifted on its blue surface. Hell to keep clean, she thought, but undeniably romantic. There was a long, low pool house tucked in among the trees and, on the other side of that, two grass tennis courts, perfectly maintained, the white of the line markings standing out starkly against the immaculately groomed turf.

"There aren't many grass courts left in Hollywood," he said proudly. "Everyone has switched to artificial surfaces. But when we had these put in—in '44, I guess it was—it was the only way to play the game. It looked so right, all the handsome men and beautiful women dressed in white, playing on those grass courts. The English colony, Niven and all those fellows, loved coming up here. They said it was just like home."

They went back inside and he showed her the rest of the downstairs, the vast kitchen, bedrooms for half a dozen servants, and the four-car garage with a chauffeur's apartment above it.

She followed him up the grand staircase to a series of bedroom–dressing room suites, each with its own sun-drenched balcony.

"We never had children, but all of these rooms got plenty of use," he said. "Sometimes there'd be a famous writer tucked away in one finishing up a script for me. Or a star who was avoiding his wife.

Sometimes I'd meet people on the stairs and wonder who the hell they were," he said, chuckling. "Yes, this was a wonderful, alive house in its day.

"Now," he said, "for the main suite, mine." And with a flourish he opened a set of double doors leading onto the biggest bedroom Mitzi had ever seen. The bed was enormous, a tented affair covered with fur rugs and huge pillows. As she rested her hand on the bed and glanced up under the tent she noted the mirror in the canopy. The rest of the space in the room was occupied by a massive desk and a grouping of low, comfortable-looking armchairs and couches set around a dark marble bar. The doors on either side of the bar led to dressing rooms, and their doors in turn converged on a white-and-gold marble bathroom with matching sunken tubs almost concealed by the masses of ferns sprouting everywhere. The bathroom was filled with natural light coming through a clear glass ceiling.

"It's . . . it's stunning," she said as they returned to his bedroom. "The whole place is so dramatic. But it's all in marvelous taste." She looked quickly at him and decided it was all right to continue. "I've seen some of these Hollywood mansions that were . . . you know . . . excessive. But this is so beautiful. I don't know how you can stand to part with it."

He bowed. "Thank you, my dear. We're not all barbarians out here, although most of the current crop of film people may be. No, I've got to let it go. What's the point of an old, lonely man like me rattling around in a place like this, supporting all those servants? And there are too many memories here for me. This room . . . so many lovely women passed through it. The things that mirror has seen."

He had clutched her hand and was pulling her toward the bed. Oh, God, she was going to lose the deal. Oaks was sitting on the bed and talking rapidly. There was a film of sweat on his forehead, and his thin cheeks were flushed. She felt his hand sliding up the back of her leg and she wondered desperately what to do. It was ludicrous, crazy, this old man coming on to her like this. But . . . she had started to pull away when she heard him gasping. He was terribly flushed and the sweat was pouring down his face. His hand fell away from her thigh.

She moved swiftly to lay him on the bed and then began patting the pockets of his jodhpurs. He managed to shake his head feebly and raised one hand far enough to indicate the bedside table. She wrenched open the drawer and found the pills. She held up the bottle and he nodded. She placed two in his mouth, then moved to the bar and found a glass, filled it with water, and returned to his side. Gently she lifted his head and held him while he swallowed the pills. His bright color began to fade almost at once and he lay back on the bed, breathing more easily. She sat there for five minutes watching him. At last he opened his eyes.

"You're . . . very competent," he said weakly. "Most women would panic in a situation like that. Or they'd let me die and curse me while I did. How did you know about my heart?"

"My husband's a doctor," she said. "Or he used to work as a doctor. It's not hard to spot heart trouble, and you look like a man who's had a history of it. What's your doctor's number?"

"I don't think I'll need him this time," he said. "I

just got overly excited. If I lie here quietly for a while I'll be okay. If you wouldn't mind seeing yourself out . . . ?"

She nodded, smiled at him, and began to move across the Persian carpet to the doors. Poor old man, she thought, his power gone and his body letting him down. She had her hand on the doorknob when she thought she heard him say something. She turned. He had painfully raised one hand to her.

"You've got the job," he rasped. "You can sell this place for me. And you can find me another one, something smaller and easier to maintain, when I come back from Europe."

She stood there looking at him. She wanted to cry, or to run over and kiss him. Instead she fixed her gaze on his.

"Thank you, Mr. Oaks, for putting your trust in Castles. You won't be disappointed." She slipped out the door and down the stairs, told the butler what had happened to his employer, and got back into the limousine.

All the way down through Bel Air and back to Rodeo Drive she let her joy surge through her.

Mitzi was often astonished by herself these days. It wasn't just the job, or Jay's confidence in her, or even Charles's grudging respect. It wasn't even the affair with Jay, which seemed somehow perfectly natural.

What surprised her was her own willingness to think about something she had steeled herself never to think about, and that was her father. Since his death and the rape and her new life in college, she had forced herself not to think about him. It might lead to a sorrow she could not fathom

and would never rise above. It wasn't safe. But
lately she found herself seeing her father on the
streets of Bel Air, in the faces of cab drivers, or
walking briskly through the market. He had come
back to her despite her resolve not to let him, and
she was warmed and grateful for his presence,
fleeting though it was. It had been such a terribly
long time.

Another surprise was her recent enjoyment of
dances and parties. She and Charles had always
had a heavy social schedule. In college there had
been those long talk parties, and Charles's endless
dinners with the other doctors from the clinic and
the doctors' wives. In Los Angeles, what had been
twice-monthly dinner parties quickly became a
demanding and, Mitzi felt, intrusive round of
charity balls and parties and hospital dances and
dinners for twenty-four. She had gradually gone
from acceptance of it all to boredom to loathing.

But since Jay she found herself liking to shop for
new gowns, liking to get her hair done, squirreling
away new eye shadows and face tints for every
time of day. And while it was Charles with whom
she danced and casual acquaintances with whom
she laughed at parties, just knowing she would be
with Jay the next day had added a lilt to everything, and Mitzi found herself sparkling as she
never had before. It was as though Jay were there
at the dance, watching her, laughing along with
her, admiring her, loving her. Jay.

Since Jay—and Mitzi began to feel her life
divided into two distinct parts, before and after
Jay—she had allowed herself an indulgence she'd
begun in Chicago, just after she and Charles were
married, but which he had scotched when he
discovered it.

Mitzi hated killing mice. She was careful to watch for animals on the road and she never put poisons around the trash cans. But most of all, she hated setting traps for mice. It seemed such an attack, setting traps around the house. When Charles had first set out two in their apartment, she had sprung them with a long-handled knife. If only the mice had disappeared Charles would never have found out. But he found mice droppings in the kitchen in a place she hadn't looked, and he suddenly understood what had been going on. Patiently and carefully he explained to her about vermin and disease, and since she could not refute anything he said, and since she was pregnant by then and her health no longer her own, she stopped springing the traps.

Her newly exuberant mood brought a strong return of feeling for other creatures besides herself, and once more she slipped the traps Charles and Dane had set in the basement. It gave her a thrill every time she did it.

As soon as she reached Castles she bounded into the receptionist's area and called for Jay. Anna looked up at her carefully, hesitating before she said, "He's gone into Cedars again."

"Cedars?" Mitzi repeated stupidly, and Anna sighed.

"It's the same problem, but I guess he's doing all right because he's called in four times already this afternoon."

Mitzi had a glimpse of her father sitting in front of the fireplace that first winter after they'd built the house. He was laughing.

"Anna," she said quietly, "what problem do you mean?"

"I'm sorry. I thought you knew. I thought everyone here knew. Jay has cancer."

It couldn't be. Jay was so strong, so generous and funny. *Not cancer.*

She wheeled around and ran back down the stairs to the parking lot and the old Pinto, driving carelessly and dangerously to the hospital, and parked her car in the "staff only" section.

She started to cry as soon as she saw him in the white bed, his face drained, his hair damp and plastered to his forehead. But he just looked at her and smiled and gestured for her to come sit by the bed.

"I'm sorry," he said, "I should have told you about this. But I was enjoying being with you too much. I didn't want you knowing what a diseased old man I am." She was sobbing and he hurried on. "It's not as bad as it looks. Most of the time I do very well. Three years now. It's just that, now and then, it catches up with me and I have to check in here. The chemotherapy is a pain in the ass but it does the job. I'll be back in the office by the end of the week and, I promise you, I've got lots of good years in me yet. Please don't cry like that." He looked at her again. "I take it your afternoon with the old lecher wasn't a success. I'm sorry, I shouldn't have exposed you to it. The whole damn project was—"

She shook her head.

"Oh, Jay, I'd forgotten all about it. But . . . we got the house! Mr. Oaks gave it to me. It's going to be so easy to sell. It's the most beautiful place . . ."

She tailed off. Jay wasn't listening.

"Did he give you a hard time?" he said. "I've been lying here all day cursing myself for sending you off to see the old goat."

She smiled. "He made a pass that he couldn't complete. I think he just does things like that because he thinks it's expected of him. Actually, I kind of like him, or feel sorry for him. He's living on the past and in the past. He was no problem."

Jay was sitting up now. He was still dreadfully pale but his eyes were excited.

"You mean you got it? You got it for Castles? That's all the therapy I need. Come here, I want to kiss you." He did and Mitzi thought, as her lips found his, that this was the real price of being over thirty—that more and more of the people you loved or admired were closer and closer to death.

She hadn't been kidding Oaks about the difficulty in finding buyers for top-market real estate. In the next five weeks she failed to turn up one client serious enough to warrant being shown the house. There were lots of queries about it, certainly, but these were all from the bored people who made a hobby of inspecting great houses. She smiled, remembering those afternoons with her father.

Jay was back in the office, although not fully recovered from the treatments.

"You just have to be patient," he explained to her. "The whole market is off right now, but all that means to us and the kind of property we handle is that it takes a little longer to move a place."

In the end it was her husband who came up with the best prospect. Charles had been unusually attentive to her lately and that made her happier than she liked to acknowledge. He had even stopped making cracks about her job, even reprimanding the children for their general rudeness and indifference to her.

Still, despite the new pleasantry at home, she was very surprised when Charles called her at Castles one morning.

"I thought you might be able to help this patient of mine," he explained. "It's Marie Blair, the rock singer, and her husband. I did a job on her nose a while back and she was very pleased with it. Well, they've been living in a bungalow at the Beverly Hills, but they have to move out because it's promised to someone else, or something."

"Oh, Charles," she said, "that's so good of you. All the clients seem to have vanished right now. If I make a sale to your friends I'll take you out to dinner."

"It's them you'll be doing the favor," Charles said. "I'll have Ned Peters—that's the husband and manager—call you in the next couple of days."

She knew all the properties on Castles's books and in the time before Ned Peters's call came she selected two or three that might be suitable. The old Thalberg-Shearer place down in Santa Monica was on the books for only three hundred thousand, and the George Hamilton place in Benedict Canyon was going for three hundred and fifty. If that was too steep, there were a couple of quarter-million-dollar properties in Holmby Hills.

When Peters called she thought at first it was a joke. He had a thick Cockney accent and his rapid speech made him even harder to understand.

"Your old man said you could help us find digs, love," he said. "So let's get to it."

"Certainly, Mr. Peters," she said. "Do you have any particular area in mind?"

"Nah. Just so it's somewhere around Beverly Hills. Marie gets driven to the recording studio so she don't care where we are. But we'd like a bit of space around us, trees and lawns, that sort of thing."

She paused. "Just how much did you intend paying, Mr. Peters?"

"I dunno. A million or so, I guess. That would get us something, wouldn't it?"

"It certainly would," Mitzi said, keeping the excitement out of her voice. "I might have just the place for you."

After the meeting was arranged she hurried into Jay's office to tell him. He was pleased but cautious.

"Rock 'n' rollers," he said. "They're the worst. They're all crazy. Their idea of fun is throwing TV sets in swimming pools. And the drugs! Still," he said, shrugging, "they seem to be the only people with money these days. And at least the neighbors are far enough away from the Oaks place not to be disturbed by rock parties. You better give them the full million-dollar treatment—helicopter, the works. I don't know what these music people drink, but champagne's always safe."

Mitzi spent the next day at the Oaks house supervising the maid service that Castles used. In the weeks since Oaks had departed for Europe, furloughing all the servants except a caretaker, the house had lost its gloss. It was dusty and unlived-in, and Mitzi brightened it up. She had it aired and dusted and polished before the day was out and then watched over the florist as he arranged fresh white roses and daisies in the main rooms. She placed a bottle of Dom Perignon in the bar in the master bedroom and another in the pool house refrigerator.

Peters and his "old lady" seemed tired and cross when she picked them up in the limousine but they brightened a little at the helicopter pad.

"I thought you might like to see the property from the air first," Mitzi explained. "It will give you an idea of your proximity to the neighbors and the surrounding roads, that kind of thing."

Peters became quite cheerful.

"We use these crates all the time," he said, nimbly swinging into the chopper. "It's the only way to get away from the fans at her concerts. They'd mob you if you tried to leave in a limo."

The star herself still hadn't said much. She contented herself with smiling vaguely at Mitzi but, once in the helicopter, she leaned across and told her confidentially, "I'm still wrecked from last night. Does it show?"

They soared up, high above the elegant bustle of Beverly Hills and into the green-draped hills around. All the houses below them appeared to be little castles, with white walls and manicured lawns. Soon they were over the Oaks place, and the pilot made several long, lazy circles while Mitzi pointed out the highlights of the property. The young people seemed impressed.

The limousine was waiting at the helicopter base and they were soon gliding silently back up into the hills. Peters was in a playful mood, rumpling Marie Blair's long black hair and grabbing at her breasts, finally bringing her out of her catatonic state.

The caretaker opened the gates for them, and the car swept up the drive. It was noon now, hot and clear with a gentle breeze. The property was at its most beautiful.

Mitzi led the couple through the house and listened to them argue about its features. If they wanted their own recording studio, would the dining room convert? Yes, the ballroom would be great for parties. And there were enough bedrooms upstairs if they ever had their band staying over after a session.

It was the master bedroom that clinched it. They both fell on the vast bed and began to romp like children. At one point Peters climbed on top of his wife and began to rub against her. Fearing what might come next, Mitzi went to the bar and opened the chilled champagne.

"I thought you might just like to sit and get the feel of the place," she said, advancing on them with their glasses.

"Right," said Peters, pulling his wife off the bed and slapping her on the fanny. "A glass of bubbly might help the way I feel. You don't have any blow, do you?"

Mitzi shook her head and made a mental note to ask Jay if they should start providing cocaine for people like this. While they drank she told them a little of the house's history and the great names who had been guests there. But she could see that the names meant little to them and that her recital was boring them.

"All right," she said brightly after they had drunk all the champagne, "how about looking over the grounds?"

The tennis courts made no impression on them, except that Peters wondered whether he could turn them into a soccer pitch. But the pool was a huge hit.

"It's lovely," Marie cried and began pulling off her boots. As Mitzi watched in wonder, Marie stripped off her shirt and wriggled out of her jeans. She wore no underwear. She stood by the pool for a moment, tall and bronzed and undeniably beautiful. Then she plunged in.

Peters was sprawled in a deck chair, working on the new bottle of champagne Mitzi had produced.

"Quite a looker, isn't she?" he said, pointing the glass at his wife doing laps in the pool. "Best body in rock, that's for sure. She's part Eskimo, you know. That's why she loves the water so much, I guess. Only thing wrong with her was her hooter. But your old man fixed that up a treat. He's an awful good knife man, considering what a swinger he is."

She stared at him. "Charles?"

"Life of the party, your old man."

"You've been seeing a little of him, then?"

"Cor, three or four nights a week he's been coming to the bungalow for our parties." Peters laughed. "He can't get enough of Marie. That's what we like about being out here. All you people are nice and open about the old drugs and the old fuckin'. Hey"—he looked at her—"maybe when we have our first orgy up here you'll come along with your old man? Then you and I can get it on."

She managed a smile. "Who knows?" she said. Fuck Charles! Fury rose higher but she kept her smile.

"So you think you'll take the place, Mr. Peters?"

"Oh, sure. It'll do us fine," he said. He called to his wife. "That okay with you, love? We take it?"

Marie was hoisting herself out of the pool, her body gleaming in the sun.

"Why not?" she said.

Going back down, Peters gave her the name of their lawyer and said he would put the purchase in motion.

"We want to move in quick as possible," he said. "They gave us the heave-ho from the bungalow because we were too noisy, some bullshit like that. At least up here there'll be no one to complain."

She nodded vigorously and for the rest of the ride all three were silent.

She felt a little guilty about old Oaks. She knew he would not approve of the new owners of his beloved house. But there was nothing he could do about it and they were the only buyers on the market.

She resolved not to think about Charles just then. Soon she would have her first really big commission, thirty thousand for her and thirty thousand for Castles. She sighed. She had earned it.

Chapter Ten _____

JAY WAS NOT RECOVERING AS QUICKLY AS HE HAD expected and it was clear that he was still very sick. No one said anything about it, but he was spending increasing periods out of the office, soon doing most of his work by telephone from his Malibu house. Mitzi, who was increasingly carrying the load of running Castles, was pressed very hard to find the time to visit him at the beach, but she still managed to make it there two or three times a week. She wished it were more.

"I think we're going to have to take on another agent," she told him one evening as they sat on the deck.

"You mean because I won't be coming back?" he asked, sipping his martini.

"No, no!" she cried. "You'll be back in no time. It's just that there's so much work now. Castles has never been busier."

"All thanks to you, my dear," he smiled. "I knew I'd picked a winner. So who have you got in mind not to be my replacement?"

"I think my friend Meredith Jackman would fit perfectly," she said. "She's got a good job with the Dorchester Agency and they're talking about making her a partner, so if she's going to move, it will have to be soon. She's a great saleswoman and she's fun to have around. You'll like Meredith."

"I'm sure I will," Jay said. "If you want her, hire her."

Mitzi glanced at her watch. It was past seven and she should be getting home. Charles was out for the evening and the housekeeper would have seen to the children, but still Mitzi didn't like to be too late. She finished her drink and stood up.

"You're not going?" Jay's voice was husky. "I had hoped you'd stay for dinner. I was going to whip up an omelet or something."

She caught the look in his eye and smiled.

"Are you sure it's dinner you're talking about?"

He grinned and shook his head. He stood up and took her hand and they moved out of the fading daylight and through the big cool living room and into the bedroom.

Mitzi was nervous and she could feel the tension in Jay. They hadn't made love since Jay's hospitalization, and his illness was there between them. It had somehow, she sensed, made Jay afraid to test his body. She had been content to wait until he gave the signal that he was ready. It was enough just to be with him. The physical love could wait.

Quickly he was undressing her, his hands moving with all the old assurance. Her dress fell away and she turned to him and they kissed long and warmly. His own body, under the tan, had a bruised look and she ran her hands over him gently.

"Poor Jay," she whispered. "You've been through the wars."

"And now I'm home," he replied softly. "Home to you."

It was gentle, satisfying love they made, terribly poignant for Mitzi because there might not be many more times. Their bodies were in tune as ever, and they came together then lay together, arms around each other, in the dark.

"I love you, Mitzi," he said. "If we'd met earlier, if things had been different . . . all I can say is thank you for the time you have given me. You know," he said with a grin, pushing himself up on one elbow, "when I first saw you I decided I was going to bed you. I'm afraid I've been a heel with women that way. Always trying for another notch in my gun. But gradually, as I got to know you, I was more concerned with earning your respect— and your love—than with sleeping with you. And then suddenly I was in love with you. A new experience for me."

"I love you, too, Jay," she said. "I guess I knew about your reputation as a . . . a womanizer . . . but you were always just good and kind to me. And so patient. Like a father. And then my lover. I couldn't ask for more happiness than our time together has given me."

Meredith was thrilled with the idea. Jay made one of his rare appearances to welcome her to Castles, and the two of them formed an instant friendship.

"You know, it's silly keeping this big office empty," Jay said to Mitzi. "Why don't you move in here and give Meredith your office?"

"I couldn't do that, Jay," she said. "Not move into your office."

"Why not?" he said. "You're running the shop now and I'd like to demonstrate that to the public."

Now that Jay had physically moved out of Castles he seemed to rally. Full time at the beach suited him; his tan deepened, he became the relaxed, witty Jay she had first known, always ready to advise but demonstrating absolute confidence in her. On the days when she could not make it to the beach, Jay would drive into Beverly Hills, stop by the office to chat with everyone, then take Mitzi to lunch. They were in Ma Maison the day Ellis Gibbons stopped to talk. Jay was affable while Gibbons was at their table but Jay seemed angry when the man finally left.

"How the hell do you know a bastard like that?" he demanded of her. "Ellis Gibbons is one of the nastiest pieces of work in this town. He's a lecherous, vicious man who'll do anything to get what he wants."

She laughed and patted his hand.

"Don't worry, Jay," she said. "I can read Mr. Gibbons's signals loud and clear. I haven't seen him in more than a year. He's one of Charles's business pals. I think he arranged financing for the clinic. He has been by the house a couple of times. Why," she added, "he even made a pass at me one night while Charles was fixing drinks."

"He makes passes at everyone," Jay snapped. "He's a rat where women are concerned."

"Isn't that what they used to say about you?" she teased and was rewarded with a blush.

"You've got me," Jay said. "Actually, it's a pity he is such a heel. Ellis Gibbons could do more for one realtor, just with a nod of his head, than everyone else combined."

"I thought he was just a hotshot lawyer," she said.

"He is," Jay said, "but he's also chief executor of

the Irwin estate. You know about the Irwin thing, surely?"

"That huge estate in Bel Air," she said. "There always seems to be litigation going on about it. I guess it's quite a parcel of land."

"It's more than that. It's sixty acres of woods and lawns and the greatest old mansion left in this area," Jay said. "It's every realtor's dream to handle that place. But for six years now the Irwin heirs have been battling each other over the terms of the old man's will. Sooner or later, though, they'll settle and it will come on the market."

"And Castles will handle it," she said firmly.

"I'm afraid not," Jay said. "It would be the greatest coup any agency ever carried off, but that's not the way it's going to be. Ellis Gibbons isn't going to let anyone, even Castles, walk away with 6 percent of a sale that could be, oh, twenty-five to thirty million bucks. No, Ellis looks down on real-estate people, but for a hunk of money like that even he would be willing to get his hands dirty and sell it himself. I don't see any realtor winning that prize. But for a sale like that I'd even break the rules and act like the other agencies do, halve the commission. Even 3 percent of thirty million would get us nine hundred thousand dollars."

"Maybe I should go to work on Mr. Gibbons," Mitzi said.

"Don't even think about it," Jay said firmly. "Mitzi, the man is a snake. I mean it. Don't go near him."

"Okay," she said, "but at least I'd like to look the place over. Is there any chance of an inspection tour?"

"We'll do it this afternoon if you like," Jay said. "I've been up there a dozen times over the years.

The manager and the staff know all us salespeople pretty well by now. We'll go right after lunch."

It was breathtaking. Jay drove the Rolls through massive stone gates and along a winding white gravel drive. They passed between perfectly matched poplars lining the drive. Through the trees Mitzi could see acres of green lawn dotted with statuary and fountains and ponds. Woodlands edged the lawns and, above the soft purr of the car, she could hear bird songs. It was a vast green oasis of peace and extravagant wealth in the middle of a bustling city. A movement at the edge of the woods caught her eye: It was a deer, stepping elegantly through the trees. A deer in Los Angeles!

They pulled up to the main house, a rambling three-story version of an English castle. Marble steps at least fifty feet wide led to massive double oak doors. She was stunned by the magnificence of it.

"It's incredible," she finally said. "I've never seen anything like it. Maybe a couple of the mansions in Newport, Rhode Island. But here, in the middle of Bel Air, that such a place could exist! It's like a dream realized."

"It's exactly that," Jay said. "The original Irwin was a cattle baron who moved out here before the turn of the century. This was all virgin land then and he took all he wanted to create his fantasy. I guess they all laughed at that crazy cattleman, building a castle in the boondocks. His son, Ben, Junior, got the best out of the place, living through the great era of Hollywood. The old-timers still talk about the parties they had here. His own polo field, where the stars would come play every weekend. All those beautiful, elegant men and women draped around his house and grounds. It's hard to imagine it now. If you asked today's stars to a Sunday party all you'd need to provide would be fast food, cocaine and hard rock."

"But what happened to the Irwin clan?" Mitzi asked. "Why isn't this place being lived in?"

"It's one of those foul-ups typical of a big family estate," Jay said. "Ben, Junior, left half of everything to his daughter, Sally, and the rest to her three cousins. But he didn't think women should handle money and property, at least not young women. So he made Ellis Gibbons chief executor with total power over the estate until Sally is forty-five. She's pushing that age now, so I guess Ellis will be looking to get the most for himself before she takes over. That's why people think this place will be sold off soon."

"What will happen to it?" Mitzi asked.

"It'll be broken up, probably," Jay said. "Even if Sally and her cousins could sort out their differences, who could afford to run a place like this now? The upkeep alone runs to around twenty thousand dollars a week. No, what you'll see here one day will be a dozen or so five-million-dollar homes. A smart developer with plenty of capital will make a fortune and we'll have lost one of our last monuments to the way it used to be. But hell, I'd love to preside over the breaking up. That's the sale we've all dreamed of. With that under your belt, you could die happy."

She glanced at him. It was all right. It was only a figure of speech. "And there's no way to get the job other than through Ellis Gibbons?" she asked.

"No," Jay said. "And Gibbons isn't about to share this pie with anyone. It will be one of those neat little deals, minimum of fuss, and Gibbons will make himself quite a bit richer."

They were on the third floor by then, in a vast, turreted sitting room. Jay had flopped down on a big, carved chest, the only piece of furniture in the room. She could see this was tiring him.

"Just rest a while," she said. "I'd like to skim through the rest of the rooms and then we can go."

"Not till I've shown you the grounds," he said. "I'll get my breath in a minute."

They strolled through the formal garden at the north side of the castle. There were roses everywhere matched in orderly, colorful ranks. Privet hedges marked the paths, one of which led to a Japanese garden where a waterfall bubbled into a beautiful pond. Fat carp were swimming lazily, not used to being disturbed. Jay and Mitzi sat together on a stone bench under a flowering cherry tree. He took her hand.

"I'm glad we came," Jay said. "It's sad and romantic, the last bastion of a grand era. Like me," he joked. There was nothing she could say that wouldn't sound false.

They walked some more, past a lake where a pair of pure white flamingos stepped delicately through lily pads and around the edge of a manicured croquet lawn to the stone and timber stables, empty now but still holding the sweet smell of horses and leather and hay.

"Seen enough?" he asked. "I don't want to keep you from work."

"My God! I'd forgotten all about the office," Mitzi said. "You shouldn't encourage me to play hooky, Jay. But it was worth it. Thank you. I'm always going to remember this beautiful place as it is, no matter what the developers do to it."

They were quiet driving back down the hill to Castles. Another of their few remaining days had been used. Life wasn't fair, Mitzi thought. Why couldn't it go on like this, driving through the cool green, the top down on the car, the sun and breeze caressing them? And then they were back in Sunset Boulevard traffic and it was time to think of business again. The Irwin estate. How could she get it for Jay? How could she secure him the one big sale that would cap his career?

She and Meredith had been close for a long time, but working together at Castles deepened their friendship. Meredith was bright and funny but also she was a bold thinker, one who could spot a trend even as it was being born. Mitzi was the more sensible one. They complemented each other. It was Meredith who sensed the danger of a downward turn in the booming real-estate market.

"What we need to do is tap a whole new pool of buyers," Meredith said late one afternoon as she sat in Mitzi's office. "There aren't any new film stars coming along—at least not the kind who shell out a million and a half for a place to hang their hat. And the industry itself is just about played out. All those 'indy prods' don't spend their money on anything but film in the can. And business in general looks like it's heading straight down the tubes, so people will be putting off buying homes for a while. Where do we look for new money?"

Mitzi didn't bother to reply because she knew Meredith would have an answer.

"The Arabs, that's where," Meredith said. "So far they've been treated like lepers in this town. Just because a couple of them screwed up, everyone treats them like jokes. But they've got all the cash, and they'll probably have it for a long time to come. Castles should be tapping that market. I think it's time we started cultivating our new masters."

It was Meredith's idea but it was Mitzi who made it work. A few days after their conversation she saw a piece in the business section of the *Times* about Adnan Sharif. He was in Los Angeles on what the paper, in the kind of prose journalists reserved for Arabs, terms a "secret investment mission." There was a lot of material about Sharif's fabled wealth, estimated at between two and four billion, which was allowing a large margin for error. The private Boeing 707 was mentioned, and the yachts. It took just a call to the Beverly Hills Hotel to find the supposedly elusive Mr. Sharif, but he sounded wary when she finally got past a secretary and spoke with him.

"Yes, Mrs. Engers," he said, "I have heard of your agency. The fact that it's the only one that hasn't been trying to sell me anything endeared you to me. But now here you are on the telephone and I'm sure you have something to sell to me, too."

"No," Mitzi said, "actually I haven't. We at Castles aren't in the business of making quick sales to strangers just for a commission. We believe in long-term relationships, which is why we are the best agency in the business. It seems to me you might be able to use someone trustworthy, someone discreet."

"Ah, discretion," he said. "A quality I value highly but one your media do not allow."

"That's what I mean," Mitzi said. "All the media hypes have made you people sound like . . . like . . ."

"Camel traders?" he said smoothly.

"OK," she said with a laugh. "It seems to me that it must be very difficult doing business with people who think you've just come out of the desert with sacks of gold you're frantic to give away."

"You've had the experience of coping with a false image," Sharif said.

"I'm a woman," she said.

They talked a while longer and Mitzi suggested a meeting. She sensed that Sharif was still cautious but was too polite to refuse her.

"Tomorrow evening?" she asked. "Just to talk, and see if there are areas where Castles can help you. In the Polo Lounge."

"No," he said, "not in public. No matter how serious our discussion, it would appear in the newspapers the next day that I had been dating yet another blonde. You *are* blond, I take it."

"How did you guess?"

"Isn't everyone in California?"

They agreed that she should come to his bungalow. He and his party, she learned from her friend at the Beverly Hills desk, had taken over five of the bungalows.

Meredith was excited.

"You're sure you wouldn't rather I went in your place?" she asked. "You know I'll do anything for Castles. Lay my body on the line, even. But you . . . the moment our swarthy mark makes a pass you'll flee, shrieking. What if he offers you a puff from his hookah? Or a sheep's eye? Mitzi, your life has been too sheltered for an assignment like this one."

They both laughed.

"Don't ever let anyone outside hear you saying things like that," Mitzi warned. "Most of the people in Beverly Hills would think you meant it."

When Mitzi did meet Adnan Sharif she was

almost dissappointed by just how businesslike he was. No flamboyance, no mystery at all. Just a sober, intelligent man who could only be taken seriously. An aide brought them cool drinks and they sat on the shaded patio and talked.

"I was impressed by your approach," Sharif said. "So many others see us as fun figures, playboys. Or as the upstarts who are bringing the Western world to its knees and need to be taught a lesson. The fault is as much ours as yours, of course. We allowed too many of our young men to wander abroad unprepared. Like the young everywhere, they made mistakes. They spent their money unwisely and created an unfortunate impression. Now the young and silly ones have been ordered home and the somber old businessmen like myself are going to try to repair the damage."

She smiled. "Your own image, Mr. Sharif, is hardly that of a somber businessman."

"The planes and ships and things?" he smiled. "All greatly exaggerated. But I have to travel fast and constantly, and I must be in instant touch with my people at home and in all the places where the decisions are made that will affect our investments. I live well, but no more flamboyantly than your own executives.

"But," he sighed, "image is everything in America, and our image is bad. We are not taken seriously. I have a list of your leading businessmen with whom I wished to meet on this visit. Those who are available at all act as if I were a child in a toy store. They add several zeroes to everything they quote me. Others are not available to me at all. One man, one of your most prominent lawyers and financiers, refused my calls for three days and then finally set up a meeting. He arrived thirty minutes late, told me very bluntly that my race and name would be a grave liability in the United States, and offered to act as my agent in all things—for a mere 20 percent commission. When I demurred he called me a stupid A-rab and suggested I get out of town. It's really rather funny because my cousin, the prince, was at Harvard Law with him and they were, supposedly, firm friends. Friendship does not, I guess, count for much with men like your Mr. Gibbons."

"Ellis Gibbons?" Mitzi asked.

"Yes," he said with a nod. "It was a great disappointment to me, alleviated somewhat by your own businesslike approach. So tell me. Just what is it you think you can do for me here?"

"We'll play fair with you, for starters," Mitzi said. "I assume you'll be getting into property dealings here—office space, residential, speculation—and we at Castles are the best. We can act for you in any real-estate capacity and you'll have our name fronting for you. We know our business and we are respected in this town."

"What do you think I should be buying right now?" Sharif asked. "What would Castles advise me to do?"

"In Beverly Hills I wouldn't be in a hurry," she said. "The market's in a slide right now but it won't hit bottom for some time. Recession, energy"—she glanced at him and he gave a little smile, almost apologetic—"all the current economic phenomena are tending to slow real estate here. The trend won't last long, not in the type of real estate Castles handles, but it will force a few very attractive properties on the market soon. No, for immediate real-estate speculation I'd advise the Sun Belt states, cities in Texas for sure, maybe

Atlanta, places like that. There's a boom in those areas in office and hotel construction and it's worth riding."

"A concise view that is very close to our own," Sharif said. "I think we may well be able to employ Castles's services in the future. I would like us to keep in touch."

It was a beginning.

She and Charles were in the kitchen, having a light supper. The children were out and Mitzi was hoping this would be one of their rare chances to talk. He was so busy these days, with the practice, the clinic, and the steady round of speaking engagements. And she was busy, too.

"Are you happy, darling?" she asked him as he leaned back in the wrought-iron chair.

"Sure," Charles said, appearing surprised by the question. "My work is going well. I'm finally getting some real rewards from it. We've got a nice house, children—yes, I'm happy."

"And my working? Are you getting used to that now?"

"I don't want to talk about that," he said. "I'd rather you were here at home but it obviously means so much to you that I have to live with it. I just hope you'll give it up one of these days."

She came around the table and put her arms around him.

"What can I give you to make up for my time away?" she asked softly, stroking his hair. He smiled up at her. His hand ran up the back of her thigh and rested there.

He stood up and took her in his arms. She moved against him, excited and happy. It had been at least three weeks since they had made love. Soon he was kissing her passionately and his hand was on her breast.

"Do you want to go up to the bedroom?" she whispered. He shook his head. His other hand had hiked her skirt up at the back and she felt the cool wood of the kitchen table pressing against her bare thighs. It was crazy, doing this in a brightly lit kitchen. The children might be home any minute. . . .

"We shouldn't," she said as his hand found her and as she struggled with his belt buckle. He bent her back across the table and pushed her skirt up around her waist. She raised her hips to help him as he slid her panties down, and then she felt him enter her. She felt so exposed there but somehow it added to the excitement. They came together quickly, and then they parted. They stood there in the kitchen, each half naked, staring at each other, and then Mitzi started laughing. Charles laughed, too, and kissed her.

"We ought to do that more often," he said. "Like being kids again."

"I don't think my back could stand it," she grinned. "But any time you like, I'll risk it."

Later, in bed, she was still glowing with good feelings. Things could be better with them if they both tried. And there was the news she had been saving to tell him. She was so proud.

"Charles," she said, "the accountant at Castles gave me my quarterly statement today. You're not going to believe this, but . . . guess how much I'm making?"

His back was to her, and he didn't seem to have heard.

She tickled his ribs playfully. "Come on," she insisted, "just guess."

There was no response.

"Okay," she crowed, "I'll tell you. Your wife is now earning at the annual rate of one hundred and twenty-five thousand dollars a year! Think of it! Me making that kind of money! Oh, Charles," she said, stroking his shoulder, "I want to do something wild and wonderful with all that money, something for *us*. What shall we spend it on?"

If she hadn't been so happy she would have noticed how tense he had become. It wasn't until he shrugged her hand away that she understood. He lunged out of bed and spun around to glare at her.

"Don't you realize what you're doing to me?" he shouted. "You're castrating me. I don't want your lousy money. *I* make enough for all of us. It's bad enough knowing you're traipsing around town, cheapening yourself to make a sale, without you throwing the money in my face. Damn you! I don't have to listen to this crap."

He was pulling on clothes and she sat up in bed, reaching out to him.

"Charles, Charles," she pleaded, "I'm sorry. I didn't mean to upset you. Please come back. Please don't go away. I'll make it all right."

"Go to hell," he snarled and rushed out of the room.

She heard the downstairs door slam and then the soft whine as the Mercedes was started up.

"You blew it," she told herself. And then she began to cry.

"I'm afraid you're going to have to make a hard choice one of these days," Meredith said. "I don't think Charles is going to change. Unless . . . have you thought about counseling?"

"A psychiatrist?" Mitzi laughed. "Charles says all the shrinks he knows are certifiably insane. Damn everything! Just when things here are going so well, something always comes along to spoil it."

"Yes, usually Charles," Meredith murmured. "Speaking of going well, your Arab was on the phone before you got here."

"Sharif?" she said, glad to put the problem of Charles out of her mind for a while. "What does he want?"

"Wouldn't say. Will deal only with you personally," Meredith said. "His direct number is on your desk."

Adnan Sharif was as businesslike as ever.

"There's a building on Sunset Boulevard I'd like you to check out for us," he said. He gave her the address. "The company that owns it is going out of business and it sounds like a property that would suit us for a couple of subsidiary companies. Again, no one must know that I have anything to do with buying it. Your real estate is inflated enough without adding the Arab factor."

It sounded to Mitzi like a very easy commission.

"*We* should be finding buildings for *you*," she protested. "You'll never know what Castles can do if your own people are out locating properties."

"There'll be plenty of time for that," he said, laughing. "If you can just give me a rundown on this place and then handle the purchase—if we go ahead—I'll be grateful to you. There is another thing, though, which is more social than business. I'm giving a cocktail party here tonight and I'd be very grateful if you could attend. It will be very dull, just businessmen, and your presence would brighten the room considerably."

The party was in one of the Beverly Hills reception rooms, and Mitzi saw at once a preponderance of men. There were only six other women in the room with over fifty men, and Mitzi figured most of the women for high-priced Los Angeles call girls: glamorous, blond, and brittle. They called everyone "honey" because there was never time to learn real names. She nodded to one of them, a girl she knew as Alana, who was, as always, on the arm of a man considerably older than herself.

"Thank you so much for coming," Adnan Sharif said softly. "I am afraid you will be very bored. We have not yet got our social activities moving as smoothly as our businesses."

He introduced her to several of his associates, all grave, courtly men who, unlike Sharif, wore Arab dress. The rest of the crowd were businessmen and she thought of them as sharks circling the fresh prey. Sharif had excused himself and left her for a moment when she felt a hand brush against her thigh. She started, turned, and found herself looking into the cold blue eyes of Ellis Gibbons.

"Mrs. Engers," he said, flashing her a smile. "What a pleasure to see you again so soon. Where's Charles?" he asked, making a show of looking around the room.

"I'm here alone," she said. "Strictly business."

"Of course," he said. "We're all here for business reasons. To meet our new masters. Not a very impressive lot, are they?" he added contemptuously.

Mitzi remembered what Sharif had said about

Gibbons. It was quite disgusting the way men could smile at each other and talk over drinks while despising each other. All for business.

Gibbons signaled to a waiter and handed her another glass of champagne.

"Poor Jay wasn't looking too well the other day," he said. "I hear he's just about given up Castles and that you are now at the helm."

"Not at all," Mitzi said firmly. "He's taking it easy while he recovers but he's still the driving force behind Castles—and he will be for a long time."

"Lucky Jay," Gibbons said, his leer pronounced. "I know what he likes to do with pretty ladies."

She blushed but it was with anger, not embarrassment. The more she saw of Gibbons, the creepier he became. Jay was right. Still, he did hold the key to the Irwin estate. He was worth putting up with.

"I wonder if Charles knows what a reputation your boss has," Gibbons continued. "A beautiful woman like you . . . no wonder people are talking."

"There's nothing for people to talk about, Mr. Gibbons," she said, forcing a smile. "Jay is the best in our business and he's taught me an awful lot. For that, both Charles and I are very grateful. Charles is proud of my working and he thinks Jay is a fine man."

"Please," he said, "call me Ellis, Mitzi. You could have fooled me about your husband. I had the distinct impression that Charles would like his wife to be barefoot and pregnant."

"Then you don't really know Charles," she said lightly.

One of the Arabs approached Gibbons and

engaged him in conversation. She moved a few paces away and surveyed the room again. Already the party was breaking up. Like most business cocktail parties, there was nothing social about it. Everyone, the call girls included, was there to make contacts, then move on to something else. Business would be transacted later.

"I hope you weren't too bored," Sharif said, edging alongside her. "A dreadful American idea, the cocktail party, but it does serve its purpose. Maybe half a dozen people here tonight will be worth getting to know better."

"I've made some good contacts myself," Mitzi said. "It was a most worthwhile evening. Thank you. The Sunset Boulevard building—"

He cut her off.

"I'll read your report," he said. "Whatever you recommend is all right with me."

She was leaving when Gibbons took her elbow, steering her across the lobby toward the Polo Lounge.

"You're coming with me for a drink," he said. It was a command. "I'm sure Charles would want me to look after you."

She was finding Gibbons really loathsome, and she had only just realized he was quite drunk. But he was powerful and might be useful. She could handle him. She allowed him to guide her into the Polo Lounge.

The maître d' smiled at Mitzi and bowed to Gibbons and led them to a banquette. They both knew a lot of the people in the dimly lit lounge. When they'd ordered martinis, Gibbons leaned across the table to her.

"I always bring my women here," he confided. "It's so public no one would ever suspect anything was going on. Always do your dirty work in the open."

She winced. He was full of himself, the smartest, toughest lawyer in Beverly Hills. But to her he was also just another drunken show-off. If he hadn't been so crude, she thought, he would be an attractive man. He was about fifty and of only medium height, but there was a virile strength to him. A full head of steel-gray hair, good eyes, a strong jaw: It was a pity he was such an out-and-out son-of-a-bitch. He drained his drink and signaled for another.

"I know quite a lot about you, Mitzi," he said. "You can cut the bullshit about your husband, for one thing. He told me he loathes the idea of you working. And I was there for that beautiful scene when he tried to take a swing at Jay Pressler. I like a woman with guts, and you must have guts to be working in a cutthroat field like real estate, especially when you don't need to. I guess it's going to pay off big for you, too. Pressler is on his last legs and you'll be the big wheel at Castles. Not bad."

"What did you bring me here for, Ellis?" she asked. "Not to talk about Charles or Jay, that's for sure."

"You're so right," he said, sliding around the table to sit beside her. "I'm used to getting what I want, and I have a feeling about you. Do you remember at your house that night?"

"How could I forget?" she said. How indeed? They had been alone for only a moment when he had made the pass, swift and sure of himself, certain no one would spurn the great Ellis Gibbons.

"I want to finish what we started that night," he said. "You and I could do great things together.

How about coming down to Acapulco with me later this week?"

"Shall I bring the children?" she laughed. "And Charles? A nice family vacation."

"I'm serious," he growled, "and I always get what I want. It would be worth your while. Apart from the pleasure of my company, and apart from the fact that I am a great fuck, there's always the little matter of the Irwin estate."

She tensed, and she knew he felt it.

"Oh, ah," he said. "That gets you going, doesn't it?" He let his hand drop to her knee.

"The Irwin estate," she said. "Jay says that won't be handled by any realtor, that you'll manage the sale yourself."

"What does Pressler know?" he said. "I'm going to have to dump the estate before that Irwin bitch turns forty-five. It'll go to a developer and the bids are in already. There's an outfit down in Texas, Lackland Properties, that wants it. I *could* handle the whole deal myself, but why cut out someone like you? A nice little commission, say, 3 percent, for handling the paperwork. I don't need the money and it would be quite a coup for you. Think about it."

She studied him for a moment.

"You mean you'd let me handle the sale . . . a sale that has already been made . . . just for being nice to you?"

"You bet," he said, grinning. "It would give me double pleasure to fuck you and have Sally Irwin paying for it."

"I don't know whether to be flattered or angry," she said. "Of course, it's out of the question. Castles should handle the Irwin estate because we're the best. I think you're kidding me, Ellis. But if you ever want to talk about a deal with Castles, strictly business, then I'm ready."

His hand was moving up her thigh and she reached down and moved it away.

"I'm serious," he said. "I plan to have you and I don't mind using Sally Irwin's money to do it. But that's the only way you and Castles are going to handle the sale."

"No deal," she said. "When you need our professional services, Castles will be there. And we are the best. But not the other thing. Never."

"Don't say 'never,'" he said. "That's my offer and I'm serious. You put out, you get the sale. You don't and you lose."

He had signaled for another drink and she stayed until the waiter was at the table. Then she stood up.

"I've got to get home, Ellis," she said. "Home to my husband and my children. I've enjoyed your little joke and I still hope you'll think of us when you're selling the estate."

He didn't stand up.

"You've heard my terms," he said. "You'll come around. They all do."

The Mercedes was in the garage when she got home and she almost turned and drove away. She couldn't face a confrontation with Charles tonight. The Gibbons encounter had left her feeling angry and tired, and the combination of champagne and martinis had done nothing to improve her mood. She took her briefcase from the seat beside her and wearily entered the house. The television was blaring in the living room, and Dane and Shana were sprawled on the floor watching it.

"Haven't you got any homework?" she asked automatically.

"Done it," said Dane, without looking away from the set. Shana didn't bother answering. Mitzi felt the anger rising. Treating her like an unwelcome visitor in her own house.

As the children grew, Mitzi's expectations about seeing anything of herself in them disappeared. They were nothing like their mother. They were Charles's children. Sometimes she wondered what they thought of her. They had begun treating her rather distantly from the time they went to school, and by the time Dane was nine and Shana eight, they had stopped asking her for help, and often for permissions, as well. It was so strange, and stranger still because Mitzi had no idea why. Dane, for example, would ask his father for a dollar even though he must have known that Mitzi always said yes and Charles didn't always. Sometimes Mitzi wanted to cry. They were her children too, but she wondered if *they* knew that.

She had never discussed her children's defection with anyone except Emily, too ashamed to trust anyone else with what she considered her horrible failing.

"Shana's barely into her teens and Dane's only a little older," she protested to Emily during one of their long talks.

"How can they have . . . have divorced me? That's what it is. They were distant, somehow, even when they were little. Now they're totally foreign. I don't understand it, Emily. They don't have to like me, I guess, but I'm their *mother*."

But this time Emily had nothing to offer her.

Now Mitzi turned away and moved down the hall. She saw Charles in the library, his long legs draped over the arm of the couch, a drink in his hand. He glanced around, saw her, and struggled to get up.

"I've been waiting for you," he said, crossing to her. "About last night . . . I just want to say I'm sorry. It was all my fault. Please, will you come and sit with me?"

She dropped the briefcase on a chair and flopped down in another. Charles was fixing himself a drink and he raised a glass to her but she shook her head. He came and sat across from her.

"That was shitty, what I did last night," he said. He was looking down at his hands, not meeting her eyes. "It's just that I've been under a lot of strain lately. The practice—I don't know, it just doesn't satisfy me. Hasn't for such a long time. You know that. I'm sick of patching up rich, spoiled bitches. And then, when you were talking so happily about your work, your success, I just saw red. I guess I'm envious. You're having fun and I'm so horribly frustrated all the time."

He was, she knew, going to start in again about the emptiness of his work here. But he had been the one insisting on the move. More important, he had *wanted* the change in his work, had railed against the clinic as taking too much out of him. These were all Charles's decisions, she reminded herself, memory gliding back to that day in Oak Brook when he had first spoken of his unhappiness with his work. Disillusioned, her mind had told her then, and it did so again just then. Disillusioned. But how had it all come about? How could Charles, always so certain of himself, be less than in charge?

She brought her mind back to what he was saying.

"I work damned hard and it's not all fun, Charles. You still seem to think of Castles as my little hobby, something to get me out of the house."

"I'm sorry," he said meekly. "It's hard for me to adjust to your job, your success. I know it's selfish of me, but I still kind of expect you to be here, wearing an apron and a smile, when I come through the door after a rotten day."

"That's a great vision," she said. "But for the past few years you've been coming through the door later and later, if at all. You've had all the stimulation of a professional life and you'd deny me the same chance. I'm sorry, Charles, but I'm not going to spend my life doing nothing, sitting around waiting until you or the children need me to scramble eggs."

"I do understand," he said. "It wasn't much of a partnership I was offering you before. But I'm really going to try harder. Spend less time away from home, maybe do some more *real* work down at the clinic, get back in touch. It used to be so good for us, didn't it?"

She softened.

"Yes, dear," she said, "it was good in the early years, in Chicago, and when the kids were little. The thing is, we've changed and grown a lot since then. We can't go back to being two youngsters playing house."

"Well, I'm going to try to be better," he said.

She thought of all the times he had made that vow, but she smiled encouragingly anyway.

"I'll tell you what," Charles said. "Let's go out to dinner tonight, just the two of us. There's a new French place on Ventura I've been hearing about. The kids can fix themselves something."

But she really was so tired. "I'm sorry, Charles,"

she said. "I just couldn't get myself together in time. Let me just fix us some eggs or something. Maybe tomorrow night."

He looked so disappointed that she decided to go out with him, but then the telephone rang. She picked it up.

"Mrs. Engers?" the voice said. "This is Barry Simons, at Cedars."

"Yes, Dr. Simons," she said. Jay's doctor, the nice young man.

"I thought you would want to know at once. Jay's just been admitted. It's very bad, I'm afraid."

"I'll come right away," Mitzi said. "Thank you."

She put down the phone and turned to Charles.

"It's Jay," she said. "He's back in the hospital, in bad shape. I've got to go see him." He turned his face away as she kissed him good-bye.

Jay lingered three weeks. On that first night he had been in a coma. He had still looked, to Mitzi, like the Jay she knew, except for the tubes and bottles. Outside the hospital room she had talked with Simons.

"Is there any hope?" she had asked.

"None," said the doctor. "Maybe a week, maybe a month."

"Will he regain consciousness?"

"Certainly," Simons said. "He'll have completely lucid periods before the end."

Two days later she sat by his bed, staring at his profile. He still seemed so strong and his voice betrayed no weakness.

"I don't like you seeing me like this, Mitzi," he said. "And it's going to get worse. Maybe a couple more visits, if you want, and then I'm going to leave orders that I not be disturbed. Please understand. I want to go remembering the good things, not the way I am now." His hand was resting on the white sheet and she took it. "That first time at the beach," he said. "Remember?" She squeezed his hand, then relaxed her grip as she felt him drifting into sleep.

She went three more times, and on the third visit Jay told her it was the last.

"In the drawer there," he said, moving his head slightly to indicate the bedside table, "is an envelope addressed to you. Read it later, after I'm gone. Now kiss me good-bye."

She bent over the bed and lowered her lips to his. His eyes were open, watching her, willing her not to cry. She wouldn't have, either, except that just as she broke off the kiss, Jay winked at her. It was such a perfect Jay thing to do. The wink brought a sob from her. Wicked, dashing, the wink said it all and it was how she would always remember him.

A week later, on the evening of Jay's death, she was at her desk—the desk that had been his—in the big, handsome office overlooking Rodeo Drive. There being nothing else of his to lay her hands on, she opened his letter. Dated six months earlier, it spelled out the terms of his will.

He left her his equity in Castles; she was, upon his death, the company president. He wished her love and success and happiness and he thanked her for their time together. By the time she got to that part, she had no more tears.

Chapter Eleven _____

AFTER JAY'S FINAL ILLNESS AND DEATH, THERE WAS
never any question of Mitzi's looking for another
love affair. That would have been beside the point,
somehow. No, she plunged herself fervently into
Castles from the week following Jay's funeral—a
hideous Beverly Hills affair with too much Vivaldi
and gray ultrasuede pews in a church Jay had
never mentioned to her, and which must have been
arranged by the cousin who flew in from Charles-
ton and took over.

From then on, Castles received the love she had
always given Jay, the time and the devotion. There
was no reason to want another romance. She had
Castles and, with it, she still had Jay.

The desk clerk at the Southern Continental
Hotel was wearing a denim suit and string tie, the
outfit all wrong for his thin frame and sallow, city-
dweller's complexion. He took his time finding
Mitzi's reservation.

"Christgau, Christgau . . ." he muttered, glancing at her several times. "No, I can't seem to find it
and we're booked up at the moment," he said.
Then, smirking, "We don't get many single women
staying here. Don't encourage it, you know."

Mitzi, with some difficulty, kept her temper.

"I'm sure you got this one," she said evenly. "It was made by my good friend Bill Jorgenson."

That stopped him cold. He straightened up, stopped smirking, and became totally servile.

"Mr. Jorgenson," he said. "Of course, of course. I didn't realize. Oh, here it is. I don't know how I missed it." He studied the card for a moment. "They've assigned you a room over the pool," he said. "That can get noisy. Let's see if we can't do better."

"Yes," she said dryly, "let's just see if we can't."

She was still angry when she reached her room, inspected it, and tipped the bellboy. She hadn't wanted to mention Jorgenson's name. She was trying to travel as discreetly as possible, which was why she was using her maiden name.

Sharif had known what he was talking about when he said that his man Jorgenson would be very helpful to her in Houston. She looked forward to meeting him, but not just then. Right then she wanted to luxuriate in being alone on the road, in a strange city using a name that was now strange to her.

She took off her skirt and blouse and flopped on the big double bed. A nice room, she thought, big and bright, decorated in earth tones, all of it in opulent but careful taste. There was a balcony through the glass doors and it overlooked a lush garden. She could hear the swish of sprinklers below. It would be a nice place to have breakfast, out there on the balcony.

It was growing dark in the room and she got up and closed the curtains before turning the lights on. She moved to the bar and fixed herself a martini, noting with approval the ice cubes, olives, and sliced lemons in the little refrigerator.

Drink in hand, Mitzi glanced through the brochures in the drawer of the light oak desk. Channel 13, she learned, would give her the Dow Jones index, quotes from all the world's markets, and the latest commodity prices. The concierge could provide multilingual secretaries, she read, and all dietary requirements could be met by the hotel's international chefs. She finished her drink as she decided on which of the hotel's four restaurants to eat in that night. She settled on the Rib Room—"Texas-size steaks, open-pit barbecue our specialties." And afterward a drink in the Alamo Terrace. She was humming to herself as she stepped into the shower.

The Rib Room was as rich and dark and masculine as the brochure had promised. The maître d' tried to sit her at a tiny table too close to the kitchen but she pressed ten dollars in his hand and he finally led her to a cozy, leather-lined booth where soft candles cast a glow on white linen and heavy silver. She ate well: a perfect avocado stuffed with fresh Gulf shrimp; and a superb rare sirloin strip. She had a little trouble convincing the wine steward that she wanted only a half bottle of the Bordeaux—it was as if no one in Houston ever ordered half of anything—but all in all it was a fine meal and the service was not in the least condescending. Glancing around, she thought it could be any fine restaurant anywhere, except that the patrons were almost exclusively male, that many of them were foreign—Arabs, South Americans, Japanese—and that everyone seemed intent on talking business rather than enjoying himself.

The atmosphere in the Alamo Terrace was more relaxed, the voices louder, heartier, warmed by alcohol. She gazed around the room for an empty table, easily ignoring the eye-signaled invitation from a group of three men. She ended up sitting at the bar.

The barstools were man-high and she had to struggle to get on one, but she made it and ordered a martini. It came promptly, with a smile, from the tall young bartender.

"I hope you're enjoying the hotel, ma'am," he said. "Are you here alone?"

"Yes," she said, surprised by his interest. "I'm here on business for a little while."

"Well, anything you need, just ask," he said. "My name's Robert and I'm here every night." He drifted off to serve another customer.

The terrace was filling up rapidly and most of the places at the bar were soon taken. She felt someone beside her and shifted a little to make room, but the pressure against her thigh continued. She looked around. He was tall and beefy and red-faced and he was leaning over her. He was one of the trio that had eyed her.

"Me and my friends were wondering if you'd come join us," he said. She could smell the Bourbon. "You look lonely sitting up here."

She smiled.

"Thanks," she said, "but I'm just having one nightcap." She was turning away when he clutched her arm.

"Let's not fuck around," he said. He held out his hand and dropped something on the bar in front of her. It was a hundred-dollar bill. It took Mitzi a few seconds to understand. When she did, she picked up the bill, crushed it into a ball, and stuffed it in the breast pocket of the man's green leisure suit.

"Please leave me alone," she said softly but fiercely. "Go away or I'll call the management."

The man's face flushed a deeper shade of red and he stepped back.

"Cock-teasing cunt," he snarled. Several heads turned to look at them.

She had gone very pale and was afraid she was going to cry. She signaled Robert for the check, signed it, and slid off the stool. The evening ruined by a jerk. She caught the eye of a young black man sitting two places away, who had obviously overheard the exchange. He smiled sympathetically and shrugged. She didn't look at the three men at the table as she hurried out of the bar.

Back in her room, Mitzi tried to get herself under control. She'd been propositioned before, of course, but never so crudely. She guessed it was something to do with the atmosphere of this city, big, busting-out Houston. Whatever it was, she hated it. She was a businesswoman, here on an important mission, yet all those men could see her as was an object to be picked up and screwed. The joy of being off on her own in a new city had gone.

Moodily she switched on the television and used the remote control to flick around the dial. Ed McMahon introduced yet another comic subbing for Carson. It brought a wave of homesickness, though she'd been away less than a day. Impulsively she picked up the phone and asked the operator for the Los Angeles number. She would speak to Charles before he went to sleep. He'd been so quiet that morning, but at least he'd wished her well on the trip and had kissed her good-bye warmly.

The phone rang a dozen times before a woman's sleepy voice answered. It was the housekeeper.

"Oh, hello, Mrs. Engers," she said. "I'm sorry, I was asleep. No, Dr. Engers isn't there. He said he had to stay over somewhere tonight and asked me to sleep in and mind the children. They're in bed but I can get them if you want. Is anything wrong?"

Mitzi apologized for the lateness of the call and said not to bother the children. She'd speak to them in a few days.

She hung up the telephone and lay back on the bed. No wonder Charles hadn't opposed her leaving town!

She slept late and awoke refreshed, ready to tackle Houston. After a room-service breakfast she called Bill Jorgenson's office and set up an appointment with him for an hour later.

The building that bore his name was big, new, and impressive, but Jorgenson himself was not in the Texas mold. He was about forty, short, slim and fair, smooth and courteous, and he was eager to help Mitzi.

"Adnan called," he told her when they were seated over coffee in his vast office. "I'll do anything I can for you but it isn't going to be easy. A whole city block! A few years ago you could have done it, but now . . . real estate's gone crazy in this city."

She smiled. "It's gone crazy everywhere, Mr. Jorgenson. But Adnan wants this package put together and I plan to do it for him."

"Call me Bill, please," he said. "Sure, I've been working with Adnan for a long time and he usually gets what he wants. How do you want to go about this?"

"Well, first thing is I'll walk around the streets for a few days, get the feel of the place, and try to decide on likely sites," she said. "Then it's a matter of title searches, finding the owners of every property on the block we select. After that we find out who holds the leases, how long they've got to run, how willing they are to move."

"You'll need some assistance for the paperwork," he said. "I can assign you a couple of people out of our own legal department, people with real-estate experience. You won't have to worry about them," he added. "Everyone who works for me is discreet."

Later, over lunch at the Petroleum Club, Jorgenson told her about Houston and the oil business— he actually pronounced it "awl-bidness"—and how he was involved in it.

"My daddy was a wildcatter who got lucky in the early fifties," he said. "In one two-year period, twelve of sixteen wells he drilled came good. That's about ten times better than average. By the time I got into the business there was damn all for me to do. Any fool could have run the family company the way oil kept gushing. So I got bored quickly. I fooled around for a few years, then I went off to Europe and worked for Shell, to learn the marketing end of the business. After that I did a couple of years in Saudi Arabia, which is how I linked up with Adnan. I guess I was lucky: I was taking the Arabs seriously before a lot of others realized what was happening. The Arabs tend to remember who their friends are, and they like to deal with them. It paid off for me. The family wells are still pumping away just down the road there, but our company makes even more money these days as middleman for the Arab producers."

"What about Houston, Bill?" she asked. "What kind of city is it?"

"Booming, of course," he said. "Growing too

fast, but you can't slow it down. It's the kind of place where if you haven't made a few million by the time you're fifty, you reckon yourself a failure. It's a very hospitable place, I think. We welcome anyone. But all that growth has brought the usual big-city problems—traffic, crime, school crowding. More and more you have to get out of Houston to relax. People have places up in the hill country around Austin, or away over to Santa Fe, to escape the heat and the problems."

While he was talking, Mitzi had been looking around the club. It could have been anywhere. Bright and opulent, its members all had that air of easy assurance that only success could bring. Many of the diners looked like John Connolly or his cousin—big, bluff, hearty Texans. But there was also a smattering of quieter, smaller men, mostly the Arabs who were an essential part of the oil business. And, she noted wryly, there were all of two women besides herself in the vast dining room.

Jorgenson was watching her survey and he grinned.

"Just about what you were expecting?" he asked. "We don't change very quickly down here. Most of us are desk jockeys now but we try to preserve our cowboy heritage. And, yes, there's not much of your sexual equality in business here. The ERA isn't a burning issue."

As if to emphasize the oddity of a woman in the Petroleum Club, a string of men had been dropping by Jorgenson's table using one pretext or another to be introduced to Mitzi. It all seemed slightly ridiculous to her, like a football weekend at an all-male college, but she tried not to be annoyed.

"Hi, Bill," one man said, clapping a huge hand on Jorgenson's shoulder. "Who's the little lady?"

She winced. Jorgenson laughed and she was introduced to "Joe Bob Armshaw, who's in cattle and a few other things."

Joe Bob inspected her as if she were one of his heifers, seemed to like what he saw, and said he hoped she would be happy in Houston. "Great stores," he said. "The shopping's as good as anywhere back East."

Then he slapped down a copy of the *Houston Post* in front of Jorgenson.

"Did you read this ad?" he demanded. "It's all that the boys are talking about today. Everyone's trying to figure whether they were at this particular shindig."

Jorgenson glanced at the advertisement, chuckled, and slid it across the table to Mitzi. She studied it, puzzled.

It was a double-column display ad headed "Public Apology" and read: "To all the injured parties in particular, and to the others involved I offer my deepest, most heartfelt apologies for the unfortunate events of last Saturday evening. Those involved will be well aware of who has placed this notice."

She handed it back, Armshaw departed, and she looked at Jorgenson. "I'm sorry," she said, "but I don't see the significance."

"That ad just tells you a little about our city," he said, grinning. "It's the old frontier mentality. Whoever placed the ad must have got himself liquored up somewhere and shot up, or beat up, the guests at whatever party he was at. What's funny about it is that half the guys in this room are wondering whether they were involved in the 'unfortunate events of last Saturday evening.' There's still an awful lot of brawling and drinking here." He was serious now. "That's one of the reasons I'd advise you to walk softly in Houston. A lot of our folks aren't used to the idea of ladies in business. They might think it was . . . demeaning. It might be best if you stayed well in the background, let my people do all the legwork."

She looked at him coolly. "Thanks for the advice, Bill," she said. "I intend to be very low-profile, but not because of the sensibilities of your cowboys. Castles might not mean much to Houston—not yet, anyway—but if anyone who knew the real-estate business knew I was here, they'd know something big was going on."

He nodded and smiled. "No slight intended, ma'am," he said. "Now tell me: How long are you going to be here?"

"Maybe six weeks," Mitzi replied. "I'll take one break in the middle to go home and see my family and check up on the office, but there's going to be an awful lot to do here."

"Well, that's fine," Jorgenson said with a smile. "Maybe you'll make the time to come down to Brownsville with me on the weekend. I go just about every Friday night. It's real nice down there. I've got a few thousand acres running up from the Gulf. I just use it for sport, fishing and shooting and riding. I think you'd like it. It's real Texas—outdoors, roughing it."

"It sounds intriguing," she said. "If I can take the time . . ."

"Done," he said. "The invitation's open. You just tell me when you want to come."

That afternoon she hired a car, a nondescript Chevy Nova, and started scouting Houston for the city block she needed. At first she was discouraged: The city had grown so fast and so haphazardly, it was almost impossible to locate any single area that would someday be the city's business heart. Huge office towers cropped up on the oddest sites. There was no sign of planning, no signals for her to follow.

It was difficult driving too. The little car continually thumped into potholes. Hugging the curb, she was continually menaced by cars driven with even more *machismo* than in Los Angeles. Huge Caddy convertibles, one sporting steer horns, the ubiquitous pickup trucks with gun racks in the rear of their cab, Buicks and Chryslers and Lincolns. There was obviously no shortage of gasoline in Houston, and its people seemed to delight in demonstrating the fact. They were cruising everywhere, fast and aggressively, and her Chevy was in their way. Finally she put the car in a parking lot and set off on foot.

It was so hot, in the high nineties with humidity to match, and she felt herself wilting as soon as she left the air conditioning of the car. She was in the northeast section of the city and by three o'clock the whole place shimmered under a heat haze. The new white spires of office blocks swam before her. For the second time since she'd arrived in Houston she felt discouraged.

There was no one else on the sidewalks, only the cars charging along beside her. She felt the sweat running through her hair and down her back. She began to panic. It was the combination of the heat and the strangeness of it all, as if she had been put down here and forgotten. Then she saw the sign: Pearl's Beauty Shoppe: Air Conditioned. She didn't think about it, she just pushed through the door and into the welcome cool gloom inside.

At first she thought the place was empty, and

then she saw the huge shape of a woman in white struggling out of a canvas chair against the rear wall.

"Just look at you!" boomed a voice as bulky as the body. "You look like you're melting away. Come and sit down and let old Pearl bring you around."

Mitzi's eyes had adjusted and she saw a woman her own age, immensely fat, maybe more than two hundred fifty pounds on a medium frame, a head of brilliant red hair over a white face dusted with freckles. She followed the woman's gaze and sat down in a big, old-fashioned barber's chair.

"I'm sorry to bother you," Mitzi said. "I don't really want anything in the beauty line today. It was just that the heat suddenly got to me. I wonder . . . could I possibly get a glass of water?"

"Sure," Pearl said cheerfully. "But wouldn't you rather have iced tea?"

"That would be great," Mitzi said with a smile. Pearl went behind a curtain and reappeared a moment later with two not-too-clean glasses filled with tea. She handed one to Mitzi, who drank from it greedily.

"You're sure enough not from around here," Pearl said, studying her. "The natives know better than to go out walking the streets in the middle of the afternoon."

"No," Mitzi said, smiling. "I'm from Los Angeles. I'm here on business. Phew! I thought I could cope with traffic and heat but I can't cope with Houston."

"It's a tough town for women," Pearl said cheerfully. "It's okay if you're one of the rich ladies living over in Memorial, drinking mint juleps and fanning themselves. But for us working gals . . . what is it you do?"

"I'm in real estate," Mitzi said. "I'm here to find a shop site for one of our clients who wants to expand into Houston."

"Well, good luck to you," Pearl said. "But if you don't already know it, real estate's gone crazy in this town. I've had to move three times in the past four years. The way they keep raising rents and tearing down buildings, it's real hard for us small people.

"Actually," Pearl said, "I've got a cousin in the real-estate business. Well, she answers the phone for this realtor. She didn't start off that way. She went to beauty school, kind of following in my footsteps. Then she got a job in one of those unisex places? You know.

"It was great at first, the tips and all. But she was always getting groped. A lot of these good ol' boys still think women are just for the taking.

"Anyway, one day she's drying this man's hair and she looked down in his lap and sees the sheet jerking up and down. Well, that did it for Maree. She took the hair dryer and smashed it in his lap. 'I'm not going to take this shit anymore,' she screams. Well, the man jumps out of the chair and the sheet falls away and it turns out he's been cleaning his eyeglasses." Pearl started laughing and the fat jiggled all over her body.

"So she had to find another job and now she's in real estate. She really likes it, says it's one job where women get a fair shake."

Mitzi had been laughing too. "Yes," she said, "it's one of the few fields we do have a chance in. But that doesn't mean we don't get hassled."

"I bet," Pearl said. "A pretty little thing like you is going to be fending off passes no matter what. And you can guarantee that in this town."

"Thanks for the warning," Mitzi said, climbing out of the chair. "And thanks for the tea and conversation. I feel a whole lot better. I think I can make it back to the hotel."

"You're welcome," Pearl said. "You come back, now, when you want your hair done. This place doesn't look like much, but old Pearl knows what she's doing."

Outside, the heat was just as fierce, but Mitzi made it back to the parking lot safely. She turned on the car and waited for the cooling blast from the air conditioner, then steered carefully into the traffic and made her way back to the hotel.

Up in her room she stripped out of her clothes, turned on the bath water, and fixed herself a long gin and tonic while she waited for the tub to fill. She slid into the cool water, the drink held carefully in her left hand. Well, she hadn't expected it to be easy. Tomorrow she'd set out again to scout the city, get an early start before the heat.

After her bath Mitzi slipped into a long cotton robe and dozed off.

It was eight o'clock when she awoke and, still feeling lazy, ordered a light dinner from room service. After the waiter had left she picked at the chef's salad, glanced at the TV listings, then tried to settle down with a new novel. Loneliness came over her. She thought about the thousands of hotel rooms across America filled with men and women like her, away from home, faced with making a living on the road. There was nothing glamorous about it. Finally, at ten o'clock, she dressed carefully and went downstairs to brave the Alamo Terrace again.

He was at the same place at the bar and he looked up and smiled at her as she entered. She had time to notice how very young and how handsome he was and how lonely he looked. She decided to take the chance.

"Hello," she said. "What's a young man like you doing spending all his time in a place like this?"

He ducked his head shyly.

"I'm kind of restricted to the hotel," he said. "I'd go nuts if I just sat in my room watching television, so I come and sit down here." He stood up. Tall, six-five at least. "Can I buy you a drink?" he asked just as shyly.

"That would be nice," she said. "Something light. A glass of wine. And do you think we could sit in one of the booths? I feel . . . exposed here at the bar."

"Sure," he said, ordering the drink. "I saw what happened last night. I should have done something, I suppose, but I'm under strict orders to stay out of trouble."

He followed her across the room, which was less crowded than the night before, and waited while she slid into a booth. Then he sat down across from her.

"I'm Tom Wyatt," he said. "Actually its Tane Wiata, Fijian, but no one here can handle the pronunciation so they Americanized it."

"Mitzi Christgau," she said. "Fijian? I never met anyone from Fiji before. What are you doing in Houston? Surely Fiji hasn't joined OPEC?"

"No," he said and laughed, flashing brilliant white teeth. "I'm here because . . . well, I'm not really supposed to tell anyone."

"'Restricted to the hotel,' 'stay out of trouble,'" she said. "You sound like you're being kept in a very expensive prison."

"Gosh, no, nothing like that," he said, looking so embarrassed that Mitzi wished she hadn't made the feeble joke. "I'd love to tell you . . . tell somebody. It's lonely enough being here without being invisible." He drained his beer.

"If you want to talk to me, please go ahead," Mitzi said. "I'm very discreet. And I hardly know a soul here. I think I'm a good listener."

He studied her seriously. "Yes," he said at last, "I would like to talk."

"Six months ago," he said, "at home in Suva, I was playing rugby for my local club. It was the day before my twentieth birthday and I played the greatest game of my life. Do you know anything about rugby?"

Mitzi shook her head no.

"Well, it's distant cousin to your own football and to soccer. Anyway, I was a fullback and on this day I won the match, kicking three field goals from long distances, one of them from fifty-five yards out.

"I was so happy. We ran off the field in triumph." His big brown eyes lit up at the memory. "Fiji is a poor country and my family are plain villagers. To shine in rugby is one of the few ways to distinguish yourself at home. It is an amateur sport but it can lead to opportunities. Already my skills had gotten me a good job as a shipping clerk for a British company.

"Anyway," he continued, "a man, an American, was waiting for me when I came out of the dressing room. He gave me his card and invited me to dinner at his hotel. Mr. Joe Bob Armshaw was his name."

Mitzi said nothing.

"Mr. Armshaw is very, very rich and a fanatical supporter of the Houston Oilers. He told me their place-kicker had been injured in the final match of the season and that if I could kick the way I had that day, I had a chance of replacing him.

"He said that, if I made it, they would give me a contract for sixty-five thousand dollars the first season," Wyatt said. "In Fiji, we have never heard of money like that. It would be enough to buy my own business, take care of my family . . . it would be all I would ever need out of life.

"But there were many conditions," he continued. "The whole thing had to be kept a secret. Their existing kicker has played out his contract and he could go to another team if he chooses—if he's fit, that is. They want me as a secret backup until they find out whether their own man can play.

"So the deal was that I would come here for two months, be put up at a hotel, given pocket money and intensive training," he said. "No one is to know I am here because Houston would then be forced either to sign me to their roster or let some other team make me an offer.

"I train twice a day with a coach who officially has nothing to do with the Oilers. And I wait to see what will happen. If the other kicker fails, then I will get my chance at all that money. If he succeeds, then I have to return home to Fiji as secretly as I came."

Mitzi was puzzled. "But if they don't sign you, and if you're so good, why wouldn't you try out for some other teams? I don't know much about football, but I do know they're always turning over place-kickers."

"No," he said. "For one thing, I gave my word. For another, Mr. Armshaw has me here on a tourist visa. And he has powerful friends. If I tried to break the deal he'd have me arrested as an illegal alien and thrown out of the country. So this is the only shot I have."

"How's the other guy, the one you're maybe going to replace, coming along?" she asked.

"No one really knows. He seems to have recovered from his injury, but he's old, thirty-nine, I think, and he could break down anytime," Wyatt said. He looked guilty. "I find myself praying that he will, and that makes me feel bad. The exhibition games are starting soon and that will decide it. If he does well in them, I might as well go home."

"That's an awful situation for you," Mitzi said. "In limbo."

"At least it's a chance," he said. "I can't ask for more than that." A waiter came by and he ordered two more drinks. "Tell me about yourself. What are you doing in Houston?"

Mitzi gave him the same story she had used at Pearl's Beauty Shoppe. She already liked and trusted the young man but there was no point in taking risks with her cover. He listened attentively.

"Maybe I could help you somehow," he suggested. "Walk around with you or something. I don't drive, but I can cover a lot of ground on foot. And I've a lot of time on my hands."

Mitzi winced at the vision of her strolling the streets of Houston with this very big, very young, very black man. But she couldn't hurt his feelings.

"That would be great, Tom," she said. "Once I've got a plan of action, some places to look at, it would be nice to have someone to help me. The city scares me a little."

"Me too," he said with a smile.

When they finished their drinks he insisted on signing the check. "It's on the Oilers," he said. He saw her to the elevator. He was staying in the old wing of the hotel, in one of the economy rooms. They agreed to meet in the bar the next night after dinner.

Mitzi went off to bed in a much happier frame of mind than she had the night before. She had made a friend.

Jorgenson's call woke her at 8:00 A.M.

"I've fixed up a couple of staff for you," he said. "And a little office downtown that one of my companies sometimes uses. It might be better if you don't work out of here. I told the people I've lent you to be there at nine o'clock today."

Mitzi groaned. She could have used a couple more hours' sleep. Yesterday had been very taxing. But she tried to sound as bright as Jorgenson did.

"That's very good of you, Bill. Thanks," she said, mustering all the enthusiasm she could. "I may be a little late getting to the office today, though. I've a breakfast meeting here with . . . Pearl, Mr. Pearl. But if you give me the office address I'll be over there right after."

"Pearl . . . Pearl . . . I don't think I know the name," Jorgenson mused. "Just goes to show how fast this town is growing. Okay then, I'll leave you to your own works. But call if there's anything you want. And don't forget about that weekend down in Brownsville. I really want you to come."

She left the car in the hotel parking lot and took a cab to her new office. It was in a small, nondescript building and there were no markings of any kind to suggest the business being carried on behind the frosted glass doors. But inside it was lush and comfortable with a paneled reception area surrounded by suites of offices. A slim brunette woman, about thirty, efficient in horn-rimmed glasses, was behind the reception desk. She looked up as Mitzi entered.

"Mitzi Christgau, right?" she said.

Mitzi nodded.

"Mr. Jorgenson gave us a briefing on you, and he described you very well," she said. "I'm Donna Graham, your secretary. A lot of the time I work directly for Mr. Jorgenson." She stood up and came around the desk.

"I'll introduce you to the others," she said. "There's Adam Spence. He's a lawyer on Mr. Jorgenson's staff. He's young and he's very bright. Carol Henson is a M.B.A. from Stanford. They've both had a lot of real-estate experience and were picked for you by Mr. Jorgenson."

"Before we meet them," Mitzi said, "do you—and do they—know what I'm here for?"

"Oh, yes," Donna said. "Mr. Jorgenson told us all about it. I think it's really exciting. Putting together a city block—like playing Monopoly with real buildings."

Her new associates also seemed eager to work with Mitzi.

Tall Adam Spence was more Harvard than Houston, brushed and polished and buttoned-down, with an air of competence and reliability. Carol Henson was a tall, blond, light-skinned woman, relaxed and sure of herself. They were both, she guessed, in their late twenties.

There was a small conference room in the rear of the office, and the four of them settled down there for the rest of the morning. Donna ordered coffee sent in and they arranged themselves around the gleaming oak table. Maps of Houston were spread out over its surface, and on a side table were piled the volumes of the city's real-estate ownership records. Mitzi was pleased by how quickly her new associates had moved, and she told them so.

"No choice," said Adam Spence, smiling. "You want to work for Bill Jorgenson, you have to move fast. He's a very laid-back guy but he expects results."

They talked about possible sites and quoted Mitzi recent prices for typical downtown lots. Even with her experience of Los Angeles's inflated values, Mitzi was impressed. The numbers were very high and that made secrecy even more important.

"Speaking of secrecy," she said, "I guess we'll need a dummy company as we start acquiring the various pieces of property. Any ideas?"

"Yes," said Spence. "I've got all the necessary company registration forms with me. I thought perhaps half a dozen companies might be needed. I have a list of people whose names we can use as company officers. None of them can be traced back to Mr. Jorgenson."

By the time they broke for lunch the operation was ready to roll.

It took seven days, a week of false starts and wrong leads, of slogging the pavements in the burning heat, of talking to salesmen and bank clerks and policemen and cab drivers, of studying the real-estate classifieds, of arriving back at the office in the evening to compare notes with Adam and Carol. Finally Mitzi knew which block she wanted. It was on the southeast side. The business district seemed to be creeping in that direction, and two new expressways were planned to skirt it. The clincher was that there was nothing taller than three stories on the whole block.

It was a mixed block. Small, shabby shops offering shoe repair and dry cleaning and adult books, next to a dozen two-family homes, most of which had been split into single-room efficiency apartments. It had a seedy look about it, a block that had failed. Almost none of the occupants would have any strong tie to the block, except for three businesses which might not want to leave. There was a restaurant which offered, from under a hideous red, white, and blue crudely lettered sign, "The Best Pit Barbecue in Texas." The boast seemed justified as Mitzi noted the stream of prosperous customers hopping out of their cars and picking up their orders every day. She ate there herself and, although no expert on pit barbecues, thought the food was fine. There was a young Chinese behind the counter. He was resting after the lunch rush, and she asked him if the owner was around.

"I'm the owner," he said, grinning. "Oh, sure, no one expects an Oriental to be in the barbecue business. But once they try the food, the good ol' boys don't mind. So what can I do for you?"

Mitzi had rehearsed her story. She had a client who wanted to open a restaurant—Continental, no competition for him, she said hastily—and she was trying to find a site. She had seen how popular his place was and she wondered what he thought of this location.

"It stinks," he said. "I got it cheap, which is the only reason I'm here. If I could afford to run this place where the crowds are, instead of forcing them to come to me, I'd make a fortune."

They talked a while longer and Mitzi knew she could have his site without much trouble. She might even offer him a restaurant concession in the office block when it was completed.

The three-story building on the block was called the Medical Center, a name far too grand for the faded brick and stucco façade. She spent a morning in its dull lobby, watching the building traffic and noting the names of the occupants from the directory. That afternoon she phoned half a dozen of the doctors, posing as a space salesman for a new office complex. The reaction was not encouraging. The only doctor who would talk to her at length explained that he and the other specialists owned the building as a cooperative and had no wish to move. Their costs were rock bottom and, even if the building was small and old, it didn't bother the patients. Doctors, he explained, were like everything else in the exploding city: in short supply. The patients had to come to them, no matter how unprepossessing the premises.

Another building which also might give her trouble was a church. It occupied a corner site on the block and its façade was, like its neighbors, faded and beaten looking. But inside it was cool and dark and well kept. Mitzi stopped there one afternoon, as much to get out of the heat as to look around. She sat in the rear pew for a while, alone. It had the feeling of a place that had been deserted hurriedly and was just waiting for its occupants to return. When she walked back out into the blinding sunlight she bumped into a young man standing on the stone steps.

"My fault," he said as she clutched his arm. "I

never expect anyone to be here during the week."

Her eyes adjusted to the light. He was wearing a clerical collar and smiling at her.

"I'm sorry," she said. "Your church is so peaceful."

"I wish more people realized that," he said. "Most of our members have drifted away. We stay here believing they will return to us as long as they know where we are. But it gets discouraging." He held out his hand. "I'm Pastor Bill Nichols," he said.

"Mitzi Christgau," she replied. "I'm just visiting Houston, looking for a place to relocate a business."

He looked at her keenly. "You're not a real-estate developer?" he asked, then answered himself, "No, you couldn't be. We've had a lot of developers around here. They look at this site and see a potential that, quite frankly, escapes me. You'd be amazed at the offers we've had. We turn them all down, of course. There may not be much of a congregation left these days but we must stay and serve the few who remain. And someday, I know, the people will come back to us. We just have to wait."

She kept her voice casual. "But if they gave you a lot of money wouldn't that mean you could build a grander church somewhere where your congregation could reach you more easily?"

"Yes," he said, "but I don't think we should move out to the comfortable suburbs. If a church is going to matter, it should be right here in the inner city." He laughed. "That's my theory, anyway, and even if it hasn't yet been proved, I'm sticking to it."

They talked a while longer and then Mitzi left

him standing there on the hot stone steps, scanning the streets for the congregation that had moved away. Money, she knew, would not persuade Pastor Nichols to move.

The days were full. There were titles to be searched and leases to be bought. The cost of buying the block, if it could be assembled as one unit, was soaring, but Mitzi was satisfied with their progress.

Most nights she ate in the hotel, too tired to venture out, and most nights she finished off the evening over a quiet drink with Tom. They seemed to have been accepted by the shifting population of the Alamo Terrace and drew only occasional looks.

Every couple of nights Mitzi called home, talking with the children and Charles, when he was there. She could feel, in those long-distance conversations about weather and meals and trivia, that things between her and Charles were coming to a head. Sometimes he was brusque with her, as if she were keeping him from something pressing. At other times he sounded lonely, genuinely missing her. Once, when she guessed he had been drinking, he begged her to come home right away. "I love you," he had said. "I need you here with me."

It was, compressed into a few phone calls, the whole pattern of their married life over again. She knew Charles did love her in his careless, spoiled way. And she loved him, too, but it was a love harder and harder to sustain. Once she exploded at Charles, on a night when he was sounding particularly pitiful.

"Damn you," she had shouted. "Why don't you grow up?" Later she hated herself for it. But, damn it, she wasn't on vacation. She was doing a job, an important job, yet Charles expected her to drop everything because *he* was feeling neglected.

It was part of the reason she so looked forward to the nightly talks with Tom. He was so young and uncomplicated, wanting nothing from her but friendship. They talked about her day and then she listened to his progress in training, sharing his fears and joys as conflicting reports were received about the progress of the man he hoped to replace. A nice, uncomplicated problem—either he got the job or he didn't. Of course, he would be shattered if he failed, but Mitzi wouldn't hear of failure for Tom.

On her third weekend in Houston she finally accepted Bill Jorgenson's invitation to Brownsville. There was going to be a big house party, and although it would not be as casual a time as usual, it was a good chance to see Texans at play, Bill said.

They flew down in his LearJet. The airport was as busy as a freeway. It seemed that planes had replaced horses in the affections of rich Texans.

"That's my spread down below," Jorgenson said, leaning across her. She looked down at the rolling terrain dotted with oaks and cedars. The plane was flying low and a herd of animals scattered wildly at the noise.

"What are they?" she asked. "Cattle?"

"Very special cattle," he replied. "One of the few herds of Longhorns still around. I've been breeding them for years. If you watch out you'll see some of my other animals too. I got deer, mountain goats, sikas—even a bunch of giraffes," he said proudly.

"The spread is only about ten thousand acres," he added, "but there's good water and it carries a lot of stock. Apart from the Longhorns, I use the place for hunting. Do you shoot?"

"No," Mitzi said. "I'm afraid I don't like guns."

"Too bad," he said. "You'll never get a better chance. There's so little cover that it's real easy to bag a deer."

They landed at his private strip and stepped from the plane into a waiting limousine, which whisked them the half mile to the ranch house.

It was not what Mitzi had been expecting. The main building was all glass and timber, starkly modern yet somehow compatible with the landscape. A flagstoned terrace swept right around the house, islands of chairs and tables nestling in the cool shadows nearby.

Two white-jacketed Mexicans came out to collect their luggage, and Mitzi followed Jorgenson inside. The main room was vast, at least sixty by fifty feet, with a floor of gleaming cedar dotted with vivid Mexican rugs.

"It's absolutely beautiful," she said. "I was looking forward to roughing it in a log cabin! Bill, it's one of the handsomest rooms I've ever seen."

"Thanks," he said. "I'm pretty fond of it myself. Let Manuel show you your room so you can freshen up. Then come on back here and we'll have a drink."

Her suite, as opulent as the main room, consisted of bedroom, bath, and sitting room, all beautifully decorated with Mexican wall hangings and solid silver objects. She quickly showered—even the faucets were silver—and dressed in white cotton jeans and a pink silk shirt.

She found Bill back in the main room sprawled on a leather chair dwarfed by the huge fireplace in the stone wall. She sat down opposite him and ordered a drink from the smiling young Mexican who appeared instantly.

"I don't know how you can bear to leave all this for the city," she said. "From the little I've seen it looks like heaven."

"I'm just waiting until I can decently retire," he grinned. "The place has everything I want: hunting, fishing on the Gulf, miles of open country for riding. We'll do some riding tomorrow, if I get rid of tonight's guests anytime before dawn. There's about seventy-five to eighty coming by," he added. "All the neighbors will be driving in and there're a couple of planes coming from Houston and Dallas."

The guests dined in one enormous, gaily decorated tent and danced in another. It seemed to Mitzi that there were far more than the expected eighty revelers present. They were all so big, so exuberant. The evening passed in a swirl of noise and stomping gaiety. She danced with tall men in black ties and cowboy boots and she suffered bruised toes. She ate venison and rare beef and fried rattlesnake that tasted like rooster. The tequila and Jack Daniels flowed and everyone got higher and higher, surrounded by music. A mariachi band alternated with a country and western group, which everyone said was "a real shitkicker band." She sat beside Jorgenson sometime after midnight and watched, dreamily, as a line of men, their arms over each other's shoulders, kicked across the floor to "Cotton-eyed Joe." It was all so American and yet so foreign. She thought she was beginning to understand what Texas was about: the fierce pride, the independence, the determination to stand up for themselves. Perhaps it was naïve, even childish, but it was endearing.

Sometime after the "cowboys" had finished their all-male routine she was aware of a tall, beefy figure looming over her.

"Well, it's the little lady from Los Angeles," the man said. "I've been looking to dance with you all night."

"You remember Joe Bob," Jorgenson said to her. "You met him the day we had lunch at the Petroleum Club."

Mitzi smiled at Joe Bob Armshaw. "Of course," she said. All the drinks were going around in her head and she felt suddenly tiny and flirtatious among all those rugged men. He reached out a huge hand to her and pulled her up from her seat, dancing her into the throng. He was surprisingly light on his feet and he held her close and guided her through the crowd of dancers. They were all hot and flushed by then and most of the men had taken off their dinner jackets. The women, almost all of whom had chosen long, strapless gowns for the evening, had finally blended into the party. Earlier Mitzi had sensed a separateness between the sexes but now, fueled by liquor and music, they were all mixing with abandon, prancing and dipping and swaying together. There was a kind of rough sexuality pervading the floor.

Joe Bob pressed her closer and closer as they danced and she didn't really mind. She just hoped his big hand wasn't leaving a mark on her white silk sheath. Then the hand was squeezing her fanny and she figured it was time to take a break. Joe Bob agreed.

"Christ, it's hot in here," he gasped, releasing

her and taking a red bandanna from the hip pocket of his black pants and mopping his brow. "Let's get out and get some air."

She allowed him to lead her off the floor and out of the tent and across the grass to a cluster of cottonwoods beside a stream. The music and the party lights were behind them now and full moonlight lit the treetops. She stood there breathing in the warm Texas night air.

"What are you really here for?" Joe Bob said between puffs of the big cigar he was lighting. "Old Billy Jorgenson's giving you the grand treatment and he doesn't do that for some little lady who wants to open a boutique or something."

"Well," she said, carefully. "I am in real estate and I am looking over the city. My agency maybe will expand to Houston. It's a boom town."

"It sure is that," Joe Bob said, nodding proudly. "And there's only one person who can help you in Houston more than old B.J. And that person," he said, flicking the cigar into the stream, "is your good new friend Joe Bob."

He moved close to her and put a huge arm around her, pulling her to him. She wanted to laugh, it was all so clumsy, but she didn't dare hurt his pride. He was trying to kiss her and she moved her face just in time. His lips grazed her cheekbone.

"I think we should go back inside, Mr. Armshaw," she said. "They'll be missing us. At least Mrs. Armshaw will be."

"No," he said, breathing hotly in her ear. "No, Mrs. Armshaw will be pie-eyed now and looking for something in pants to give her a thrill." His hands were all over her and Mitzi's head began to clear. The man was becoming a menace. She tried to slip out of his grasp but he held her even more tightly with his left arm, his right hand on her breast, squeezing. Then he moved the hand down to her thigh and began hiking up the flimsy material. She was starting to panic and he was breathing fast and pushing against her. Then, in a minute, her dress was up over her hips.

"Stop it! Stop it!" she cried. "Please let me go!"

"Not till we've done what we came out here to do," he said, panting. His hand was clawing at her underwear, and she felt the delicate fabric rip. She panicked.

She raised her spike heel and brought it down as hard as she could on his toe. There was a crunch and something snapped. The heel had broken off on the steel tip of his cowboy boot.

"Fiery little thing, aren't you?" he said with a giggle. "Joe Bob's just the man to put out the flames."

Panic was replaced by cold white anger. The hand that was up her dress moved away from her and she heard him unzipping himself. Then he forced her left hand down onto him. She had only meant to wrench her hand away and perhaps slap his face but, as her hand touched the huge weapon he was forcing on her, she recoiled. She forgot that around her wrist was an evening bag made of silver mesh. When she wrenched herself away from him, the steely strap of the evening bag was yanked tightly around his member, cutting deep into the flesh. Joe Bob's grip lessened and he stood stock-still, big wet mouth flopping open for just a second before he screamed, falling to the ground, clutching himself. The bag dropped and she picked it up and took a couple of steps away from him.

They all arrived at the sound of the scream, the cowboys and their ladies, standing around the fallen Joe Bob and hooting with laughter. But Joe Bob was impervious to them because of his pain. A tiny, faded blonde in a red dress pushed through the crowd and stood over Joe Bob.

"I guess my husband won't be bothering *me* this weekend," she said, with satisfaction. Then, turning to Mitzi, she said, "You did real good, honey. Old Joe Bob is built like a bull and he has all the sensitivity of one. Now I guess we'll have to treat him like a steer."

The crowd roared. Mitzi, white and shaking, pushed her way through them and ran toward the house. It was an hour before she was calm enough to undress and crawl into bed.

A maid, small and dark and smiling, brought her breakfast on a tray, and a few moments later there was a knock on her door and Jorgenson entered wearing jeans and boots and a checked shirt.

"If you're coming riding," he said, "you'd better be up real soon. This time of year it's too hot to ride later than noon."

She drank some coffee and stared at him over the rim of the cup.

"Bill," she finally began, "that scene last night . . . I'm sorry your party was disrupted. I . . ."

He was laughing. "Hell," he said, "it was the funniest damn thing in ages. Old Joe Bob is always coming on heavy to the ladies and this time he got what he deserved. I guess I should have warned you about him, but I figured you could take care of yourself. And you sure did!"

Then he turned serious. "Joe Bob was so mortified he just stomped out of here, woke up his pilot, and flew straight back to Houston," he said. "I think you've made some kind of enemy there. Joe Bob's got a lot of influence and he could do you harm. Maybe if you apologized—"

"Damn it, Bill!" she said, angry now. "I've got nothing to apologize for. That ape attacked me. I didn't mean to hurt him. That was an accident. I was only trying to get away. But he brought it on himself."

"I know, I know," Jorgenson said with a sigh. "It's just that a man like Joe Bob doesn't like to be made foolish. And," he said, laughing, "he's going to be feeling what you did to him for weeks. I'll talk to him when he's simmered down, see if I can't smooth things over."

Back in Houston, Mitzi managed to put the incident out of her mind. The real-estate scheme was finally falling into place. Adam Spence was worth his weight in gold. He had done all the following-up work on the block, quietly and diligently tracing the owners of the sorry little properties and securing commitments from many of them. Only the medical center and the church, he said, seemed to present real problems to their acquiring the whole block.

But the absence of either of these properties would sink the project. It was Carol Henson who solved the church problem. She came across a magazine article describing the manner in which Citicorp had picked up a whole block in midtown Manhattan where a church had adamantly refused to move. The church elders had finally agreed to compensation plus a sparkling new church, built on the same site, set right into the new Citicorp headquarters. St. Peter's thrived, a vital part of the rebuilt city block. Mitzi went back to see Pastor Nichols and tried the idea on him obliquely. He allowed that, yes, if the church could get some money, be rebuilt, and still remain where it was, he would think that was fair.

There was only the medical center left. The doctors were an arrogant lot: What did they care if their building was old, cramped, and uncomfortable? They owned it free and clear, and their patients had to come to them. No one knew how to solve that problem.

Chapter Twelve _____

THE WEEKEND AFTER THE BROWNSVILLE FIASCO Mitzi flew home to Los Angeles for a short visit. She got in on Friday afternoon and went straight to Castles because none of her family would be home before evening. It was with real joy that she embraced Meredith.

"You don't know how much I've missed you," Mitzi said. "To have someone who understands, someone to talk to . . ."

They sat in the office above Rodeo Drive while Mitzi told of her Houston experiences. She winced when Meredith burst into laughter over the Joe Bob story.

"It wasn't a damn bit funny," Mitzi said. "It's not right that we should have to put up with that kind of thing."

"I know," Meredith said. "It's something all woman have to cope with. At least you have the satisfaction of being successful. They try to screw you, then you screw them by being smarter. Just think of all the poor women stuck in jobs they have to keep, and all the sexual harassment they take. You and I aren't so badly off."

"Still, it's demeaning and infuriating," Mitzi said. "And—I hate to confess this—sometimes it makes me want to give up and just rush home to safety, back to the nest."

"Apart from the groping," Meredith said, "how is the grand scheme developing in Houston?"

"Pretty well," Mitzi said. "It's all coming together." She told Meredith about the final holdouts and how she was handling them. "I wish I could get it all wrapped up, though," she said as she fixed them a drink. "I don't like leaving Charles and the kids for so long."

"Send me, if you like," Meredith laughed. "Frank is in the middle of his great novel and I might as well not be there. Still, I can't complain. He comes home from that madhouse publicity department at night and half the time I'm still out selling houses. He's a good guy—he really wants me to do what I want." She studied her friend. "How's Charles standing up to your absence?"

Mitzi sighed. "Sometimes he's not there when I call, out with his buddies or whatever. At other times he sounds like a little lost child. He makes me feel so guilty, like I'm letting them all down. Maybe I am. But I can't believe my children need me for anything. It's been ten years since they have."

It was one of their better weekends. Charles told her, proudly, that he'd cleared his schedule for her whole visit. He'd even done the marketing, laying in vast slabs of steak for barbecues. She never wanted to see another piece of charred beef after her sojourn in Texas but she didn't tell him that. Dane and Shana were pleased to see her, but nothing was going to interfere with their social lives, and on that first night back she and Charles were left alone.

They ate by the pool under the stars. There was a

lot that she wanted to raise with Charles but she decided to leave it, to enjoy this peaceful time together. She watched him as he filled her wineglass. They were both lucky, she thought. Despite all the tensions, they were well and, she supposed, as happy as anyone expected to be.

Later, when Charles sat by her and gently stroked her arm, she spoke to him about being back.

"I really missed you," she said. "At first I thought it would be wonderful to be free, on my own. You know, it seems I've always been looking after someone else, instead of just looking out for me. But in Houston, in the damned hotel, I found I missed you so much. I know we can make this work if we both try."

"Sure, sure," he said absently. "I love you, too. Always." He stood up and pulled her gently from her chair. "Come on upstairs," he said. "It's been so long."

In the bedroom he undressed her and she moved against him, feeling his masculine strength, the currents he gave off. Their first lovemaking was furious and swift and they climaxed together. Then, like people just getting to know each other, they started again, a long, drawn-out courtship and acceptance. It seemed to go on forever and it left Mitzi pleasantly sleepy and fulfilled.

Later Charles sat back in bed, smoking a cigarette and grinning at her.

"Maybe we should spend more time apart," he said. "The coming together afterward is so much fun."

She smiled back at him and let herself drift off to sleep, happier than she had been in a long time.

* * *

The good mood lasted until she returned to Houston on Tuesday. Carol was waiting for her in her office.

"I've been seeing one of the young doctors over at the Medical Center," her assistant said. "Just to keep an eye on the situation, looking for a way to get through to them. Well, I was out with him last night and he let slip that the building was sold late last week. He doesn't know who bought it, just that the board sent around a note saying they'd had an offer they couldn't refuse. We've been working on it ever since and we'll know who the buyer is soon enough. But it's damn sure our cover was blown. Whoever has that building will be able to hold us up for ransom now."

It was a bitter blow. All their scheming, the intense organizing, the slipping around and buying up leases, all for nothing.

In midafternoon Bill Jorgenson called her.

"It was Joe Bob," he said bitterly. "And I think it was all my fault. After your little set-to with him I tried to patch things up, told him you were down here on a big real-estate deal for Sharif and that was why you were so uptight. I shouldn't have done it, I know. He must have got his people working right away, found out what you were up to, and got to the people who run the Medical Center."

She fought to control her anger.

"So what do we do now, Bill?" she said. "Just give up? I'm not used to being beaten like this. I think you better call Mr. Joe Bob Armshaw and see what his terms are."

"I already did," he said, wearily. "He wants twenty million for the building."

"He's got to be joking," she cried.

"No, he's vengeful," he replied. "The building's not worth a million as it stands and it might be worth ten million as the key to your assemblage, but that's it. Joe Bob wanted to screw you one way or another, and he's succeeded. Either you pay his price or you end up stuck with a bunch of buildings you can't do a thing with. I tried everything with him—appeals to friendship, threats, everything I could think of. I brought Adnan's name into it and he just said that while I may jump when the A-rabs whistle, he is his own man. And the son-of-a-bitch is, you know. He can do as he pleases."

She left the office early, furious. Tom Wyatt was walking away from the hotel newsstand when she came through the lobby and he greeted her with boyish enthusiasm. She wanted to escape to her room but she allowed Tom to steer her into the coffee shop.

"Everything's looking great," he told her, grinning hugely. "Mr. Armshaw came by when I was working out today and he told me to keep at it, that he thought there was going to be a place for me with the Oilers. He was in a great mood, really nice to me."

I bet he was in a good mood, Mitzi thought. She hadn't told Tom that she knew his mentor because she hadn't wanted to upset him.

"I'm glad it's looking up for you, Tom," she said. "I'd love to stay and talk, but I'm just so tired from the flight. I'm going to eat in my room and get an early night."

"Okay," he said, still buoyed by his own good news. "Maybe tomorrow night? I really missed our talks while you were away."

She came to appreciate more than ever her nightly talks with Tom. His enthusiasms, his unhidden admiration of her, the lessening of his shyness, all these things helped her through the bad time that visiting the office had become. Each day the figures come out the same: She had laid out four million dollars already for a group of buildings that were worth a fraction of that figure, unless they could be grouped together and razed. She had made commitments for another six million dollars, commitments that would now have to be broken. And they had been so close to success! It would have required another year of waiting for leases to expire, for contracts to be exchanged, but they could have done it, all of it.

She had been back in Houston a week when Charles called.

"I wanted to tell you myself, before you read it in the papers," he said. He sounded scared.

She felt something icy in her stomach. Something awful had happened. The children?

"There was an accident last night," he said. "Nothing serious," he added hastily. "I was driving the Mercedes down Laurel Canyon. I'd been to a party—no one you know."

She listened and waited. So Charles had gotten himself in trouble somehow. She had been expecting this.

"I gave a lift to this woman, an actress," he said, letting it all spill out. "Moira Johnson, actually, from Chicago, you remember her. Anyway, the car slid off the road and hit a tree. I wasn't hurt but she was a little banged up around the face. She'll mend all right but when the police arrived she was hysterical, screaming that she was maimed for life. And, of course, the bastards from the press were right behind the police. They got pictures of her and the car and me. It'll all be in the *Herald Examiner* this afternoon."

She kept her voice cool. "Is that all? Are you going to get sued?"

"No, no," he said quickly. "Moira is okay today and doesn't blame me for what happened. There'll be no trouble there. But . . . the police did take us back up to the house where the party was, to wait for the doctor and, well, it turned into a raid. There was quite a lot of cocaine around and the hosts were arrested. The press got that, too," he said, sounding bitter and persecuted.

"So," she said, "the headlines will be all about the prominent plastic surgeon, the starlet, and the wild party. Right?"

"Yes," he said miserably. "Mitzi, I'm so sorry. There was nothing to it, just a little accident, but you know how the media play these things up. It was just rotten luck."

"Stop whining, Charles," she said. "You just take care of it all. I've got enough to cope with here without a husband carrying on like a teenager." And she hung up on him, slamming the phone down.

Troubles did come in threes. That night when she went to her room she found Tom Wyatt pacing the corridor outside. He looked strained and nervous.

"Tom, what are you doing here?" she said. She couldn't keep the edge out of her voice. She was angry and beat.

"I came to say good-bye," he said, scuffing the carpet with the toe of his shoe. "It's all over, everything. They told me today that I'm not going to make the team. I'm supposed to be on a bus for

Los Angeles now, then a plane home. There isn't even a room for me here anymore. They canceled everything, as if I never existed."

She was fumbling with her door key.

"Come inside and sit down and tell me about it," she said. For the moment her own troubles were forgotten.

He followed her into the room.

"I couldn't go without saying good-bye to you," he said. "You've been so patient with me, listening to all my woes when I know you must have so many more important things to do."

He sat on the edge of a floral-patterned armchair.

"Do you want a drink?" she asked, moving to the bar. His reply was muffled and she turned to see him hunched in the chair, weeping. His broad shoulders were heaving.

She moved to him and took his hands from his face. She held the hands and talked gently to him, soft, reassuring words. He looked so young and helpless and, without thinking about it, she kissed him on the lips.

She led him to the bed, turned off the light, and undressed him, reaching up to his great height to fumble with his shirt buttons. She didn't think about what she was doing. It was giving comfort and it felt right.

She slipped out of her own clothes and took him in her arms, shivering as she felt him against her, so huge and yet so vulnerable, so young and hurt.

They made love in silence, gently at first and then rising to a shattering peak as all the frustration and disappointment in both of them came out. Afterward he slept like a child while Mitzi lay in the dark smoking a cigarette and thinking. It had been a different kind of love for her, totally giving, selfless. She was glad she had been there for Tom's sake. No shame. It had been the right thing to do.

She awoke at dawn, still thinking. A plan had formed.

"Tom, wake up," she whispered. "You and I have a lot to talk about."

He was shy then, trying not to meet her eyes, and she slipped into the bathroom to shower and dress and give him time to get used to the change in their friendship. When she returned he was dressed and sitting in the same armchair by the curtained window.

"I'm going to order breakfast," she said cheerfully. "I'll have cereal and you can have eggs and bacon. Room service is going to think I've suddenly developed a big appetite."

He stayed in the bathroom until the waiter had left and then they sat across from each other at the small table.

"Have you got all the documents you signed with Mr. Armshaw?" she asked without preamble.

"Yes," he said, pulling a thick brown envelope from his inside jacket pocket. She took them.

"I want to make copies of these as soon as the secretarial service opens for business at nine," she said. "After that, I want you to go to Los Angeles and see a man I know there. I'll call him. He'll be expecting you. Have you got any money?"

"Two hundred dollars, plus my bus and plane tickets," he said.

She fished in her bag.

"Here's another two hundred. You'll need it. The man I'm sending you to see will be able to give you more if he decides to work with you."

He started to protest but she laughed.

"No, Tom," she said. "It's I who owe you. You'll see."

Joe Bob Armshaw kept her waiting an hour in his outer office. It was noon before a secretary led her in to the vast paneled room where Armshaw conducted his business.

"Come to beg, have you?" he said with a sneer, rocking back in his chair and putting his boot-clad feet on the big oak desk. "It won't do you any good. I want this lesson to be a long and painful one for you. You don't make a fool of Joe Bob Armshaw."

She sat down uninvited and spoke.

"No," she said, "I've come to bargain, not to beg." She reached into her bag and removed the copies of Tom Wyatt's letters of agreement and slid them across the desk.

"You're familiar with these, I think," she said. "What they comprise is everything from restraint of trade to the most blatant of recruiting violations. All done to an innocent victim, an unsophisticated kid from a Pacific island."

Armshaw was sitting up straight, looking very nervous.

"Tom Wyatt is now on the way to Los Angeles," she said. "But not back to Fiji. I've sent him to an old friend of mine, the best sports agent in the business. Depending on what you decide today, that agent will or will not release the whole story to the press.

"And it's a great story, isn't it, Mr. Armshaw? How the mighty Oilers played with the career of a trusting kid and then threw him out."

He was on his feet.

"It's nothing to do with the Oilers," he protested. "I was acting on my own. I love that club so bad, I just wanted to help them if they needed it."

"You and I know that, Mr. Armshaw," she said, "but who is going to believe it? It's going to be a very dirty business and a lot of that dirt will rub off on your beloved club. They're going to be in a lot of trouble, and you are going to be mud around the clubhouse. I don't think you'll get to use that fancy box of yours again."

"What do you want?" he asked, and she knew she had won.

"One: Tom Wyatt is free of all agreements he made with you. That's easy, anyway. The deal would never stand up in court," she said. "Two: you'll sell me the Medical Center building for a reasonable price. Two and a half million."

He flushed.

"I paid five million for that, plus throwing in three floors of prime space in one of my own buildings," he said. "Ten million's the least or else I lose too much on the deal."

"You can afford a small loss," she said. "It's the price of my silence and Tom's."

He looked at her with loathing, then shrugged.

"Looks like you've won," he said. "This time." Then he fixed her with his gaze. His eyes were a cold, deadly blue. "There's just one thing I want to know," he said. "You've obviously been screwing this kid. Why would you fuck a nigger and not me?"

She stood up.

"That, Mr. Armshaw, is something you will never understand."

She walked out of his office without a backward glance.

Chapter Thirteen _____

THEY WERE ALL SO PLEASED TO HAVE HER HOME that Mitzi wondered all over again if she was right to spend so much time away from them. Dane and Shana went out of their way to be polite and helpful, even loving. After all the years of rudeness or indifference, it was a dramatic change.

And Charles. She guessed it was shame over the Moira Johnson fiasco, but he was touchingly eager to please her, embarrassingly grateful that she had come home. Charles and Dane and Shana had been waiting for her at the airport, an unprecedented greeting, and they had fussed over her and competed for her attention. She luxuriated in all of it, knowing it could not last and that there were still some very grave matters to be dealt with between her and Charles.

During that night's meal of endive salad and artichokes, broiled chicken and fresh raspberries, Shana very proudly announced that she had helped the housekeeper with the dinner. Then Dane, with a glance at Shana, said he had something to say.

"Mom, Dad," he began, "Shana and I have been talking things over while Mom's been away. We both figure we've been real pains in the ass lately. We know you've both got your own problems."

Mitzi stole a glance at Charles, who was staring down at the tablecloth. "We figure we've been adding to them."

"Out here," Shana broke in, "the kids are all trying so hard to be cool. That's all that matters, being cool and dope. Everyone's parents are divorced, and well, it's hard to be normal. It's hard."

"So what we decided, Shana and I," Dane said, "was that we'd like to go back to Chicago, go to school there. We can get into Millbrook because Dad went there, and it's coed now and it's not far from Grandma's place. We don't see any point in staying here," he finished somberly.

After a stunned silence, Mitzi asked, "Shana?"

"Yes, that's what I want," she said. "I'll miss you both terribly, but I don't want to grow up like a lot of kids here."

"Charles?" Mitzi asked. "Did you know about this?"

"No," he said. "First I've heard of it. But it makes sense. Millbrook's a great school and my mother would love to have the children close by. Chicago is a real place to grow up in. And we'll get together every few months, what with vacations and all. To tell you the truth, I feel guilty that I didn't think of it myself."

"We'll have to think about it," Mitzi said. "I hadn't realized how much you hated it here." She knew she had been putting off doing something about the children, just as she had been putting off having the showdown that must come with Charles. Sending the children away to school would be an admission of failure, an admission that, as a happy family, the Engers just weren't working out. But it was time to face those facts for Dane and Shana's sake.

She and Charles were left alone in the library a few hours later, the children gone to bed. There was a silence between them. He was waiting for her to speak and she let him wait. Finally he had to make the first move.

"The business with Moira Johnson," he said. "I'm sorry I caused us all so much embarrassment. It was just one of those things, a piece of damn bad luck."

"Was it, Charles? 'Bad luck'? Moira Johnson and you have been turning up together for years now."

"But Jesus, I swear there's never been anything in it," he said. "I knew her before, and in a town this size I can't help running into her now and then. But that's all."

"I don't believe you," Mitzi said simply. "I know you've been leading another life away from me and the children. You started to find me too . . . predictable, not dramatic enough for you. I can guess what you and your friends do at night. Remember, I see life in the fast lane every day, selling houses to those people. And why should you be any different from the other people who are leading the fast life out here? That's one more reason I went to work. Maybe I was wrong, but I thought our marriage would have a better chance of surviving if I were doing something, if I made myself more interesting to you. Instead all you've ever done was resent it like hell and sleep around with two-bit actresses."

He grew red and his voice was angry.

"I'm not sleeping around!" he snapped. "Maybe if you were home more often you'd know that." Then he looked at her appealingly. "Please, Mitzi, give me a chance. I'm trying so hard."

They made love that night and it was good. But later, just before falling asleep, she found herself wondering why Charles was so insistent that he wasn't sleeping around. Maybe he'd stopped. Maybe they could work things out. She finally drifted into sleep, a little optimistic.

"The cash-flow problem is quite grave," Mr. Tuckwell said, closing the books and rubbing his long nose.

"You mean we're in the shit," Meredith said, lounging in the seat by Mitzi's desk.

The accountant blushed.

"No, Mrs. Jackman," he said, "that's too extreme. Castles is prospering, but the nature of the business, the long delay between a sale and its completion, the general slowdown in the trade mean that you are experiencing a liquidity crunch."

"But what can we do about it?" Mitzi asked. "This is the best agency in town. Our volume's down, but not as badly as that of most of the others."

"The first thing to do is cut back on staff," Tuckwell said. "Cut overhead, retrench until times improve. When interest rates go down again you'll be selling more houses, faster, and you'll also be able to get more bank credit to tide you over."

"I can't just tell our people, 'Sorry, we have a liquidity problem and you're out of a job.'" Mitzi was adamant. "That's immoral and I won't do it. And anyway, our people are Castles's greatest asset. If we laid them off now we'd never get them back when we wanted them."

"I see no other way . . ." he began.

"Yes, there is a way," Mitzi said, sitting upright.

"Expand. That's the way. That's what Jay would have done. I saw it in Houston, the growth that's going on. All the Sun Belt cities, and Washington, D.C., and New York. They're the sort of markets Castles should be getting into now."

In fact, business soon picked up at Castles. If some of the business community had laughed at "a couple of women" running the agency, Mitzi and Meredith were now taken very seriously. Castles, it was acknowledged, performed its task better than any other agency, and Mitzi kept raising the minimum on properties they handled: from one hundred fifty thousand dollars to two hundred thousand, then finally to a round quarter million. And there were an awful lot of houses selling for a quarter million dollars or more in their territory.

Sharif, well pleased with the way the Houston project was going, paid her two hundred thousand dollars on account, and Mitzi used the money to set up a Castles office in Houston with Carol Henson in charge. Bill Jorgenson hadn't been happy to lose the young woman but Mitzi won him over.

She also had her sights on a small agency in Atlanta. But it was the nation's capital that she really wanted to be established in: Even compared with Los Angeles, Washington was a crazy real-estate town, with properties doubling and tripling in value in a couple of years.

Jorgenson came through for her there. The Texan was in Los Angeles for a week and during lunch at La Scala she said to him, "The Washington thing is so tantalizing and so frustrating. Real estate is booming there, but if you're not connected in Washington, forget it!"

"I might be able to help you," Jorgenson said

casually. "Willie Bladen's wife, Joy, used to be a realtor in Corpus Christi, a damn good one. Then old Willie got himself elected to Congress and now he's a big wheel on the House Foreign Relations Committee. I saw them down home a few months back and Joy was complaining then that she's going nuts with nothing to do but go to embassy parties. She said she wanted to go back to work but Willie was against it. She'd be worth trying—open all the doors for you and maybe even head up your new branch office. I'll call her if you're interested."

A week later Joy Bladen called Mitzi at the office and the two women arranged to meet in Washington on the first of the month.

Joy Bladen was tanned and blond and exuberantly Texan. She came striding across the lobby of the Hay Adams and pumped Mitzi's hand.

"It's great to meet you," Joy said. "Bill gave you a hell of a build up. I know we're going to get along together just fine. Let's go over to my house and sit down and have a good talk."

Mitzi followed her out to the car. Joy seemed to know everyone in Washington, and their progress was slowed as she stopped to exchange kisses with several women. Finally they were in the limousine and sweeping through the streets to the green quiet of Georgetown. The Bladen house was a handsome three-storied Victorian mansion set among cherry trees.

"It's beautiful," Mitzi said when they were sitting in the parlor. "I didn't realize Washington had so much old character."

"It's recent old character," Joy laughed. "For a long time this was a city in which all you wanted to do was get away from it. People stayed Monday through Thursday, then went home. But in the past few years D.C. has developed a life of its own and some of us really love living here. Of course," she said with a laugh, "that's if you can afford to live here. We bought this place for a song ten years ago, when Willie first came up. I reckon now, with the market so crazy, it would go for eight or nine hundred thousand. Which is why you're here, right?"

"Yes," Mitzi said. "I never thought anything would top the Los Angeles boom, but everything I've heard about Washington says it's the place to be. I'd love Castles to have a place here."

"No reason why you shouldn't," Joy said. "About half the congressional wives have taken out real-estate licenses, but most of them are just playing at it. And there's always room for one more. The thing about the market here is that there's a constant turnover. Every two years a new crop of congressional faces, every four or eight years a whole new administration. As Bill told you, I've been thinking about getting back to work myself. If you wanted me to come in with Castles, I think we could work something out. I know the business and I know this town. Being married to Willie doesn't hurt, either. A lot of people are going to think that by dealing with me they're getting brownie points with him. They won't, of course, but that doesn't matter. This place operates on images, images of power, and if they think you've got power they come flocking around you."

Joy held a dinner to celebrate the setting up of Castles East. She gathered four senators, six congressional representatives, three Cabinet Secretaries, two key White House staff members, and four ambassadors, plus representatives of what she called the fun crowd.

Mitzi was nervous before the dinner, and more so when she saw the newspaper. A columnist led off with an item about the new enterprise.

Joy Bladen, the Texas whirlwind, is forsaking the round of parties, parties, parties to return to her first best love, selling stately mansions. Joy's husband, the revered Foreign Relations honcho, Willie, is none too happy about Joy re-entering the work force. He'll be even less happy when he learns that his wife's new partner is Mitzi Engers, the woman who set the Los Angeles real-estate market on its ear. The redoubtable Ms. Engers just happens to have as her best customer Adnan Sharif, the Saudi moneybags. Shades of the Marion Javits-Iran flap?

Mitzi called Joy.

"Willie just got off the phone," Joy said, laughing. "He was sputtering. I calmed him down and reminded him that down in Texas we do more business with the Arabs than anyone else does. Don't worry about it. It'll blow over."

Certainly no one at the dinner seemed concerned with the gossip column. She might have been back in Los Angeles: It wasn't matters of state they discussed, but matters of scandal. Who was sleeping with whom, who was drinking too much, who was the heaviest loser in the Senate's longest-running, highest-stakes poker game. And they talked, as did the residents of any big city, about real estate, boastful stories about how much they had been offered for their homes, hard-luck stories about the little place they could have bought for a song just two years before.

It was, Mitzi noted, a harder-drinking crowd than in Los Angeles, the white wine revolution apparently not having reached Washington yet. And as the drink flowed in the paneled drawing room and the voices rose, Mitzi felt excitement rising in her. Castles was going to make it in Washington. Jay would have been so proud.

Senator Hocking was already drunk, but he carried it well. It was only the slight lurch when he passed Mitzi a fresh glass of Dom Perignon that gave him away. He seemed to have been sizing her up during their small talk and soon he gave her his personal stamp of approval.

"You're going to do just fine here, little lady," he said, bending closer to her and staring down the front of her dress. "This isn't a male chauvinist town anymore. We really like to see you gals getting out and doing something. If I can help in any way, you just call on me. Maybe you'd like to stop by my office and we'll talk. There's not much goes·on in Washington that I don't know about."

"Thanks," she said, wishing she could politely get away from the old bore. "But I'd have thought you people would steer clear of me and my notorious 'Arab connection.'"

"Hell, no!" he said. "That's all bullshit. The Saudis are okay, and they've helped finance the campaigns of quite a few men in this room. Now, if you were tied up with those crazy Libyan bastards, or the PLO, or, God forbid, the Iranians, you might have a problem. But we should be getting closer to the Saudis instead of letting those goddamned Hebes dictate our foreign policy."

"I'm Jewish, Senator," she said easily, without rancor.

"Oh . . . ah," he muttered and turned away.

Going into dinner, Joy took her arm and whispered to her, "We're home free, everyone thinks we can't miss. And I see you're charming the pants off old Hocking. Did he ask you up to his office?"

Mitzi nodded.

"You ought to go just for the experience," Joy said. "He got me up there when I was a new congressional wife. The office is set up like a bordello. All red plush couches and oak bars. He tried to get me into his private sauna. I don't think the old fart can get it up anymore. He drinks too much. But still, he tries."

"How does he get away with it, the drinking and the carrying on?" Mitzi asked. "And the bigotry?"

"Oh, we're very tolerant of human failings here in Washington," Joy said. "Better to have an old rogue like Hocking, someone we know, than some raving young reformer who might make waves."

Mitzi was seated beside Willie Bladen. He had greeted her gruffly earlier in the evening but he seemed to have softened.

"I didn't want Joy getting back into business," he confided to her after the turtle soup. "It doesn't look right for a man in my position to have his wife running around town selling. But that's what she wanted and she is a very determined woman. At least linking up with you makes sense. I know quite a lot about you, not just what Bill Jorgenson told us. You're a lot tougher than you look."

She grinned. "Thank you. I guess that's a compliment."

"It was," he said. "That stunt you carried off in Houston, putting together that whole block, that really shook up some of the boys back home. Strangers aren't supposed to come onto their turf and pull tricks like that. George Dana, he runs

Lackland, he was mad as hell. Wanted me to have you investigated for operating on his territory. You really stirred them all up."

The name stirred something in Mitzi.

"Lackland," she said. "I think I've heard of them but I don't know anything I've ever done to upset them. What are they, exactly?"

"Lackland's probably the biggest developer in the Sun Belt," Bladen said. "But they keep a very low profile, working through dummy companies. They're real sharks, real tough guys. So when you come along and make it look easy, they lose face with their clients. Old Joe Bob Armshaw has a piece of Lackland, and of course the story of what you did to Joe Bob still has them laughing right across the state of Texas."

"I'd rather forget about that, thank you," Mitzi said. "Just tell me more about Lackland."

"They're a shadowy sort of crowd. They need to be, given some of the deals they've pulled," Bladen said. "Joe Bob and a few other locals have money invested with them, but they're not principals. In fact, the rumor in Houston is that the company is really owned by an outfit in your town, an investment company called Hartford or something similar. In turn, it's supposed to be the more or less respectable child of all those old Los Angeles land robbers. After they had plundered all the land there was around Los Angeles they started branching out, and Lackland is one of their extensions. Or so I've heard."

The man on Mitzi's other side started talking to her then, telling her a dull story she hardly followed. She smiled and nodded occasionally, but she let her gaze roam around the elegant tables. The people all looked so sure of themselves, so prosperous, so knowing. Yes, this was exactly the place for Castles.

Branching out had its disadvantages, Mitzi was quickly finding. Everyone seemed to have a problem they thought only she could solve. The morning after Bladen's dinner, Barry Metter called her from the Castles New York office, which he was managing. He was usually a confident, aggressive young man. That day he sounded very nervous.

"We've got a big problem with the Gloria Raynor deal," he told her. "The board of the Riverside meets tomorrow and I'm told by a good inside source that they are going to reject Gloria. She's got a million and a quarter in cold hard cash ready to plunk down for that duplex, and those bastards plan to reject her just because she's an entertainer."

"Have you told Gloria?" Mitzi asked.

"No," he said. "I wanted to talk to you first. I know she's one of your valued star clients out on the Coast, and I figured you'd want to handle this one yourself."

"Yes," Mitzi said. "Gloria needs gentle treatment. She's got her heart set on the apartment. She told me that when she was a kid starting out, she lived in a walk-up a few blocks from the Riverside. She'd go by in the evenings and watch the beautiful people arriving in their limousines for parties in the Riverside. She promised herself that someday, when she'd made it, she would come home to New York and buy the grandest apartment in that building."

"That's the trouble," Metter said. "She's made it too big. Those assholes on the board of the Riverside are all old-money WASPs and they hate the idea of someone 'notorious' moving in there. This happens a lot with other top buildings. Actors, musicians, even artists get turned down. It's a disgrace in a city that's supposed to be liberal."

"They can get away with it, legally, is that right?" Mitzi asked.

"They always have," he said. "No one's ever really tested the law. It's clearly discrimination, but who wants to go to court and publicly admit that people don't consider you and your money good enough for them?"

Mitzi took the evening shuttle to New York. Metter was waiting for her at LaGuardia.

"I've been calling people all day," he said. "The board isn't going to bend. They feel they got burned last year when, against their better judgment, they accepted Alex Restac's application to buy a co-op. You remember Restac? He was bouncing around the networks and Hollywood for years, failing upward, moving from one higher-paid production job to another. Anyway, the board finally decided that since he was in the production end he might just meet their lofty standards. What they didn't know was that old Alex is a pederast. At first the other residents couldn't figure out why there were so many young boys and girls in the elevators, heading for Restac's floor. They thought he must have been some kind of one-man Big Brother outfit. Then all hell broke loose when Restac picked up this thirteen-year-old boy on Fifty-third Street and took him home. The kid's father and uncles had been searching everywhere for the boy and apparently they spotted him getting into Restac's car. They followed them to the Riverside. By the time the cops got there the father and uncles were up in Restac's apartment beating the shit out of him. They would have killed him if the police hadn't gotten there in time. The thing was hushed up, no charges made, nothing. Restac still lives in the building and he still procures children and brings them home. He smiles at the other residents. He seems proud that they know what he's up to and that there's not a damn thing they can do about it. I tell you, those people spent millions of dollars to get away from the ugly side of Manhattan and now they have it move in on them. It's hardened their opposition to people like Gloria."

"Did you tell Gloria I was coming in?"

"Yes," he said, "but not why. She's staying at the Carlyle and is expecting you to come by."

"Let's go straight there," Mitzi said. "She might as well know what's going on."

Gloria Raynor's suite was sumptuous, with a breathtaking view of Manhattan's night skies. A bottle of Roderer Crystal was cooling in a silver bucket, and a buffet of caviar and smoked salmon was laid out on a gleaming oak table. But after she had kissed Mitzi warmly, the star declared, "I can't wait to get out of this dump. How quickly can we get all the paperwork done and get me moved into the Riverside? There's so much to be done. I've got the best decorator in New York on standby. Oh, Mitzi, you don't know how much this means to me."

"Sit down, Gloria," Mitzi said gently. "There's a problem."

"They want more money?" Gloria interrupted. "Shit, I don't care. Pay 'em anything. Just get me in there. It's my last dream, and the only one that looks like ending happily. Three husbands, two live-in lovers, and now I'm all alone again. I've failed at everything. Well, I'm damn well not going to fail at that one dream. I've had this dream too long."

"I'll tell you as directly as I can," Mitzi said. "They don't want you. The board meeting tomorrow, when we were going to get you approved? Well, it's not just a formality after all. They're going to vote you down because you're in show business. It's nothing personal, but it's their policy."

Mitzi waited for the famous Raynor temper to erupt. Mitzi glanced around the suite nervously, looking for objects Gloria might start throwing. And then she looked back at Gloria. The tall, defiant-looking star was changing before her eyes, crumpling onto a sofa, making an agonized, whimpering sound.

Mitzi refrained from touching her but said, "It'll be all right, dear. We'll find you another apartment, a better one. Those people can go to hell. They're not good enough for you."

"That's been my dream all these years, to come home and live in the Riverside," Gloria sobbed. "I've tried to do right. All those free concerts in the park, every New York charity I've supported, the politicians I've backed . . . everything. I tried to give so much back to this city and now it spits in my face. I know I've been a bitch to the people I work with, but that was only because I was always so scared, so insecure. And now I'm being punished for it." She was crying harder.

"It's not you, Gloria," she repeated firmly. "It's policy, not anything personal. A lot of the older buildings are scared that if they have prominent people, artists like you, they'll be bothered by fans in the lobby and noisy parties and that kind of thing. They're just silly old people who don't understand. It's not personal."

"But can't we fight them?" Gloria asked through her tears. "Isn't there anything we can do?"

"I'll go along tomorrow and argue your case for you," Mitzi said doubtfully. "But, legally, it could be an expensive and dirty fight. These people are awfully determined. Do you think you could handle the kind of publicity a court fight would bring?"

"Oh, God, I don't know," she said. "All I know is that I want that apartment. Please, please, Mitzi, try to save it for me."

"I'll do what I can, Gloria," she said. "But my hopes aren't high."

Mitzi was staying at the Pierre and as soon as she was in her room she started working the phone. There was a feature writer on the *Times* she knew well; Mitzi had helped him with a series on selling to stars, and they had become good friends. Finally she tracked him down in Sardi's.

"Josh," she said, "this isn't a story—yet. But I need to know all the grubby little secrets of the Riverside and particularly its board of directors. They're about to blackball a client of mine and I want to go in there armed."

"I can make some calls for you," he said. "And I know quite a bit about that place already. A woman I sometimes date lives there. I suppose you know the Restac story?"

"Yes," she said, "but I don't think it's much of a weapon, not for our side."

"Okay," he said. "Why don't you meet me for dinner up at Elaine's—say, nine-thirty. I should have something—if there is anything—by then."

There was a crowd waiting at the bar for tables when Mitzi arrived at Elaine's. Josh was sitting with a small group at one of the premier tables. When he saw her, he got up to take her in. She sensed the envy of the others, those not so favored, and she smiled to herself. They must be wondering who she was.

"Stick this in your bag," Josh said, slipping her an envelope as he took her arm. "Don't look at it here and forget who gave it to you. It's not the kind of information the *Times* peddles, but it's better than gossip. It could be proven, if anyone had a mind to. My source has been sitting on it, looking to make some money with it, but he owes me."

She was introduced around the table to a couple of well-known writers, a director, and two beautiful girls whose faces she recognized from glossy magazine covers. The talk was not quite what she had expected. The writers were busy arguing tax shelters and complaining about the parsimony of their publishers and the incompetence of their agents.

"If you want literary debate," Josh said to her, "find a table of stockbrokers. They'll be arguing the merits of Hemingway or Faulkner. These guys," he said, gesturing to the writers, "just worry about making a living."

All Mitzi wanted to do was examine the envelope, which was burning a hole in her bag. Distracted by it, she glanced around the restaurant and saw a very familiar face. She smiled and nodded and the man winked back. Only then did she realize it was Frank Sinatra. She'd made a fool of herself.

The wine and the talk flowed and they didn't get around to eating until midnight. New York was so different from Los Angeles. New York was a real nighttime city. It was one o'clock in the morning when she finally thanked Josh, said good night, and went out to find a cab.

The beat-up Checker was jouncing from one pothole to another and she couldn't have read Josh's notes even if there had been a light to read by. She had to wait until she was back in her room.

She kicked off her shoes and tore open the envelope. She read:

William Z. Morbray is the driving force on the board of the Riverside. The others are mostly old or indifferent and Morbray can get his way about most things. He is extremely wealthy, having taken the modest fortune left him by his grandfather and parlayed it into perhaps five hundred million with a series of dashing Stock Exchange coups. Mr. Morbray is a pillar of rectitude, consulted by the city fathers on fiscal matters, a man who gives often and generously to charity. However, he has certain vices, which he indulges only in the walled privacy of his Hamptons beach house.

Last July 4 weekend, at one of his regular parties, Morbray was entertaining a group of eight men and three women. There was a large amount of cocaine and hashish being used in the house. The guests were, it appears, all regulars except for the youngest of the women. An aspiring actress, an extremely beautiful young woman, she had been brought to the party by one of the male guests. All present consumed drugs and alcohol through the evening. They then repaired to the basement "games room," where Morbray indulges his habit of "discipline." The guests all undressed, except the budding actress. She, though affected by drugs, was not cooperative. She was forcibly stripped. Morbray then administered a spanking with a riding crop, drawing blood on the young woman's buttocks. He then raped her, as did three of the other men. The other two women also sexually assaulted her. The revels continued through the night.

Sometime around dawn the young woman escaped from the house and found her way to the local police headquarters. They were dubious about her story—Morbray is a major contributor to the local police force—but at her insistence a doctor was summoned. He established that she had recently had a number of sexual encounters, that she displayed the signs of a severe beating, and that, until the very recent past, she had been a virgin.

When the police rather diffidently approached him, Morbray denied all. A search was made of the house and a quantity of drugs seized. At that point a fix was put in. A large amount of money, rumored to have been more than a hundred thousand dollars, was spread among the investigating officers and their superiors. The doctor was ordered to change his report under the threat that the excessive number of prescriptions he had issued for amphetamines would be revealed to authorities. The whole case was closed and no word of the scandal leaked out, except for one thing. Another pleasure of Morbray's was, unknown to his guests, videotaping the activities in the games room. On the morning after the party a disgruntled manservant decided to leave the house. He stole a considerable amount of cash, some priceless silver, and the videotape of the night's proceedings. Only Morbray knows the tape exists and he does not know where it is. My source knows and intends to use it at the appropriate time, presumably to blackmail Morbray. At least two of the police officers who were bribed are thought to be uneasy about their involvement. It is felt that should the case be reinvestigated they would turn State's evidence. Morbray would then be facing bribery and corruption charges, charges that—unlike the rape and drug raps—he would not be able to beat. Please, and I'm not kidding, *I mean it*—burn this after you've read it.

Mitzi read it four times, then, rather self-consciously, burned it in a large ashtray, flushing the charred pieces down the toilet.

It was 9:00 A.M. before Mitzi had talked her way past the Riverside doormen and was confronting Morbray's maid.

"Just tell him it's vital that I see him," she insisted. "Tell him it's about Gloria Raynor."

Eventually Morbray appeared in the entrance hall. A large, florid man dressed in a conservative dark suit, he appeared angry.

"Madam," he said, "you are seeing me now only because I must pass you to reach the elevator. If you do not remove yourself immediately from these premises the staff will be summoned to do so."

"Why don't we find somewhere private to talk," Mitzi said. "It will take only a moment."

"There's nothing I have to talk about to you," he snapped. "I presume you represent Miss Raynor. That is a matter the board will take up at its meeting this afternoon. I will say one thing: By pushing in here like this you have gravely damaged any hope that woman had of being permitted to live here."

"Oh," said Mitzi casually, "it wasn't *just* about Miss Raynor. I also wanted to talk about video-tapes. And riding crops. That kind of thing."

Morbray deflated before her eyes, the ruddy glow of success and power vanishing from his plump cheeks.

"Oh, my God," he whispered, looking frantically around. "Come in here, the library, quickly."

She followed him. The library was all leather chairs and gleaming old oak. Books in fine bindings marched along the shelves, and through the window she could see ships moving on the river, close enough to reach out and touch. Morbray slumped in one of the leather chairs.

"How much?" he whined. "How much do you want, damn you? I've been waiting for this. I knew it had to come. Oh, God." And he slumped forward in the chair and began to sob.

Mitzi waited for him to control himself.

"I'm not here for money, but for justice, Mr. Morbray," she said. "At this afternoon's board meeting I am going to argue the case for my client. I am going to threaten to take the whole issue to the city's Human Rights Commission and, if there is no satisfaction there, into equity court and to the media. At that point I expect you to turn to your fellow board members and say that my argument is a convincing one and that it would be better to let Miss Raynor buy into the building than to risk a test case and all the publicity that will go with it. They will then, of course, approve the application. If they don't I will tell them all about the events of last July 4 and challenge you to sue me for slander."

"I'll do it," he said quickly. "But will that get me the videotape back?"

"No, it won't," she said sweetly. "All it will do is buy *my* silence. You still might have to face up to the evidence, sooner or later. This way, at least, it's not sooner."

The next day they celebrated over lunch at 21. Mitzi had never seen Gloria so happy, so bubbling. She couldn't have been more gracious to the two middle-aged, giggling women who hesitantly asked for her autograph.

"I'll owe you forever, Mitzi," Gloria said. "You beat those bastards for me. Tell me, what can I do for you? Name anything."

Mitzi looked around the handsome dining room at all the wealthy, probably powerful people there. She waved her hand, encompassing all of them.

"They're all potential Castles customers," she said. "All I ever want you to do is steer as many of them to me as you can. And," she laughed, "keep buying and selling houses as often as you do, Gloria. You're my best customer."

"Bad luck for you, then," Gloria said. "Now that I've got Riverside I'm never going to move again. But I'll tell you what I can do. You know Roger Fairfax? The meat-packing heir? Well, Roger and I are very old friends. He helped me a lot when I was starting out, singing in the Village. He had a little arts magazine then—just one of the hundred schemes he's failed at—and he pushed and pushed me. We've stayed close over the years." She leaned across the table and dropped her voice. "I think I'm the only person the poor old guy can still get it up for. Anyway, Roger's been through two fortunes. Luckily, he inherited three. Now he lives in this great old mansion in Palm Beach. Acres on the waterfront, worth two, three million dollars. He wants to sell it because, he says, the girls he takes down there think it's like a museum. Poor old Roger. He picks up these awful little hookers and installs them in his mansion, and a month or so later, after they've bled him dry, they leave. The mansion's a dream and he doesn't much care what he sells it for. It should be a very easy commission. If you want it, I'll call him now and you can go down and see him."

"It sounds too good to be true," Mitzi said. "Of course I want to handle it."

"Okay, then," Gloria said, and she signaled to the captain. "Bring me a telephone."

Mitzi landed at West Palm Beach at four o'clock in the afternoon. The chauffeur found her waiting by the baggage carousel.

"Mrs. Engers?" he asked, touching his uniform cap. "I'm from Mr. Fairfax. He sends his apologies. He would have met you himself but he's . . . tied up. I'm to drive you to the house."

The man took her bags and she followed him through the holiday crowds to the gleaming white Rolls-Royce defiantly straddling the No Stopping zone. The Rolls purred away from the airport and soon they were sweeping down Worth Avenue, sparkling in the sun, majestic palms overhead, and shops almost the equal of Rodeo Drive. The car turned between two big stone pillars and moved up a pink gravel drive through stands of wildly flowering trees and acres of trim lawn. The house was a vast, sprawling monument to the thirties, pink stucco with statuary tucked in its corners. A butler, incongruously clad in a black tailcoat, hurried down the steps to meet the car.

"The Coconut Suite has been prepared for madam," the butler said. "Please follow me."

Inside, out of the brilliant sunshine, the mansion did indeed have the musty air of a museum. As Mitzi followed the butler up the sweeping marble staircase to the second floor she glimpsed into the rooms and noted the dust covers on the furniture.

But her own rooms were bright and cheerful, with flowers set everywhere. She stepped out onto the wide balcony and gasped at the view: The blue Atlantic stretched before her, ringed at her feet by a snow-white beach. The lawns of the mansion ran down to the sand and merged there gracefully.

She heard the butler cough. She knew not to tip him, but wondered what was keeping him.

"Dinner is at eight-thirty, madam," he said. "We will be dressing. If you wish to talk with Mr. Fairfax, he will usually be found in the Hibiscus Library at seven-thirty for cocktails before dinner. The Hibiscus is to the right at the foot of the main staircase. A maid will be up in a moment to unpack for you. If there is anything you need, the bell by your feet will summon the staff." He bowed and left the room.

The maid who arrived minutes later was a happy contrast to the butler. A cheerful blond

Irish girl, Katie was happy to chatter on about the house and its occupants.

"It's so nice to have guests again," she said enthusiastically. "This place has been like a morgue. Mr. Fairfax usually has a lady staying here but not for the past few months. Anyway," she added, "we didn't think much of the ladies he was entertaining. They weren't. Weren't ladies, I mean." She giggled. "They were always falling out of their dresses at dinner."

"What about Mr. Fairfax?" Mitzi asked. "What's he like?"

"Oh, he's a very nice man, really," the girl said. "It's just that he's lonely here in this big old house. No one ever comes to visit anymore. He just sits around by himself and I'm afraid he sometimes takes a little too much to drink. It's not good, to drink on your own." She lowered her voice. "That would be why he didn't meet you himself. He always has a little nap in the afternoons, to get over the champagne at lunch. And why shouldn't he? The poor old dear has had too much grief in his life, for all that money."

After the maid had gone, Mitzi took off her clothes and lay down on the bed. The only sound coming through the lace curtains was the sighing of the trade wind and the soft boom of the long Atlantic rollers on the beach. She dozed there, pleasantly relaxed for the first time in days.

At seven she awoke, showered, and put on a long blue silk gown. Descending the main staircase, she found Fairfax in the library. He was standing at the bar, carefully going through what must have been a time-honored ritual, mixing martinis in a silver shaker. He stopped when she entered, and he bowed to her. He was a tall, thin man, beautifully dressed in a black velvet dinner jacket. Only the tremble of his hands as he put down the shaker gave him away.

"Mrs. Engers," he said, crossing the room to her. "This is indeed a pleasure. Gloria, Miss Raynor, speaks most fondly of you. It is so nice to have a guest here, and one as charming as you. Will you join me in a cocktail? I always think this first drink of the day, when one's work is done, is so pleasant."

Mitzi nodded, crossed to the couch he had indicated, and smiled her thanks when Fairfax brought her drink.

"Your house is so beautiful, what I've seen of it, Mr. Fairfax," she said. "I don't know how you could bear to part with it."

"Please call me Roger," he said. "It suggests a degree of intimacy, even if I am old enough to be your grandfather."

There was a little gleam in his tired old eyes and she grinned to herself. The old roué might have faded a little, but the spark was still there.

"Certainly, Roger," she said. "I'm Mitzi."

For the next hour they talked, or rather, Fairfax talked and Mitzi listened. He seemed so hungry for company, for an audience. He told her of the early days in Palm Beach, the polo tournaments, the tennis and sailing, when Palm Beach had been America's premier resort. He talked about his own life, the dashing young playboy he had been, sailing the world on the great ocean liners, always being at the right international playground, always with the most eligible debutantes, gambling until dawn and sporting through the day.

"And now, in my twilight," he said, "I look back

and it seems such an empty life. Nothing to show for it but a string of ex-wives and a couple of children who despise me and can't wait for me to die and leave them what is left of my dissipated fortune."

"I find that hard to believe," Mitzi said lightly. "It's a life out of a romance novel. Anyone who has to grind away at a nine-to-five job, doing something he hates, and living in terror of being fired . . . would be sick with envy."

"Oh, I concede that," Fairfax said. "It's just that I had so much and did so little with it. And now it's too late. That's why I want to get rid of this house. For me it can never be what it was, when it rang with the laughter of handsome young people who knew their future was golden."

She was afraid he was going to get even more maudlin, but the situation was saved when the butler appeared to announce dinner. Fairfax snapped out of his mood and became the dashing, courteous host. He gave her his arm and they strolled through the halls to a magnificent dining room.

The table would have seated at least twenty-four and with just the two of them at either end there was a vast space between them. Mitzi was seated facing the full-length windows, which opened out onto the terrace. The moon was coming up and it glowed on the ocean.

The meal was superb, served by two maids under the supervision of the butler. There was conch chowder followed by Gulf shrimps and a baked, stuffed pompano. Then Key lime pie. She saw that Fairfax barely touched his food but that he continually emptied his wineglass.

"I like to take coffee and brandy on the terrace,"

he said when the meal was finished. "I think you'll be warm enough out there without a wrap."

It was beautiful outside, the stars out by then, and a gentle, warm breeze moved through the palms flanking the terrace.

"I suppose I will miss this lovely place," he said with a sigh. "But it's too big for me now. I rattle around in it and sometimes it depresses me. From what you've seen, do you think you could sell it for me?"

"Easily," Mitzi said. "It's a dream house, and dreams are very simple to sell. It's just that . . . I'm not sure you should sell it. You don't need the money. And where will you live?"

"I have other places," he said. "New York, the South of France. But in fact what I'll probably do is live aboard my yacht down here. You see, I have this one abiding passion, oceanography, marine biology. The last great frontier. I already fund a marine laboratory just down the coast and I might use the money from the sale of this place to set them up in better quarters. At least it would be a better thing to do than I've done with the rest of my fortune. It would make me feel somewhat worthwhile, even at this late stage of my life."

And then, to Mitzi's intense embarrassment, Fairfax began to cry. At first she could barely hear his sobs over the sound of the surf and the breeze, but when she stole a look at him she could see the tears on his cheeks, bright in the moonlight. She knew they were drunken tears, but still her heart went out to him. A man coming to the end of a wasted life, a life that had once promised so much, it must be awful for the poor old man.

She put down her glass and crossed the terrace to sit beside him.

"Please," she said, "try not to be so unhappy. There's still time to make a new start. You have so much. Concentrate on what you can do, not on what you haven't done."

He reached for her hand and they sat in silence for several minutes until he had himself under control.

"I'm sorry for that display," he said finally. "I don't know what brought it on. Getting ready to sell this house, I suppose. Admitting that the happy times are finally over. Oh, to hell with it, just get rid of it for me for whatever you can get."

"No, I don't think I'll do that," Mitzi said. "I won't handle the sale."

He was surprised. "Why? What's wrong? You said yourself you could sell it easily."

"I could," she said. "But I don't think you really want to sell. You love this place and it's just that you're feeling guilty about not putting it to good use. I've been thinking about it while we've talked. This marine place that you fund. You say they need better premises. Why not turn the mansion into the fanciest marine biology station anywhere? You could go on living in your own wing and your scientists would have a wonderful place to work out of. And you'd have their company and their gratitude. You'd even," she said with a laugh, "have a whopping tax deduction. Why don't you think about it? It would, most of all, get you involved more deeply in something you really care about. You need that."

Fairfax was sitting up straight and staring out to sea.

"By God," he said, "I think you just might have hit on something. The place would be very suitable. Lots of rooms for the staff, guest cottages for visiting scientists, a deepwater dock—I don't know why I didn't think of it."

She stood up.

"It's late and I've got to travel tomorrow," she said. "You sleep on it and we can talk over breakfast. In the meantime, thank you for a fascinating evening."

"Thank *you*, my dear," Fairfax said. "You may have just started me on one last, wonderful lease on life." He bent, took her hand, and kissed it. "You are a very special woman," he said, gravely. "I am in your debt."

Breakfast was on the terrace at nine o'clock, and as Mitzi crossed to the white wrought-iron table she saw that Fairfax was looking far brighter. He rose to greet her.

"It's a wonderful morning, thanks to you," he said, smiling. "I sat up half the night going over your suggestion and, you know, it's going to work. I feel like a new man."

She took coffee and juice and watched with amusement as Fairfax ate a hearty breakfast. When he caught her watching him, he grinned.

"The start of the complete cure," he said. "Good food, cut out most of the drinking, make myself useful. I don't suppose," he said, "you'd consider staying on here and helping me set this thing up?"

"No," she said with a laugh. "I couldn't do that. You don't need any help. Anyway, I've got a family and a business."

"Ah, yes, your business," he said. "This is rather delicate. Last night, by thinking about my needs rather than business, you deprived yourself of a handsome commission. I want to make that up to you. Perhaps a check for—"

"No," she said. "I won't take anything. At

Castles we've always believed that it was better to make a good friend than a bad sale. If we part friends, I'll have been more than sufficiently rewarded."

After breakfast he saw her out to the Rolls. He was walking taller and more proudly, and he seemed impatient to get on with things.

As he helped her into the car he leaned down and said softly, "You are a wonderful woman. I shall always be in your debt." He kissed her on the cheek and stood there waving as the car rolled down the wide driveway. He was still waving when it turned off onto the street.

Chapter Fourteen _____

"JESUS CHRIST!" MEREDITH YELLED WHEN MITZI told her about the Fairfax deal. She was genuinely angry. "Don't you realize how much trouble we're in? The market is nose-diving, but we've expanded all over the place and now we're stuck. We need every commission, every cent we can get our hands on, and you turn down a huge sale because you feel sorry for some old man?"

"I couldn't do it, Meredith," she said miserably. "It would have been wrong for him to sell."

Meredith softened. "I didn't mean to yell at you," she said. "Hell, you're the boss. If you want to send us into bankruptcy, that's your right. Anyway, something will turn up. It always has, so far."

But when they went over the books that afternoon with Mr. Tuckwell, the picture looked very black indeed.

"There's no advice I can offer you," the accountant said. "I have already suggested a retrenchment of staff. The offices in Washington and New York and Houston . . . they're just draining off all your profits. I concede that someday they could be very lucrative, but for now . . . they have to go. We are in a recession and until it's over we all have to tighten our belts."

After that depressing session she and Meredith felt they had to get out of the office. They left early and stopped by Chasen's for a drink. The restaurant had a reassuring air about it, prosperous and stable, and they both brightened up.

"No one thought a couple of women could make it this far," Meredith said. "We'll get by. If I can clinch the sale on the Field place this week . . ."

Someone was looming over their table. Mitzi looked up into the hard gaze of Ellis Gibbons.

"I've been missing you around town," he said. "Time's running out. My offer still stands, but I'm running out of patience. What's it going to be?" He was staring at her insolently, challenging her, laughing at her. "I hear you need a big deal in a hurry," he said. "Mine's the biggest you'll ever have a shot at." He was ignoring Meredith entirely. "I don't know what's holding you back. It can't be Charles. He's too busy smashing up cars and faded starlets."

Something snapped. Mitzi turned very carefully in her chair so that she was facing Gibbons squarely. She was pale and she could feel herself trembling but she kept her voice calm and just loud enough for patrons nearby to hear her.

"Mr. Ellis Gibbons," she began. "The hotshot lawyer, the wheeler-dealer, the ladies' man. For three months now you've been pestering me, offering me a huge commission if I'll climb into bed with you. You shouldn't have to pay that much to get laid. Beverly Hills is alive with whores who'd put out for less—even for you. I really feel sorry for you, Ellis. You've got a very big problem. But I have problems of my own and I can't waste time on a creep like you. Just go away and leave me alone."

The people around them were all listening by the time she finished. All other conversations had stopped.

Gibbons stood there, an angry flush spreading from his cheeks to his forehead. He moved forward as if to strike her, then stopped himself.

"Lady," he hissed, "you just made the biggest mistake of your life. You are through in this town." He turned away quickly and strode out of the restaurant, leaving a deadly silence behind him.

"That's all, folks," she heard Meredith announce. "The show's over."

Mitzi was trembling violently but she willed herself not to cry or to get up and run.

Meredith reached across the table and held her hand for a moment.

"Phew!" she said. "I guess we can kiss the Irwin estate good-bye. Hell, I think we both need another drink. I think you're very dumb, but I'm proud as hell of you, kid."

It hadn't been an easy week, and Mitzi was glad it was Friday. She wrapped up early and left the office before four o'clock, planning to beat the traffic home and relax in a hot bath before the family got home. The prospect of a couple of hours of peace and quiet made her smile to herself as she reached the driveway. The garage door was closed and she climbed out to open it. It was stuck.

She started to walk away when she heard the sound inside the garage, the low, regular purr of the Mercedes engine. At first it didn't register. Charles must have left the car on and gone inside for something. Then she knew. She ran up the steps and wrestled the front door open, dashed through the house to the kitchen and through the connecting door to the garage.

He was sitting upright in the front passenger seat, fully dressed and looking as if he were waiting for someone to come and drive him away. She began gagging.

Mitzi ran to the main door of the garage, unbolted it, and swung the door up and open. Then she sprinted back to the car, crashing into one of its rear fenders, and opening up a long gash on her leg.

She tugged open the driver's side door and, reaching in, turned the engine off. Through all this Charles sat immobile, his eyes closed, his face stony. She grabbed him and tried to drag him across the seat and out her doorway but he was too heavy. She put her ear down to his lips and felt him breathing in short, rasping gasps. She tried again to move him, then gave up and ran into the kitchen to call for help.

Frank Denman, their family doctor, and the ambulance crew arrived within seconds of each other. Charles was placed on a stretcher, and the ambulance men gave him oxygen while Dr. Denman worked on him. She watched numbly until the ambulance sped away, whooping loudly. Then she and Denman went to the kitchen and sat there talking.

"It was close, but he's going to be all right, Mitzi. A few more minutes, though . . ."

She was crying then, tears of shock and sorrow and . . . yes . . . furious anger.

"Try to relax," the doctor said gently. "It's all going to be okay. And there'll be no fuss, either. We get . . . incidents like this all the time in Beverly Hills. There'll be no trouble with the police or the press. The report will just say that Charles was overcome with fumes while giving the car a tune-up. It happens all the time."

"But why?" she finally asked. "Things have been tough, bad, but not that bad. I've failed him. That's what it was." And she cried again.

"Blaming yourself is all wrong," Denman said. "It could have been anything. We'll find out soon enough. I'm going down to the hospital now but I know Charles will be all right. He'll be out of emergency this evening and spend just a couple of days in the hospital. Do you want to come with me now?"

"No," she said. "I should be here when the children get home. The neighbors will have seen the ambulance."

She didn't visit Charles until the next morning, Saturday. The children had accepted the story of his "accident" calmly, although she had caught the glances they exchanged. They knew Charles had never even cleaned the Mercedes, much less attempted a tune-up.

When she arrived at the hospital, he was sitting up in bed, in a bright, cheerful room filled with the early-morning sun. He looked pale and thin but little the worse for his experience. She walked across to the bed and kissed him on the cheek.

"Thanks for coming," Charles said and ducked his head in that boyish gesture which had once so charmed her and which now brought a flash of anger. She sat down in a chair a few feet away from the bed.

"Okay, Charles," she said, her voice low, "what in the hell was that all about?"

"My grand gesture?" He gave a little grin. "I

even screwed that up, didn't I? I've screwed it all
up, everything."

"But why now?" she demanded. "What suddenly got so bad that you had to try a thing like
that?"

"I'll try to make it as brief and simple as
possible," he said. He lay back against the pillows
and stared at the ceiling, avoiding her gaze.

"You remember, of course, the accident I had
with Moira Johnson," he began. "Well, she came
out of it all right, with just a couple of scars around
the eyes. They were healing and would have
vanished completely in time. But Moira was impatient and she got this fixation that she was
going to be scarred for life. She kept nagging me to
do something for her, plastic surgery. She seemed
to think I could just wave a scalpel and they would
vanish.

"I argued with her for weeks, told her the
operation wasn't worth the risk. I'd have to work
on the eyelids, which is risky, delicate stuff. But
she insisted that she wanted to take that risk and
that I do the operation. Well," he shrugged, "I owed
her. The accident was my fault. So against my
better judgment I operated. One side was perfect
but there was some nerve damage on the other side
and the operation made it worse. Now she's got a
little tic, a slight droop in the eyelid. For anyone
else it wouldn't matter a damn, but for an actress
. . . well, it's pretty bad.

"At first she was really good about it," he said.
"She didn't blame me for any of it. Then, about a
week ago, I suddenly heard from a lawyer. They're
going after me for everything—malpractice, the
ruined career, the trauma she suffered. They want
a million bucks out of court or there'll be a trial and

they'll go for even more. Whatever happens, I'm ruined."

"And this is the woman you swore to me you weren't having an affair with?"

He raised a hand, almost wearily, from the sheet.

"Of course I lied," he said. "I don't know why it happened. I used to blame you. You were so tied up with your job, so involved, that I seemed to have taken second place in your life. I guess I was searching for attention, or love, or something. Now I know better—I'm just a weak man. It's too late now, but I'm sorry. I know now that it's you I love and that you were the best woman I would ever meet. But I've ruined it all, haven't I?"

"What about malpractice insurance?"

"There's none," he said. "A lot of specialists stopped carrying it when the rates went through the roof. We're all very clever out here," he added. "We put everything in our wives' names so that if we get sued, there's nothing for the victims to recover. But it means bankruptcy for me and the end of my practice. I'm ruined. So that's why I did what I did last night. It seemed the best way out. And I've dragged you down with me, Mitzi."

"It was stupid," she said. "It's no answer. Somehow or other we'll be able to straighten this out. If you'd only talked to me . . . I could have helped. Maybe I still can."

"Would you want to?" he asked, eager, his eyes begging her.

"Yes," she said, not softening. "I still love what you were once, even if I can't love what you have become."

"Mitzi, please," he said. "I've made so many promises to you before. Now I see what a fool I've been, how weak and childish and spoiled I am. I'd give anything for another chance with you. I've learned my lesson."

"We'll think about another chance later," she said, "after we've cleared this mess up. We're going to need time to work this out. God, a million dollars! Is there any chance they'll accept something more reasonable?"

"No," he said, "I don't think so. You see, Moira would be reasonable. She's not a bad woman. But this lawyer has his hooks into her and he is a real tough bastard. It's funny," he added, not laughing, "he was a friend of mine once. Even came to our house a few times. You might remember him. Ellis Gibbons."

Charles recovered physically but in the following weeks she knew that he was still deeply depressed. He saw few patients and spent a great deal of time around the house. He was always there when she got home, always attentive, trying to be helpful. It was as if he were trying to make up for all the years of his selfishness. At any other time she might have welcomed it but now, with so many problems to cope with, she had even less patience with him.

Once the shock subsided, she knew she shouldn't have been surprised. She knew how thoroughly he hated his work and for how many years he had despised himself for the miracles he couldn't perform. That *no* doctor could put people back together perfectly meant nothing to Charles; he clung to his disillusionment and had begun clinging to liquor as well. She wondered just how unhappy he really would be if he couldn't practice anymore. This malpractice suit wouldn't make Charles his old self again, but if it forced him into another field, would it be so bad? Charles had turned on his practice years before. Now it seemed to be turning on him.

Mitzi talked to Meredith about it. "I feel sorry for him, I guess, and I do still love him," Mitzi said. "But—deep down, I think I almost despise him now."

"Just take it one step at a time," Meredith said. "You've both been through a hell of a lot. And there's still a lot of crap to come. How's the legal situation looking?"

"No better," Mitzi said. "His lawyers say we can stall for time, up to a year even, but that sooner or later we're going to have to settle. And they think we'll be lucky to get out of it for a million! I find myself wishing we'd never left Chicago. Maybe I was just a housewife there, but at least I didn't feel like the whole world was waiting around the next corner to ambush me.

"And our so-called friends here," she continued. "They call offering sympathy, and you know all they want is to find out how we're taking it so they can gossip about us. The invitations have stopped, too. They couldn't talk about us if we were there, could they? I'm starting to hate this town."

"Just hang in, dear," Meredith said. "Something will turn up. We've both been down before. Things will work out, they really will."

The first thing to do was to get Charles out of Beverly Hills, as much for her sake as for his. She couldn't cope with his hangdog, beaten attitude and his awful dependence on her. And the horror of crushing public humiliation after the triumphs he had enjoyed in California was destroying him.

"I want you to go back to Chicago for a while,"

she told him. "The house in Oak Brook isn't being rented now. Stay there and put the children in school. You could look the situation over, maybe think about going into practice there, at least until the mess here is straightened out."

He grasped at the idea joyfully.

"That's a wonderful idea," he said. "Get out of this stinking town, make a fresh start. I'm still very well thought of in Chicago. And as soon as I get settled there, you'll come and join me, right? You could work there as easily as you do here. It's a big market, Chicago."

"One thing at a time, Charles," she said, wearily. "We'll see about that."

"Please," he said, "say you'll come. We'll start over again. It will all be wonderful and I'll make up to you for all the shitty things I've done."

"We'll see," she said again, just as wearily.

Chapter Fifteen _____

WITH CHARLES AND THE CHILDREN BACK IN Chicago, Mitzi plunged full time into her work at Castles, knowing now that she not only had to reverse the firm's fortunes but also, somehow, pull off the kind of financial miracle that would get Charles out of hock.

"The Irwin deal would have done it," she told Meredith bitterly. "If only Ellis Gibbons weren't in charge."

"Why not try an end run around Mr. Gibbons?" Meredith asked. "Maybe we can represent the buyer instead of the seller. There would be a few dollars in that. Who's he setting up the deal with—Lackland or something?"

"Yes, Lackland," Mitzi said. "A Texas outfit. I don't think there's much hope of dealing with them. Willie Bladen told me in Washington that they were mad at Castles for coming onto their turf and setting up the deal for Adnan to buy his block. But I suppose it's worth a try. Anything is better than sitting around here waiting to go broke."

She called Jorgenson to see if he could help with Lackland, and he got back to her a couple of days later.

"Sorry, Mitzi," he said. "Nothing doing there. I checked with a couple of people who are supposed to have a big say in running Lackland and got the brush-off. They were very polite but definite. No outside help required, thank you. As I told you, it's a very shadowy operation. No one really knows who these people are, and they like it that way. So they're hardly going to take in an outsider. I'm surprised Gibbons even mentioned their name to you."

"He was drunk at the time," Mitzi said. "And he wanted something from me. Anyway, Bill, thanks for trying. I'll just have to look for something else to save the ship."

A couple of days later Mitzi was in the lobby of the Gruzman Building in downtown Los Angeles. Hartford, Lackland's parent company, was listed on the building directory and she took the elevator to the fourteenth floor. It was not a busy office and the receptionist seemed almost pleased to have a caller. Mitzi gave the girl her card.

"I'm interested in doing business with Lackland down in Houston," Mitzi explained. "I understand your company is affiliated with them."

"Gee, I don't know about that," the girl said. "You'll have to talk to Miss Langshaw. She's our managing director. If you want to sit down I'll buzz her and see if she's got time."

Two minutes later Mitzi was shown into a big corner office. A tall redhead, probably in her early thirties, got up from behind a desk and came around to shake Mitzi's hand.

"Hi," she said. "I'm Joan Langshaw. Grace said you wanted to talk about Lackland. I don't know that I can help you much, but let's sit down anyway. You want coffee?"

Mitzi nodded and sat down on a long leather

couch, looking down at the freeways already clogging with traffic in midafternoon. Joan Langshaw brought their coffee on a silver tray and sat across from Mitzi.

"I'll get right to the point," Mitzi said. "I understand Lackland is about to buy the Irwin estate and I want to represent them in the transaction. My agency is the best in the business and for a deal of this size they're going to need the best. So I thought I'd come straight to the top, which, I understand, is Hartford. The fact that the managing director's a woman will, I hope, give me some slight edge."

Joan Langshaw smiled.

"I'm the managing director, all right, but I'm not quite sure what I'm managing," she said. "I've been in the job four weeks now and you are only the third caller. I'm damned if I know what the job is supposed to be."

"But I thought Hartford was a big holding company," Mitzi said, frowning into her coffee cup.

"No, I'm afraid you've got it wrong," Joan Langshaw said. "I was hired by Lackland to run this office. We are very much their subsidiary. So I don't see that I can help you at all. You'd have to approach Lackland directly."

Mitzi shrugged. "It was worth a try, anyway," she said. "Business is so lousy right now I'll do anything to get something moving."

"You too?" she said. "Surely real estate is still booming in L.A.?"

"Oh, it'll come back in time," Mitzi said. "But these downturns are hell to live through. Your overheads stay the same but there's nothing coming in."

"I've always been interested in real estate," Joan Langshaw said. "I took a masters in business administration at USC but for a few months it looked like I'd have done better to have gotten a realtor's license. I was pretty desperate when this Lackland job came along. Actually, I thought it was going to involve property dealing. That was the line they gave me when they flew me down to Houston for the interview. Instead, I ended up sitting in this nice office, making coffee and waiting for the phone to ring."

"If it gets too boring, give me a call," Mitzi said. "Business won't always be bad. And I think you might do really well selling. There are three hundred thousand doing it now and, somehow, women do it best."

"I might just do that," she said. "Right now I feel like I'm taking their money under false pretenses."

They had more coffee and talked for another half hour until Mitzi checked her watch. She was due back at Castles. It had not been a fruitful meeting but she felt she had made a new friend and did not begrudge the time.

It was two weeks later when Joan Langshaw called her.

"Hi," she said. "I don't know if you remember me . . ."

"Of course, Joan," Mitzi said. "The woman whose phone never rings."

"Don't joke," Joan said. "Things have suddenly gotten *too* hot over here. Look, I know you're busy but I badly need to talk to someone about the spot I'm in and—I know we met only that one time— I feel I can confide in you. Please, may I come see you?"

It was late Friday afternoon and Mitzi was

about to go into another gloomy session with the accountant. "I'm afraid today is shot," she said, "but if you feel like it, why not come by the house tomorrow afternoon? We can have a swim and sit in the sun and talk."

"That's very kind of you," Joan said. "I'd rather talk away from an office atmosphere."

Mitzi gave her the address and wrote a reminder to herself to shop in the morning. With Charles and the children away she seemed to have been living on takeouts.

Mitzi was watching a Rams game when Joan arrived. "I'll just leave it on for a couple of minutes, if you don't mind," Mitzi said.

"I didn't pick you for a football fan," Joan said, taking the coffee Mitzi offered her.

"I'm not," Mitzi grinned. "I just have a special interest in the team."

The Rams had just scored seven points and Mitzi watched the screen intently. The tall, dark young man moved forward to kick off and sent the ball spiraling downfield and into the end zone.

"Another fine effort from young Tom Wyatt," she heard the play-by-play announcer say. "This kid is tremendous—what a find for the Rams!"

Mitzi was smiling broadly as she turned off the set.

"I'm glad someone's happy," Joan said when Mitzi had sat down across from her. "I've just come through one of the worst weeks of my life and I pray you can help me somehow." She took a deep breath. "I had to quit my job."

Mitzi was surprised. "I hoped things would improve for you. What happened?"

"Well, it was all kind of strange," Joan said. "Just after you came to see me things started picking up. There was a real flurry of work—property deals going ahead, people from Houston here, rushing in and out of the office. I was really starting to enjoy it. By the way," she said, "you were right. It seems Hartford *is* the parent company of Lackland. For some reason they want it to appear the other way, but I've seen all the papers and met the principals and there's no question that it's the L.A. people who are running the show."

"So what went wrong?" Mitzi asked.

"As things hotted up I got to see more and more of the head honcho, a real tough guy," Joan said. "He's one of those high-pressure businessmen and I was kind of impressed. Anyway, we had a few working sessions together, and a couple of nights ago he called me and asked me to come over to his place. I suppose I was a bit uneasy about it but I thought, what the hell, if I were a male executive there'd be nothing wrong with it."

Mitzi nodded sympathetically, sure she knew what was coming.

Joan continued, "It was all perfectly normal at first. We went over some papers. Remind me to tell you about them later. I think you'll be interested. Then he fixed drinks and came and sat down beside me. God, I almost laughed. It was so juvenile, this guy, this hotshot businessman, trying to make out on the couch with me.

"But it was no joke," she said bitterly. "He started to get physical. You know, pinning my arms and feeling me up. After a struggle, I hauled off and hit him square on the nose." She stopped and giggled nervously. "I grew up with five brothers in the house and they taught me how to fight. Anyway, there was blood all over the place from his nose and for a moment there it looked like he was going to punch me out. Then he just started to walk out of the room, saying over his shoulder that I could either quit the next day or be fired. I let myself out and went home and drank too much and cried myself to sleep. So much for my M.B.A. and all the dreams of making it in a man's world."

"It's happened to all of us," Mitzi said gently. "I know that doesn't make it any better, but you're not alone. And of course most men aren't like that. It's just a few *macho* bastards who still think women in business are on the make. You can't quit after one job. So what are you going to do?"

"That's where I hoped you could help," Joan said. "I'm not short of money right now but I do need experience and I wondered if you'd take me into Castles as a trainee or something. I love real estate and after this experience I'd like to be working in it with other women."

"Hell, it's a rough time to be starting out," Mitzi said. "I told you how slow things are right now. But I suppose we can work something out."

"It would be great if you could," Joan said. "And maybe I can give you the inside track on that Lackland thing you were asking me about. That's what the papers were that we were supposed to be working on, a deal for Hartford and Lackland to buy the Irwin estate. Maybe you can cope with that bastard where I couldn't. His name is Ellis Gibbons."

Mitzi couldn't stop herself. She began laughing, so hard that tears came to her eyes. Joan just sat there watching her, at first puzzled, then resentful.

"I'm sorry," Mitzi finally gasped. "I'll explain it all to you in a minute. But in the meantime, Joan, you've just earned yourself a job at Castles. You've just delivered me Mr. Ellis Gibbons on a platter."

Sally Irwin was not an easy person to reach. Her secretary in Los Angeles would say only that she was traveling. Mitzi finally tracked her down in Palm Beach, at one of her winter residences, but that didn't help. A bored-sounding aide listened to Mitzi's request to speak to the heiress about the estate and firmly told her that all inquiries had to be addressed through Ellis Gibbons, the executor. The rich were so insulated, she thought bitterly, that you couldn't even get to them to do them a favor.

Well, she did have one good friend in Palm Beach, and on an impulse she called Roger Fairfax. She was relieved when a butler answered and confirmed that it was, indeed, the Fairfax residence. So he had taken her advice and held on to the place.

He sounded well when he came to the phone. "My dear," he said, "it's so wonderful to hear from you. I've thought about you so often. Everything has been going wonderfully for me since your visit. The plans for the ocean research station are going along well and the old mansion is just humming with life. Why don't you come visit me now? I'll send a plane for you."

"Thanks, Roger," she said, "but I'm just a working girl and I'm trying to hustle some business. I need help, if you can help me. Do you by any chance know Sally Irwin?"

"Sally? Of course I do," he said. "We're really a very tiny colony here. We all know each other. I was talking to her at the polo on Sunday and I think I'm seeing her at the Hibiscus Ball tomorrow night. What do you need?"

"Just for her to talk to me," Mitzi said. "I've tried to reach her through regular channels but her body-

guard of servants treats me like a brush salesman.
I know something that will be of *great* benefit to
each of us. If she'll just talk to me . . . would you put
in a word for me and give her my number here and
ask her to call me?"

Fairfax said he would be delighted to do Mitzi
any favor and that this one required no effort at
all. He assured her she would be hearing from
Sally Irwin.

Fairfax was as good as his word. It was only two
hours later when the call came. Sally Irwin was
apologetic but guarded.

"I get so many calls about the estate," she told
Mitzi. "Everyone wants to handle the sale. But if
you've followed the case at all, you'll know it's out
of my hands. For better or worse, Ellis Gibbons is
running the show. I'll gladly give you an introduc-
tion to him but I warn you right now, it won't do
you much good. Mr. Gibbons and I are not exactly
the best of friends."

"I've already had the dubious pleasure of dealing with Gibbons," Mitzi said. "That's really what
I'm calling about. I have some information that
will get Gibbons out of your hair—and mine—for
good. I don't want to talk about it on the phone. It's
dynamite. I promise you won't be wasting your
time if you'll just see me. I can fly there tomorow."

Sally Irwin said no, that she was leaving Palm
Beach in a couple of days and was going to be busy
until then. "But," she added, "I have booked into
the Alton Retreat for a week of repair work. If you
really want to talk with me, maybe you could fly
down there for the weekend."

Normally the prospect of a few days at the Alton
Retreat would have thrilled Mitzi. It was the
newest and most popular of the jet-set health spas,

set in a luxury compound just outside Scottsdale, Arizona. She had read in the glossy magazines of its sumptuous facilities and had seen, in her friends who had been there, the amazing results of the Alton treatment.

But her own visit would be strictly business, she told Meredith. "I'll be working on my mind, not my body," she said. "There'll be no time to be pampered."

"Oh, you'll find a spare hour or two," Meredith said. "I've heard all about the masseurs at the Retreat . . . all tall, blond, and handsome, and not one of them over twenty-five. One hour's rubdown with one of those boys and you emerge a sexually liberated woman. And the food and the skin treatments and everything, it's what every woman is supposed to dream about—a place where the only men in sight are there to serve you. And at five hundred dollars a day you should get a little pleasure as well as business out of the experience."

When Mitzi did check in there was a note from Sally Irwin inviting her to her suite for cocktails before dinner. Mitzi was given a brief tour of the gleaming white adobe-style buildings that made up the spa, then shown to her own suite. It had a balcony looking out over lush green gardens to the surrounding Arizona mountains.

"Would madame care for a massage to initiate her into the spirit of the Retreat?" the pretty young girl who was her escort asked as they surveyed the suite. "It will help madame forget the cares of the city and prepare her for the unique ambience that is fostered here."

Mitzi glanced at her watch. It would be a couple of hours before she could see Sally Irwin. Why not?

"Then if madame will prepare herself and lie

down on the massage table," she said, pulling a long, narrow table down from its hiding place in the wall, "one of our men will be along shortly."

Mitzi quickly showered and put on the soft white toweling robe that was in the bathroom. She smiled nervously at her reflection in the mirror, then stepped out of the bathroom and lay face-down on the massage table, the robe soft and reassuring around her.

She lay there for about five minutes, gently drowsy, listening to the soft sounds of the breeze in the trees outside the suite. She heard a soft knock on her door and it opened before she could say anything. Mitzi turned her head to look. She could have been dreaming. He was a tall, slim young man, deeply tanned, with a mane of fair hair, dressed all in white—short shorts, a T-shirt, sneakers, and socks. He looked like a young and gentle Viking and when he quietly introduced himself as Jens the illusion was complete. He was carrying a white leather Adidas bag and he swiftly unpacked a range of bottles and tubes, at the same time talking quietly, reassuring her. She turned her head away from the room and toward the soft glow that came through the curtained window. Soon she felt him beside her, gently easing the robe from her shoulders and removing it from her body. At first, as the strong young hands soothed a sweet-smelling oil into her limbs, Mitzi thought she was drifting off to sleep. The sensation was one of tranquillity, as if all the strains and stresses were being eased out of her body, coaxed along by Jens's experienced hands. It seemed to go on forever and it was only when the hands were moving between her thighs that she felt the new sensation. She tried to fight it and she heard him murmur to her to relax. Then he gently asked her to turn over.

The room seemed much darker now and Mitzi, through half-closed eyelids, could see her masseur only as a gold-and-tan glow in the dusk of the room. She felt the hands again, moving all over her body, serving her, soothing her. In some kind of trance she felt herself nodding yes to him, and she sensed him slipping out of his all-white uniform.

She must have slept later because the room was quite dark when she was first aware of the gentle buzzing of the telephone. There was no one else in the room and, just before she picked up the telephone, she wondered if it had all been a dream. Sally Irwin's voice brought her fully awake.

"Hi," she said, "welcome to the Retreat. Don't hurry yourself, but when you're ready, I'm in Suite 101. That's one floor up from you and on the northwest corner."

Mitzi showered quickly, slipped into a silk wrap dress and sandals, and left the room to meet the woman who could save Castles and solve almost all of Mitzi's own pressing problems.

"You look very . . . relaxed," Sally Irwin said. "What was it? A nice therapeutic massage?"

Mitzi felt herself blush as she walked across the room and shook hands. Sally Irwin was tall and big-boned, with straight blond hair and an almost masculine jaw. She wasn't pretty, but she was very striking.

"I love this place," the heiress said. "I don't come to lose weight, just to have a rest and be pampered. That's why," she added, "I break the alcohol rules. I'm going to fix a martini. Will you have one?"

Mitzi nodded.

"I've learned quite a lot about you," Sally told

her. "You've made a real friend in dear old Roger Fairfax. May I call you Mitzi? And call me Sally. I feel I know you already."

"Well, I've done my homework on you, Sally," Mitzi said. "I guess everyone in my business has. I've been hearing about the Irwin estate forever. The man who started me in this business, Jay Pressler, dreamed for years of handling the sale. But in the end, everyone gives up that dream."

"Yes, that damned trust and all the complications about it," Sally said. "My father never realized just what a monster his male chauvinism would create!"

"I take it you're not enamored of Ellis Gibbons?"

"He's a creep," Sally said flatly. "But it looks like he's going to get his way with the estate. Daddy's will was ironclad. Until I'm forty-five, Gibbons can dispose of the estate as he sees fit. And now that the magic number is almost upon me, I hear he's about to sell to some outfit in Texas. The three cousins who share half of Daddy's estate are all pretty dotty. They think Gibbons is God Almighty."

They took their drinks out onto the terrace.

"Still," Sally said, "I suppose he'll get us a fair price. I'll just be glad to be rid of the whole mess, though I'll miss the estate."

"I'm here," Mitzi said slowly, "because Gibbons isn't going to get you the best price, but he is going to make himself several million dollars. You see," she said, pausing to enjoy the moment, "Mr. Gibbons has set up a sweetheart deal. He is the hidden power behind Lackland, the outfit that's going to buy your land. He's selling it to himself at a bargain price and, incidentally, ripping off the estate for a commission on top of all his other fees."

Sally Irwin was studying her in the dim light.

"Can you prove it?" she finally asked.

"Yes," Mitzi said.

Sally Irwin's rage was impressive. No longer the languid rich woman, she began pacing the terrace as though stalking prey.

"The son-of-a-bitch," she said. "I could get him disbarred for this. Even Los Angeles lawyers aren't supposed to have conflicts of interest as stinking as this!"

"I'm not so sure you can do anything to him yet," Mitzi said. "Until the sale actually goes through, that is. And it would be an awful shame to see that wonderful property in the hands of those sharks as the only means of getting revenge on Gibbons."

"So what should I do?" Sally asked.

"Get confirmation of what I've told you," Mitzi said. "Somehow, get proof that he intends the deal to go through. Then confront him with it. I think Gibbons would be pleased just to turn the estate over to you rather than have you go public on him."

"Okay," she said. "I'll get on the phone tonight and have my own lawyers start digging. If they find what you say they'll find, Gibbons is out. I'll need a real-estate agent, won't I?" She grinned at Mitzi.

Mitzi grinned back. "That's the idea," she said. "Or part of the idea. I'd almost work without a commission just for the joy of screwing Ellis Gibbons."

And then she told Sally about her dealings with the lawyer. At first Mitzi spoke angrily, recalling the threats and coercions, Gibbons's brutish sexual come-ons. She glanced up when she heard Sally's laughter.

"We're going to leave him the way he deserves," Sally said. "With his prick in his hand, looking stupid."

Two weeks later, Sally Irwin strode into Castles flanked by two gray-suited attorneys. They were shown into Mitzi's office.

"It's all here, chapter and verse," Sally said, tapping the Gucci briefcase in her lap. "We staged a little break-in at Lackland." The lawyers winced and turned away. "We found letters of intent signed by various officers of Hartford. After that it was only a matter of delving into the records to establish that Gibbons is the beneficial owner of Hartford, which in turn owns Lackland. We have an appointment with the man in one hour. He was very affable when I called. He's looking forward to a session of being patronizing with me. He's got quite a shock coming, Gibbons has."

They had been gone a couple of hours and Mitzi was just getting ready to leave her office when the phone rang. She picked up the receiver.

"You cunt. You'll pay for this," she heard. Then the phone went dead.

Chapter Sixteen _____

IT WAS THE LEAD ARTICLE IN THE REAL ESTATE
section of the *Los Angeles Times*. Castles was
made the sole agency to dispose of the Irwin estate.
There was speculation about the asking price
for the fabulous parcel of land, and the consensus
was that the estate would be split up into several smaller blocks. Several developers were
interviewed for the article and they all agreed it
would be the most impressive land deal ever
consummated in the Los Angeles market.

There was even a comment from Ellis Gibbons,
the prominent attorney and executor of the Irwin
estate.

"A deal of this magnitude requires the employ-
ment of the finest professionals," Mr. Gibbons
told the *Times*. "I would be failing in my duty to the
legatees if I didn't get the best. I am confident that,
in Mrs. Engers and Castles, I have done just that."

Meredith brought her down to earth. "Now all
you've got to do is sell it," she said as they poured
celebratory champagne in the Polo Lounge. "That
ain't going to be so easy, kid."

"I know," said Mitzi. "It's like nothing we—or
anyone else in the field—have ever handled before.
God, I wish Jay were here to help us."

Meredith leaned across the table and patted

her hand. "You don't need Jay, love," she said. "You're a real professional and if anyone can pull it off, it's you."

Some of Meredith's optimism rubbed off on Mitzi. "Yes," she said, "we won't let this overwhelm us. Just treat it like any million-dollar sale and forget that it's thirty times that. You think we could start the sales campaign with a little ad in the *Hollywood Reporter*?"

They both laughed, then became damp-eyed, not from the champagne but from all the memories of their times together, striving to survive in the cutthroat world of Beverly Hills.

"We've come a long way, baby," Meredith said, raising her glass. "A long way from Mrs. Scanlon's."

In the end, they advertised the estate in all the world's leading newspapers: the *New York Times*, the *Wall Street Journal*, the *Times* of London, *Le Monde, Asahi Shimbun*, the *Australian*. The ad copy was brilliant but the response was slow. The estate was surely a prize but no one, in those times, had the courage to compete for it.

She saw Ellis Gibbons once during that period, at a cocktail party in Bel Air. He crossed the room and stood uncomfortably close to her.

"I didn't think you'd have time for parties like this anymore," he said, smiling. "Such a big responsibility you've taken on, for a little woman. I do hope you'll move the property soon. I have my clients' interests to consider. But then, I'm sure it's in the very best of hands."

He smiled again and it chilled her. "You always did say you were the best, didn't you? Now's your chance to prove it." He started to walk away, then turned back to her. "By the way, if you're speaking to your husband—where is he, skulking in Chicago?—you might ask him to call me. That other client of mine is getting impatient for a settlement. We'd really hate for that nasty matter to end up in court, wouldn't we?"

The next day she told Meredith, "That bastard's up to something. He was positively gloating last night. He knows the estate isn't pulling any buyers. But why isn't it? The price is fair. The size of it, sure, will have deterred a lot of people. But where the hell are the local developers? Why aren't they beating down our door?"

Because, she learned later in the day, it was Ellis Gibbons's door the developers were going to. Gibbons phoned her, sounding just as smug and oily as he had the night before.

"I've had several companies approach me directly about the estate," he said. "Of course, I've told them to go to you, that that's what you're there for—to handle all the little details. But in the course of our talks I did notice that the figures they were mentioning were nothing like the price you have on the place. Could it be that you've set your sights a little high? Far be it from me to tell you your business, but really, my dear, all the developers—and I guess they represented every major firm in Los Angeles—were talking around the eighteen-to-twenty-million-dollar mark. I could have gotten more than that from Lackland if you hadn't interfered. I wonder if Sally Irwin's going to be so high on you when she finds out."

"The bastards!" Meredith said. "So the developers have set themselves up a nice little cartel to keep the bidding down on the property. It makes me so mad. They think just because we're a bunch of women they can rip us off."

"No," Mitzi said with a sigh. "Being women isn't what's caused the developers to gang up on us, although I grant you that Ellis Gibbons and his hatred of me is part of the reason it's been so well orchestrated. The thing is, it *is* a cartel, and what are we going to do about it?"

"Isn't the government supposed to outlaw rigged bidding?" Meredith asked. "Let's complain to our congressman."

"It wouldn't help," Mitzi said. "These guys are smart, tough. They've been raping Los Angeles for a hundred years and they know how to do it. There's nothing in writing, no agreements signed. They all belong to an invisible club. Maybe we've just got to accept it and take what they're offering."

"To hell with that!" Meredith snapped. "Even if the same thing would have happened to any other realtor, I'm not going to have us known as the little ladies who got stomped by the male developers. There must be something we can do."

"You can get as mad as you like," Mitzi said. She was very weary and Meredith's anger wasn't helping. Mitzi felt herself near the breaking point. "There's no one to protest to. If the land barons decide that eighteen or twenty is what they'll pay, that's what we're going to have to take. Christ, don't you think I find it humiliating? I'm the one who went out and won us the sale. I'm the one who's going to look like a fool. You only work here."

Even as the words were spoken, she realized what a cruel thing she had said. She saw Meredith blanch and recoil slightly. Then her friend was standing and turning away from her.

"If that's all you think of our relationship, you

can go to hell," Meredith said bitterly. "You've always been the leader, the driving force here, but I thought we had something better than a master-servant relationship. Hah! I thought it was you and me against the world. Well, you can—" She stopped then, because Mitzi was slumped in her chair, sobbing, her shoulders heaving. Meredith crossed to her and took her in her arms. "It's okay, love," she said. "I know what a strain you're under. You can call me anything you like. I understand."

"But you don't," Mitzi sobbed. "Everything's so much worse than you suspect. I had Charles on the phone for more than an hour last night. He was begging me, pleading for me to quit Los Angeles and join him in Chicago. All his promises . . . how he loved me, how the children needed me. And you know, a big part of me wants to do just that, just settle back into the bosom of my family, be a loved wife and mother."

"Do you think you can do that?" Meredith asked carefully. "With Charles?"

"I know I could," Mitzi said. "When you've been together as long as we have, even with all the deceits and the broken promises, you get to be one person instead of two. Charles is a part of me. He does love me, I know. It's just that he's been . . . careless. So have I, I guess. While he was talking last night I was remembering the good times. It's funny, but when the chips are really down it's not the bad times you remember. Instead I was thinking about having Charles to talk with. It's like you sleep so long with one person, you never feel whole again sleeping with yourself.

"It's not a matter of forgiving him anything," she continued. "It doesn't matter who did what first. The point is what you are today and what you are both going to be tomorrow. At this moment Charles is at the lowest point of his life. He needs me, and part of me says I must go to him and start over again. But the other part of me wants to finish what we started here. I'm so scared. Whatever I do will be wrong. That's why I'm just about resigned to rolling over and playing dead for Gibbons and his cartel. The fight's just gone out of me."

Meredith hugged her again. There was nothing to say. This time her friend had to fight alone.

It didn't take long for the story to get around town. In the men-only business clubs and at the bars and bistros where the movers and shakers gathered, they talked about it with knowing grins. "Just like a woman," they said. To run out in the middle of an important deal just because her family beckoned. That was why women would never really make it in a man's world. Women didn't have their priorities straight. Gibbons would be well advised to look for another realtor.

There *was* a TWA flight to Chicago and Mitzi *had* booked a first-class seat on it. But there was another TWA flight that day, over the pole to London. And when the big Europe-bound jet lumbered down the runway of LA International, Mitzi was on it. The martini sloshed alarmingly as the plane gathered speed, and Mitzi quickly drained the drink. She needed all the courage she could muster for what lay ahead. At eighteen thousand feet the "No Smoking" sign went off and she lit the first of many cigarettes. She'd been so good about cutting down but now she was back to two packs a day. She would give up completely as soon as things settled down. She managed to smile to herself. When would that be? The year two thousand and what?

No one knew she was coming, so there would be no one to meet her at London's Heathrow Airport. Yet Mitzi still found herself scanning the faces waiting at the barriers outside Her Majesty's Customs. They all looked so happy, so expectant, waiting to be reunited with their loved ones. She just felt tired, jet-lagged, and nerve-jangled, not quite sure why she was here or whether she should have come. There was, of course, no friendly face in the crowd, and Mitzi wearily dragged her one large case through the crowd. The porters were on strike again and there was no one to help her.

She moved to the currency exchange and swapped five hundred dollars' worth of travelers' checks for British money, the strange sterling notes she received too big for her wallet. She tucked them in the side pocket of her beige suede jacket.

Outside the terminal the day was dank, a thick mist hanging over everything. Three of the odd-shaped black London taxis were parked there, their drivers standing together under the shelter of a concrete balcony. They were in uniforms of sorts, shapeless cloth coats and soft peaked caps. Each of them had a damp, stained cigarette dangling from his bottom lip. They showed no interest whatsoever as she stood by the front cab and stared at them.

"I want to go to the Waldorf Hotel, in the Aldwych," she announced. "Are any of you gentlemen on duty?"

The trio looked at each other. Then one of them shrugged, grinned at his mates, and started toward her.

"Okay, luv," he said, "I'll take you to your pub. But it'll cost you twenty quid."

She made a quick calculation that the fare was

going to be about fifty dollars. She was being ripped off but she was too tired to care much. She nodded and climbed into the rear compartment of the high-roofed cab. The driver placed her bag in the open compartment next to him, carefully relit the stub of his cigarette, and sent the cab lurching off into the mists.

Mitzi's depression grew heavier as they moved down the highway to London, crawling along at thirty miles an hour, stopping for long minutes as the traffic around them choked on itself. At least there was no blaring of horns, as there would have been in America, and for this she was thankful. A dull, persistent ache was building just behind her eyes.

"First time here, Yank?" The driver had slid back the glass partition that separated them and was speaking to her over his shoulder. The accent was so thick—Cockney, she supposed—that she could barely understand him.

"Yes," she finally replied. "It's my first time in London."

"You bloody Yanks are the only ones who can afford it," she heard him say. It wasn't a challenge, just a statement about the way things were. "You and the Arabs," he continued. "It used to be that we could go anywhere in London, afford it, you know. Now it's priced so that only toffs and Arabs and Yank tourists can use the city. Bloody shame. I'd get out of here, migrate to Australia, except I can't stand the bloody Aussies either." Mitzi was grateful when the traffic started up again and he slammed the partition shut.

She could just barely see out the windows to the houses clustered along the highway. There was no sign of life in any of them. There was a uniform grayness about the tract, unrelieved by flowers or trees. So much for the green fields of England, she thought bitterly. Another illusion shattered. Would the whole trip be like this?

By the time they reached the City of London proper, both Mitzi and the weather had brightened a little. She got a glimpse of Buckingham Palace to her left, smaller than she had imagined from photographs but still solid and regal, reassuring her that she was in London. Then a stretch of brilliant green parkland before the bustle and rush of Piccadilly Circus. Her confidence was beginning to come back. Maybe, just maybe, she would bring this off.

The Waldorf Hotel was old and had a pleasant, homely look about it. It was only six floors high, but the building curved with the sweep of the Aldwych, and Mitzi stood on the pavement for a moment admiring the grubby white façade. A small boy dressed in a tight black jacket took her bag and she followed him up the steps. Inside it was all red plush and old crystal and, yes, they did have her reservation. Her room was small but adequate. Mitzi unpacked quickly. Then there was nothing to do but sit by the window, look out at India House across the street, and think.

Being away from any familiar scene allowed her mind to roam freely, and she came to see how desperate she really was. She was nearly forty, and it looked as though she had had all the good times she was going to have. Jay was gone, and even if, by some wild chance, she did sell the Irwin estate, it wouldn't be the triumph she and Jay had talked about so often, not without him there.

Her choices seemed hollow everywhere. If she went back to Charles she could try to make things all right again, but they would never be more than just all right. Dane and Shana never would really be hers again, had not been hers since they were little. And Charles never was going to change. She had come so far, not "far for a woman," but done wonderfully. Giving it all up and creeping back to Illinois seemed all wrong, but her achievements gave her very little boost anymore.

At long last she understood Charles's disillusionment. How sad that she felt no closer to him because of that.

She was awake before dawn, her biological clock still running on faraway Los Angeles time, and she forced herself to linger over a vast breakfast of kippers and sausages and bacon and kidney and eggs until it was time to make the call.

She gave her name to the secretary, and Sharif came on the line at once.

"I couldn't be more pleased to hear from you," he said. "Business has kept me from your city for so long but I have often thought of you and I have followed your activities with great interest. Congratulations on the Irwin coup. You must be very proud."

"Thanks," Mitzi said. "Actually, that's the reason I'm here in London. To talk to you about the Irwin estate. I think—"

He cut her off. "Just wait until I see what the day holds for me," he said. She heard him speak rapidly to an aide and then he came back. "The day has been cleared," he said. "Would you like to come to the hotel? We'll talk, then go on to lunch."

"That's wonderful," Mitzi said. "I know how busy you are and I promise I won't be wasting your time."

"I know you won't be," he said. "I look forward to seeing you."

She walked to the Dorchester Hotel, going against the flow of businessmen in their dark suits, umbrellas, and attaché cases, and entered the hotel's ornate lobby. The desk clerk looked up quickly when she asked for Adnan Sharif's suite and, when she gave her name, he spoke softly into the telephone beside him.

"Certainly, Mrs. Engers," he said, his voice respectful. "I'll have one of the footmen show you to the Imperial Suite."

Mitzi grinned. The way the Arabs were buying up London property, she thought, Sharif is probably this clerk's employer by now and anyone associated with Sharif was to be pampered. It made a nice change, she mused, from being treated like a pariah just because she was an unescorted woman.

The massive double doors to the suite were opened by a short, strong-looking young man in a dark suit. He bowed and indicated that she should follow him. They moved through three anterooms, each occupied by male and female staff working telexes and talking on telephones. Finally they reached the main room, a vast, sunny space dominated by a highly polished antique desk. Sharif sat behind it, a telephone to his ear. He rose as she entered, then he smiled and waved a greeting. She sat on a brocade couch near the full-length windows while he finished his conversation.

As he talked, she stole a glance at him. He was, she thought again, a most handsome man, tall and dark, his face highlighted by soft brown eyes and gleaming white teeth. As always, he was impeccably dressed. A dark blue silk suit, soft white shirt and Gucci tie was the costume that day. In London, with its vast international population, he seemed much less a foreigner to her than he had in Los Angeles.

At last he was finished with the telephone. "I'm sorry," he said, crossing the room and sitting beside her. "There shouldn't be any more calls to disturb us."

"I'm very grateful to you for making time for me," Mitzi said. "I'll try not to waste it." She took the briefcase from its place beside her. "In here are all the facts and figures on the Irwin estate. At thirty million dollars, it's a steal. In ten years, the way Beverly Hills real estate is going, it can be subdivided and will bring anything up to one hundred and fifty, two hundred million. In the meantime, the buyer gets the last, greatest estate in the most sought-after residential area in the world. It's a great prospect, but I've got a cartel working against me and the developers are keeping the bids way down. So I came to see if you and your principals are interested."

Sharif smiled. "I heard about your problems, of course," he said. "And I hoped you would eventually come to me. I've had our own people do a study of the property and I agree with what you've said about it. In fact, I think you've been somewhat conservative in guessing its future worth. Our own projections suggest a higher figure in 1990. Perhaps five million an acre. I'm quite surprised that your local developers are so undervaluing the land. It is, as you say, the last chance to purchase the best land in the most volatile area in the world."

"Oh, they know its true value," Mitzi said. "But they think that by banding together they can beat me. And they know Sally Irwin doesn't really care about the money. She just wants to get rid of the estate. They're just playing the old game of ripping off people they think are weaker than they are. That's the way Los Angeles was developed, really, and they think the old rules will apply forever. I want to prove them wrong."

"So you are formally offering it to me?" he asked, and she thought she caught a twinkle in his eye.

She gulped. "I wouldn't have presumed on our . . . friendship," she began, "if the property were not priced fairly. I think it's a good deal, but you know all the circumstances, so you may choose to make an offer less than the asking price."

"We don't like to do business that way," Sharif said. "Taking advantage of a situation, I mean. If we were going to buy the Irwin estate, we would want to pay the fair market price for it, not take advantage of the cartel against you. A great deal of prestige is involved here. A few extra million dollars are worth it if they bring us a reputation for fair trading. Now," he said, rising and pacing the room, "the estate itself does not fit in with our investment structure. It's too big, too unwieldy. We would have to develop it immediately, and that would bring an outcry from your fellow Americans. I can see the headlines now: 'Oil-Rich Arabs Tear Down Historic Mansion.' No, we can do without that kind of publicity."

Mitzi listened to him, dismay mounting. That was it, then.

"However," he said, "there is someone else for whom I am acting—more as a friend than in a long-term capacity—who has empowered me to buy for her just such a property. It must be big and secure, a place where she can be protected from the public and safe from those who would wish to harm her. I will not tell you her name but will just say that she is in exile, her husband has died, and she must find a permanent refuge. It may be some time before the political climate allows her to take up residence in America, but we have been assured that that time will come. The Irwin estate will suit her ideally, and I am now offering you thirty million dollars for it."

She sat there, stunned. Sharif was smiling down at her, waiting. She clutched the briefcase to her.

"That's . . . great," she finally said. "We've got a deal."

The next hours sped by as Sharif summoned lawyers and financial advisers and the bill of sale was prepared. He placed a call to Cairo and took it in another office, returning to Mitzi after several minutes to say that the purchase was confirmed. Finally he sat at his desk and took out a gold-embossed ledger. He wrote quickly in it, tore out a sheet, and carried it delicately to her.

"The check," he said, bowing and passing it to her.

Her fingers trembled. It was hard for her to read the words and figures. The zeroes seemed to go on forever. "The sum of thirty million dollars. $30,000,000," she finally read.

They lunched in the Dorchester's elegant dining room. He ordered for them both, caviar and Scottish salmon, raspberries with clotted cream. And a bottle of Crystel champagne to start. "After all," he said, smiling at her, "even I don't spend thirty million dollars every day."

She was so exhilarated that she had no need of

the champagne. They talked of business trends and politics and she warmed further to him. There was no condescension in the man. He was incredibly knowledgeable, and he made it clear that he respected her judgments and opinions.

It was over coffee that he reminded her of her other crisis.

"Your commission," he said. "It will make you a rather wealthy woman. Have you any plans for all that money, or will you just continue as before, building Castles?"

She now so trusted Sharif that she did not hesitate to tell him everything—Charles's accident, the unsuccessful operation, the ferocious malpractice suit that had followed.

"So you see, after taxes and everything, the commission plus the capital I take out of Castles and the sale of our home, will net me the million I need to pay off that woman and put Charles back on his feet."

"And what will you do then?" Sharif asked.

"I'm still wrestling with that decision," Mitzi said. "But I don't really have much choice. I'll be broke, with a husband who needs me. So I suppose the career of Mitzi Engers in real estate is finally over. At least Charles will benefit," she added, without any bitterness.

"There is another option," Sharif said casually, after a pause. "Of course, it would mean the gravest disruption of your home life, constant travel, being headquartered here in London. I do not think your husband would like it."

"Like what?" she asked.

"Taking over all the property investments I am now handling," he said. "There are other areas in which I should be working full time. Until now I have not found anyone who had both the ability and the personal bearing to take over what is, by anyone's standards, a massive portfolio. I know you could do it. I would like you to think about the prospect. It would be, on the surface at least, a most glamorous job. A salary of, say a quarter million dollars a year, private planes at your disposal, a residence here and suites in New York, Los Angeles, and anywhere else that generates business. You would be buying and selling everything from hotels to office blocks to tropical islands. It would also be a nerve-racking job, one that would leave you little or no time for home and family. It would be a lot to ask of anyone, but particularly of a woman. You know how executives live and work in this age. It is scarcely possible to retain any family life. I know," he added, "from personal experience. My own marriage foundered years ago because of my commitment to business."

She hadn't known. She saw a new depth in him then. "What you're talking about . . . it's so much bigger than anything I ever thought about. It makes running Castles seem like a hobby."

"Just think about it," he said. "There is no great hurry. I have waited long enough to find someone who could do it. I can wait a little longer for her reply."

That night she flew from Heathrow to New York and on to Los Angeles. She couldn't sleep. Too much was running through her. There was the exhilaration of the deal, of winning the prize that dear Jay had talked about hopefully. Several times she rummaged in her purse, among the papers and the passport and the TWA ticket and the crushed

pack of Kools and the roll of Lifesavers and the
Kleenex and the lipstick. She took out the check
and examined it in the dim light. The figures were
the same each time, but they did not give her an
answer.

Chapter Seventeen _____

"THE *NEWSWEEK* GUY'S DEMANDING A PRIVATE session with you," Carol said. "They've upped you to a cover!"

Mitzi continued to gaze out at the late-afternoon traffic on Rodeo Drive. She was very tired, jet-lagged, and anxious about the decisions she'd made. They involved so many people she loved and cared for.

"I haven't got time," she told her secretary wearily.

"But it's fabulous publicity, for you and for Castles," Carol insisted. "You can't pass it up."

"All right, I'll try to fit him in right after the press conference," Mitzi said. "If I can just relax for a while now."

The sun was setting behind Beverly Hills, bathing Rodeo Drive in a soft pink light. The stately palms moved gently in the evening breeze, and the handsome shops were closing for the night. She was going to miss all this. Her head was nodding when Meredith came striding into the room.

"It's a madhouse out there," she said cheerfully. "Reporters waiting for you, flowers by the truck-load, the switchboard backed up with calls. We're famous!" She glanced at Mitzi fondly. "You're really beat. I'll fix us both a drink."

"Thanks," Mitzi said. "I still don't feel anything, certainly not the sense of triumph I expected. But listen, I don't want to talk about the Irwin estate right now. There's something more important."

Meredith stopped moving and stared at her, hard. What could be more important than a thirty-million-dollar deal?

"As of tomorrow," Mitzi said slowly, "you are the president of Castles. I'm taking my share of the profits and turning the company over to you."

"You really are tired," Meredith said after a moment. "You sleep on it and we'll talk it over tomorrow." She looked at her friend closely. "It's Charles, isn't it?" she said. "You'd sacrifice all this for Charles."

"Charles is part of it," Mitzi said. "But there's another part, too, that I can't tell even you about. Not yet. Just believe me. If you want it, Castles is yours."

Suddenly Meredith was crying.

"You stop that right now," said Mitzi, close to tears herself. "We can't meet the media looking all weepy. They'd think we were just a couple of silly women. Please, give me a few minutes alone and then we'll get the press over with."

Meredith left her alone.

Mitzi had told Meredith. Now she must tell Charles.

She dialed the house in Oak Brook and he answered on the fourth ring, sounding almost embarrassingly grateful to hear her voice.

"Darling," he said, "I've been trying to reach you for two days. I know how busy you are, but I've had great news. I'm going back on staff at the hospital, where I used to be. And they want to fund a new clinic for me. Everything's going to be like it was at the start. You and me and the children . . . please, say you're coming home. I know what a sacrifice it will be for you, but I'll make it up to you. I love you so. I've changed at last, grown up, really I have. All I have to do now is somehow get that damned malpractice suit off my back and we can start a whole new life. Please, Mitzi. Come home."

"I'm glad for you, Charles," she said carefully. "I know what a good person you are and how much good you can do. And you don't have to worry about the damages suit anymore. I just sold the Irwin estate and with that commission, plus what I get from pulling out of Castles, we've got the million dollars to buy that woman off."

She heard him gasp. "Jesus! That's wonderful, Mitzi," he said. "You're incredible. I'll never be able to make all this up to you." He paused. Then, "Pulling out of Castles? That means you're coming home to us! You won't regret it, Mitzi. I promise you."

She swallowed. "No, Charles," she said gently. "It doesn't mean I'm coming home. I tried, but I can't just walk away from everything I've fought to achieve, from all those years. I'm leaving Castles but I'm taking on a far bigger job, one that will take even more of my time. I'll be traveling all the time, living far away from here."

"But—what about us?" he asked. He was pleading. "We need you. *I* need you, more than ever before."

"You're going to have to make it on your own for a while," she said. "You can do it, Charles. Later, maybe, we can work something out. I don't know what, exactly, but something. But for now I must do what seems right for me. I'll miss you terribly, Charles, you and the children."

"I think I understand," he said after a long silence. "I don't blame you. I screwed up everything, didn't I. I never meant to, you know. I love you and I'll be here when—if—you need me."

"Charles"—she found the words coming more easily—"I can't say anything right now except thanks. I was afraid you wouldn't understand, but I almost think you do. I'll call early tomorrow when the children are there so we can all talk."

She wanted to hang up but didn't want to be abrupt, so she rushed on. "How is the house?"

"Wonderful. You were right, as usual. It was a marvelous buy." And he hung up, leaving her not quite sure whether he'd meant to be sarcastic.

As she sat at her desk, Charles's image quickly faded. She found herself looking at the portrait facing her on the opposite wall. Close to tears, but grinning despite herself, she winked at Jay's face and gave him a smart military salute.

"Okay, Carol," she said into the intercom, "you can send in the press now."

Three Novels from the
New York Times Bestselling Author

NEAL TRAVIS

CASTLES   79913-8/$3.50

A woman reaches for her dream when she joins Castles, a prestigious international real estate firm, and follows her driving passion for life from the playgrounds of Bel Air to the boardrooms of New York. On her way to the top, there would be men who tried to keep her down, but one man would make her see the beautiful, extraordinary woman she was.

PALACES   84517-2/$3.95

The dazzling, sexy novel of a woman's struggle to the heights in Hollywood. Caught up in the fast international scene that burns up talent and dreams, fighting against power moguls who have the leverage to crush, she achieves fame and fortune at Palace Productions. Yet amid all the glamour and excitement in the celluloid world of illusions, she almost loses the one man whose love is real.

And now...

MANSIONS   88419-4/$3.95

Her first success—as Washington's top TV news personality—was ruined by a lover's betrayal. As wife to the young scion of the Mansion media empire, she was expected to sacrifice herself and her dreams. But if the world gave her a woman's choice between love and success, she gave the world a woman's triumph. And when real success was hers, she was ready for the man who offered her love.

AVON PAPERBACKS